Literary editor of the *Irish Times* for sixteen years, Terence de Vere White is also a highly acclaimed novelist and contributor to various journals.

TERENCE DE VERE WHITE
PRENEZ GARDE

Futura

A **Futura** Book

Copyright © Terence de Vere White 1961

First published in Great Britain in 1961 by
Victor Gollancz Ltd, London

This edition published in 1986 by
Futura Publications, a Division of
Macdonald & Co (Publishers) Ltd
London & Sydney

*All characters in this publication are fictitious
and any resemblance to real persons, living or dead,
is purely coincidental.*

All rights reserved

No part of this publication may be reproduced, stored in a
retrieval system, or transmitted, in any form or by any means
without the prior permission in writing of the publisher, nor
be otherwise circulated in any form of binding or cover other
than that in which it is published and without a similar
condition including this condition being imposed on the
subsequent purchaser.

Printed and bound in Great Britain by
The Guernsey Press Co Ltd, Guernsey, Channel Islands

Futura Publications
A Division of
Macdonald & Co (Publishers) Ltd
Maxwell House
74 Worship Street
London EC2A 2EN

A BPCC plc Company

For
Billy and Eleanor

It is usual—particularly when they are clearly identifiable—to proclaim in this place that all the characters in the book are fictitious. I refrain. Not because my characters—the boy not excepted—are other than creatures of fancy, or that the events here described ever took place; but because the scene and the mood of the story, the manners and opinions of the characters are as true to the little world of my childhood as memory can make them.

It was a peaceful little world. There were no shootings, no raids; and the local schoolmaster, whom I distinctly remember, was an elderly, innocuous man of sedentary habits. Clearest of all in my recollection of those days is the thrill of horror with which I read the newspaper on the morning of the twenty-second of November, in the year one thousand nine hundred and twenty. I feel it still.

It was never the same after Miss Morris came. Our home had been the most predictable place, each of us moving in his predestined groove; but after Miss Morris came we were all at sixes and sevens. I remember my first view of her. I had come into the hall from the back, through the kitchen, a way forbidden to me, but very convenient as it avoided the necessity for brushing and scraping shoes and enabled me —with luck—to get to the schoolroom without being observed. (To be observed meant so often to be sent on a message.) As I came into the hall the drawing-room door opened and a young woman came out. She was, perhaps, two-and-twenty. I stared at her. And she gave me a quick and (I thought) rather slighting look. She had small, rather pert features and large, disrespectful eyes. I fell madly in love with her at that first meeting.

"You ought to know me the next time," she said. I did not answer. I could think of nothing to say. And then she walked upstairs humming a tune to herself. Unable to speak, enormously excited, I rushed into the drawing-room where my mother sat behind a tea tray.

"So there you are," she said. "I have been looking for you everywhere. I wanted you to meet Miss Morris. She is coming to be your governess; and you must promise to be very good because she has never been a governess before and we must make it easy for her."

"I saw her," I said. Then I went into the bay window at the other end of the room and hid myself behind the curtain where I had a book ready beneath a cushion. My heart was full; but nothing would induce me to disclose the strange excitement that ran through me at my first encounter with the new governess. I was a connoisseur of the breed, having had seven. One angel who was unable to stay, followed by six unhappy women whom my parents found they could not put up with. Miss Morris had nothing to do with the dim world of governesses. I saw that at a glance. She came straight from the romantic kingdom of which I had had only glimpses: at Christmas pantomimes when we went up to Dublin, in book illustrations, and in real life only in the person of Mrs Heber who lived in what was formerly the rectory and with whom I used occasionally to spend an afternoon playing snap. I stayed until after tea which we drank from cups of great rarity (so Mrs Heber told me). It spoiled the tea worrying about the cups. I went home always at six o'clock so as to avoid Mr Heber. I had been in love with Mrs Heber until I saw Miss Morris. But she put everyone out of my mind. It was quite overwhelming. I had never known anything like it. I was nine years old.

*   *   *

We were a happy family until Miss Morris came, but happy in an uneventful way. I kept out of sight so that I might be allowed to read in peace. My mother was busy in the house and garden. Sometimes neighbours came to play bridge with her or she went out to play with them. My father, who had some job in the Courts, came home an hour before dinner. When he came into the house he went into the dining-room, poured himself out a small glass of whiskey, and sat reading the evening paper until it was dinner time. When I went in to see him he gave me two pennies as a bribe to leave him alone. I had my supper in the schoolroom with the governess. But I was allowed to go in at the end of dinner and sit with my parents. There were coloured crystals for the coffee which I liked eating, and I usually got a helping of pudding. Then my parents moved into the drawing-room, and it was time for me to go to bed.

Supper in the schoolroom was never very pleasant. Most of my governesses had strange ways of eating. They complicated the process from excessive gentility. Watching them chewing slowly, I was crazy with impatience to get down from the table and join my parents in the cheerful dining-room with the red-shaded lamp low down over the table and the twinkling glass and silver. The schoolroom table was covered with oilcloth. And I disliked the china decorated with rabbits and bears which seemed to be miraculously durable. I was no longer a baby. If necessary I was prepared to steal plates more worthy of Miss Morris from the china cupboard and to hide the baby stuff I was made to use and which could only lower my importance in her eyes. With such a companion I would no longer want to manufacture excuses to leave the table. I would prolong meals indefinitely. It was going to be an effort to find subjects she would like to talk about.

But it was not to be.

From the first Miss Morris took her meals in the dining-room and a place was laid there for me. At any other time I should have been delighted with this promotion, but now it came as a bitter disappointment. I had looked forward so enormously to our tête-à-têtes. This was the first way in which the change brought about by Miss Morris's arrival showed itself. Not only were there four of us in the dining-room, but conversation which had been gentle and intermittent when my parents were alone, now raced along. Everyone was laughing all the time. When the laughter was loudest Miss Morris looked at me and said something in French. That meant, as I knew, from long experience, that she thought I ought not to be allowed to listen to what was being said. It seemed extraordinary that she should be so concerned to keep me out of the conversation when she set the tone of it. Before she came my parents laughed, but never giggled, or talked about people, or made fun of them, as they did now.

I noticed that my father had given up his quiet hour in the dining-room before dinner. Now he came into the schoolroom and asked about my lessons. He even offered me help for which I was grateful. I never understood arithmetic. I don't think my father was good at it either, because he used to take up my book and start to work out the sums by himself at the table. Sometimes Miss Morris joined in, and the two of them used to laugh over the sums and forget that I was waiting to get the book back.

It was symptomatic of all Miss Morris's treatment of me. I could not get her to pay me any attention. She offered to play cricket and tennis with me. But I was very feeble in my efforts, and she got bored and flung away the bat and racquet and made some excuse to get away. We played tennis once and cricket once.

My mother who used to avoid the schoolroom while I was doing lessons with governesses now began to come in for elevenses with Miss Morris. The tea drinking sometimes took so long—they both talked and laughed so much—that it was time for luncheon before anyone realised how quickly the morning had gone. I who had hated lessons now resented these interruptions of the morning sessions. I could see that Miss Morris was bored. She was more and more inclined to put something before me to be learnt by heart while she manicured her hands or talked to my mother, or read letters which she took out of her bag.

It was not only our household that was affected by Miss Morris's arrival. She became a centre of interest in the neighbourhood. She was invited to tennis parties and to all the local entertainments. I watched her play, lost in admiration, but saddened by the widening of the gulf between us. For it was only too plain that Miss Morris was my governess only in name.

I heard my mother say: "He reads too much. It will do him good to take it easy for a bit." There was something in this remark to cause a pang in my over-apprehensive heart. "For a bit" meant that some lease had been given to Miss Morris. After that there was to be a change. But what? I was intelligent enough to realise that no one would ever expect us to get down to work together. It must mean that after Christmas Miss Morris was to go. To my sadness caused by her high-handed treatment of me was added the awful prospect of parting. It was like the shadow of death on us.

I resumed my weekly visits to Mrs Heber. It had been so long since my last call I felt guilty and more than a little apprehensive about the greeting I should get. And if Mrs Heber guessed the reason for my infidelity I expected she would be wildly jealous. As it turned out my fears were groundless. She received me, as always on fine days, under the weeping-ash in the garden where she sat among white garden furniture with bright cushions and rugs on the grass, and beside her on a marble-topped table all the weekly social magazines and several novels in new dust-wrappers. Her large blue hat cast a shadow like a veil across the top part of her beautiful face. In winter, or on cold days, she was laid out on a sofa in the drawing-room in an elaborate gown not unlike a kimono and of a deep blue which brought out the colour of her eyes.

"I am so glad to see you, Brian," she said. "I have missed you. I hope your father and mother are well."

When I said they were, she went on talking just as if it was one week instead of four since we had met. She never talked down to me or adapted her conversation to my age, but told me about the past and her childhood in Dublin. I was flattered by this and the subject did not bore me as a rule, but today I longed to talk about Miss Morris. At the same time I felt too shy to introduce her name into the conversation. We were having tea when Mrs Heber said very casually: "I hear you have a new governess."

The cake which I was eating almost choked me. But the distraction was useful. I made the most of the ensuing fit of coughing, and hoped that the subject would be forgotten.

"I think it is much nicer for you to have someone young than to have some old sorrowful person looking after you." Mrs Heber, as her manner was, launched into an account of the governesses she and her sister had when they were children.

"I believe she plays a good game of tennis," said Mrs Heber after a short period of silence. And I who had but one thought in my mind did not need to ask to whom she was referring.

"She—Miss Morris, I mean—is playing with Daddy in the American Tournament at Raheny Castle on Saturday," I said. I did not think Mrs Heber looked over-pleased at this piece of information.

"I hope Doreen will be able to play in that," she said. "I am expecting her on Friday. I rang up Lord Swords and he very kindly said he would partner her if she were."

Doreen Hailey was Mrs Heber's niece. Her annual visit to our neighbourhood was one of the events of the year. Her father was someone of tremendous importance, and everything about the girl was given a consequence which her personality hardly justified. She was very fashionable and well-cared for, but without any vitality, and only moderately pretty. Perhaps it was the striking beauty of the aunt and her almost theatrical presence which made the niece seem so anaemic. But we all took our tone from Mrs Heber, and none of us ever admitted to ourselves that Doreen was not the most interesting of topics for conversation. So much so that I should not have been surprised to hear that she was going to marry the Prince of Wales, or Admiral Beatty, or Georges Carpentier, or a nephew of the Archbishop of Canterbury. In fact, we never heard about any engagement although Doreen was now twenty-three.

"Perhaps Doreen will marry Lord Swords," I said.

Mrs Heber looked at me suddenly and then looked away again. Once again I had the feeling of not having pleased her.

"Mummy said she expected you would get Doreen over when Lord Swords came to live at the Castle," I said, to lend weight to my theory.

"Did she?" said Mrs Heber, and added after a few seconds: "That was rather naughty of your mother."

"I saw him—Lord Swords I mean—the other day. He is very small and he has no hair. I thought lords were usually handsome," I said. "But I am sure he is very rich," I added hastily, remembering Doreen.

Raheny Castle was the great house of the neighbourhood. The last lord lost his son and heir at the beginning of the war. He had gone out in August 1914 and was reported missing at Christmas. The old man then locked himself up in a wing of the castle and saw nobody. He never came outside the grounds from that time until he died. That was a year before Miss Morris came. His heir was a cousin who lived in England. I heard him described as 'young', and as my ideas of a lord were based on the illustrations to the *Idylls of the King*, I thought of a young, unmarried lord as a thing of wonderful beauty. Lord Swords was thirty-five, prematurely bald, very stout, round in the body, and bandy in the legs. I burst into tears when I first saw him.

It surprised me that anyone should want to marry him, but from what I heard my mother say I was forced to the conclusion that because he was a lord a great many people would overlook his plainness; and I rather liked the thought of Doreen coming to the Castle if she could put up with such an ugly husband.

"Is it because Lord Swords is so ugly you don't want Doreen to marry him?" I said, anxious to get my mind clear on this topic.

"Brian, I want you to listen to me very carefully"—Mrs Heber took my hand in hers and looked at me earnestly. She had a charming voice, high but full of laughter. When—as now—she became solemn, her voice became as deep as a 'cello. If she was angry her voice would be hard. I guessed that; but I had never known her to get angry.

"You must not talk about people marrying one another like that or ask questions about it. You will understand when you are older. It is one of the things—like money and religion—people don't talk about. It would upset Doreen very much if she heard what you had said. Lord Swords is quite young in spite of his bald head, and he is naturally pleased when a girl of Doreen's age comes into the neighbourhood. They have friends in common. But that is all there is to it. They enjoy one another's company. Wouldn't you be pleased if a boy or a girl of your own age were to come and stay with me? So promise me you won't ever say such silly things again."

I promised, looking into her eyes which were the colour of a pansy in our garden, deep blue and dark in the centre. Mrs Heber's treatment was soothing to my vanity which Miss Morris had bruised so often in recent weeks. I would have died for Mrs Heber. And it never occurred to me to question what she said. I determined then and there to put my mother right if I heard her talk lightly about marriages in future.

I embarrassed Mrs Heber once again that afternoon. She mentioned a dinner-party which she was giving in Doreen's honour. Lord Swords was coming.

"Are you asking Mummy and Daddy?" I said.

"It's only a small party, a sort of family party really," said Mrs Heber. But I noticed that she had reddened a little and I decided not to mention the party at home.

"I must have you all over when Doreen is here. And perhaps your nice governess will come. I will ring your mother up about it," said Mrs Heber as she poured out tea from a silver tea-pot. I had a vague premonition that if Miss Morris met Mrs Heber no good would come of it. I felt that my little world was in some invisible but deadly peril.

"That would be too much trouble," I said. "Miss Morris can stay at home with me. It's her job to, really."

I thought Mrs Heber looked at me rather searchingly when I said this. But she murmured something about 'the whole family' which raised my hopes that I might be invited as well. But I knew this was most unlikely.

"Here comes Harry," she cried out. Her voice had so many shades that it seemed to convey pleasure and, for me, a warning.

Suddenly I felt inexpressibly sad. I saw Mr Heber walking slowly up the drive, thin and stooped, years older than his wife.

"I must go home," I said, sick with gloom.

"Have some more tea," said Mrs Heber.

"No thank you. I don't think Mr Heber derives any pleasure from my society," I added. It was a phrase I had been storing up for use for some time. This seemed as good an opportunity as any. I was always surprised when Mrs Heber laughed. She had not the joking manner of my mother who was constantly on the look-out for something to make up a story about. But Mrs Heber laughed now until tears came into her eyes and her cheeks were flushed. "Good evening, my dear," said Mr Heber who had now come up to us. He kissed her lightly on the forehead. "You seem to be amused," he added in his school-mastering way.

"Take the white cake, Brian," said Mrs Heber gently, as if to console me for the blight of her husband's presence. I had been eyeing the cake since tea began, having refused it from politeness the first time it was offered to me. I did not make the same mistake again.

"And how are you, young man?" said Mr Heber, giving me his neutral look. I had been told he had a bad heart and for that reason was permanently on the verge of ill-temper.

"I saw your father on the train," he added. Mrs Heber gave me a conspiratorial smile which I recognised as a signal to go. If her husband had not been there my leaving would have presented no difficulty, but I was miserably aware of his anxiety to see the last of me and unable to think of a suitable formula for departure.

"I think I had better go home," I said at last. "God forbid that I should come between man and wife."

I shook hands with Mrs Heber, and glanced in her husband's direction. He was apparently lost in contemplation of his shoes, so I walked off without attempting to catch his attention. I heard them laughing when they thought I was out of earshot. I did not like the thought that Mrs Heber was capable of this.

When I got home I found my father practising croquet with Miss Morris on the lawn. My mother was making an omelette in the kitchen. Jane, the raw-boned cook, was trying to sharpen the carving knife in the scullery. Through the drawing-room window I saw Alice, her younger sister, who was called the housemaid, trying to stick a Dresden figure together with soap. Everyone was busy. It provided a contrast with the house I had just left, where Mrs Heber never seemed to move, and the staff only appeared from the kitchen in answer to a bell.

Alice did not see me; Jane asked me 'for the love of God' to keep away from the knife. My mother asked me where I had been, and when I told her said: "It's well for her" in a tone that implied criticism of Mrs Heber's way of life. I resented this.

Miss Morris and my father seemed to be enjoying the croquet enormously. It had always seemed to me a dull game. But they were laughing away. And whenever Miss Morris missed, my father said it was because of the way she held her mallet. And then he showed her how to use it properly, and gave her the shot all over again. I had never seen him so pleasant about a game. And I asked if I could join in.

"I'll take you on next," said my father.

"There is sixpence at stake," said Miss Morris, "so please don't interrupt us."

They made no effort to hurry; and I knew that at any moment my mother would appear at the top of the garden and say the omelette would be ruined if we didn't come in at once to eat it. And as I predicted, this happened just when Miss Morris took her last shot at the stick, to win her the game despite the way she had been going on, as though she was a child playing for the first time. I knew she was very good at games, much better than my father.

"Will you play with me after dinner?" I said.

My father looked guilty and said 'yes'. But I knew when the time came we would have a quick, perfunctory game because it was after my bed-time. And everyone would be bored by my bad shots, and not at all inclined to think them amusing.

I had hoped to attract some attention at dinner by giving

the news that Mrs Heber's niece was coming to stay. I had kept it to myself until then. But as soon as we sat down my father said: "You were right, Dorothy. You always are. Doreen Hailey is coming to stay. Heber dropped it out in the train."

"I wish her luck," said my mother.

"I hear the castle is almost falling down," said my father. "The old man never lit a fire in it. Heber went round it with Swords the other day."

"As soon as the new man puts it in order the Sinn Feiners will burn it down," said my mother.

"For God's sake, be careful what you say in front of the servants," said my father, hastily looking round to see if Alice was in the room.

It was taken for granted that the servant class as a whole were in the confidence of the Sinn Feiners, and that any criticism of their activities would be reported and punished. All over the country houses were being burnt down, but in our immediate neighbourhood there had been no trouble as yet.

"Brian was having tea with Mrs Heber," said my mother to change the conversation.

Everyone looked at me now. Miss Morris as usual seemed to be mocking me. I was determined to win her good opinion.

"Mrs Heber is having Lord Swords to dinner," I said. "She wants you all to come. I specially impressed on her that Miss Morris should be invited. I said she was not an ordinary governess. Please ring up Mrs Heber and arrange about it. She is dying to meet Miss Morris. And she says Doreen is longing to meet her too."

"Heber never mentioned it," said my father dubiously.

"Are you sure you got the message right?" said my mother.

"I think I should wait for Mrs Heber to ring up," said my father.

"No. No. Go on. Ring her up at once. She will be very disappointed if you don't," I said.

It had occurred to me that if my mother rang up, Mrs Heber from politeness would be unable to contradict my message. In this way I would get my parents and Miss Morris to the party. Afterwards I could tell Miss Morris that she owed the evening to my ingenuity. She would, I felt sure, be impressed and deeply grateful.

Miss Morris was anxious to hear about Lord Swords.

"It reminds me of *Pride and Prejudice*," she said. "The young lord coming to the quiet neighbourhood and all the girls expecting to find a husband."

"That is not my recollection of *Pride and Prejudice*," said my father, who rather liked to tease Miss Morris.

"Oh, well. It was roughly like that," she said.

"Exactly," said my mother, who was not a reader of books. "Every unmarried woman for miles around will pursue him. And in the end he will marry some frump in England. Unless he is not the marrying kind. He won't meet much temptation in his own circle. I wonder why girls of good family so often have that underdone look. It is quite extraordinary, as though there was a curse on the Irish peerage."

"Mrs Heber says it is very rude to talk about people marrying," I said.

"Prenez garde à l'enfant," said my father, looking anxiously at my mother.

"It's time you were in bed, Brian," she said.

"What about our game of croquet? You promised to play with me," I implored my father.

"Come along, I will play with you," said Miss Morris.

"We will all play," said my father.

He and I played against my mother and Miss Morris. It was really the greatest fun. No one minded my bad play.

Mother cheated all the time. No one seemed to mind that either. We played until Alice came out to say 'the Mistress is wantin' on the telyphone.' It was Mrs Heber, she added. My heart knocked inside me. I was strongly tempted to beg my mother not to mention the dinner party. But I hesitated. And then it was too late. It seemed an hour until my mother came out of the house again. By then everyone except me had lost interest in the game.

"Go off to bed, Brian. It's long after your bed-time," said my mother. She did not appear to be upset. I longed to know what had been said.

"What is the news from the Palace?" said my father.

"I will tell you," said my mother. "Run along, Brian. I will come up and see you when you are in bed."

I saw the three grown-ups looking after me walking as slowly as possible across the lawn and the gravel sweep and into the house. I stopped at the door and looked back. The grown-ups were still looking in my direction, their faces in shadow, cigarettes glowing, waiting to talk when I was gone.

Mrs Heber called next day. It was most unusual to see her out of her own domain, unusual indeed to see her moving. She walked, I noticed, quite swiftly, holding herself very straight. I had observed her arrival from my hiding place in the laurels, and I was beside her before she could knock at our door.

"Hello, Mrs Heber," I said.

"What are you up to now, Brian?" she replied. But she had her laughing look on, so I did not take offence at her question.

"I wonder if your mother would care for these," she said. It was then I saw that she carried a brace of pheasants in a basket.

"It is very good of you, but I am sure she doesn't need them," I said. I had a complex about people giving things away, and thought it was one's duty to refuse gifts except at Christmas and on birthdays.

"They might be a treat," she urged. "We were sent two brace, and Mr Heber is forbidden to touch game. It does dreadful things to him."

"Go on, keep them. Eat them yourself. We have plenty to eat here," I protested.

Mrs Heber laughed and rang the bell.

"The door is open," I said. "Mummy is sorting out the hot-press. It's in a mess."

I turned the handle and let Mrs Heber in. Alice was settling her cap in the hall preparatory to answering the knock. Our arrival nonplussed her. But I ran past her calling out "Mrs Heber is here" with the vigour of an angel on the last day. Alice had recovered sufficiently to show Mrs Heber into the drawing-room before my mother appeared to see what the row was about. I noticed how ruffled and red-faced she looked in comparison with Mrs Heber, who was powdered and wore a veil. As she came forward to greet my mother she looked like the good fairy in the pantomime.

To my embarrassment the present of game was accepted by my mother without demur. I hovered in the background anxious to see how she got on with Mrs Heber, anxious also, I must confess, to see how my mother would acquit herself. Was there the vaguest hint of condescension in Mrs Heber's manner to my mother? I assumed that Mrs Heber came from some exalted sphere and that this was her manner towards every woman. My mother was by no means a plain woman, but she was not a beauty, and she had a very natural, democratic manner. With Mrs. Heber she was always a little ill at ease. In those days people were not so apt to use Christian names as they are now. My father called other men by their surname as a rule, and Mrs Heber and my mother were always "Mrs" to one another. Alice produced cups of tea, and a tin of shortbread. Mrs Heber, though originally she declared she was merely stopping to give us the game, showed no signs of hurrying away. Indeed, she and my mother after the inevitable "Prenez garde à l'enfant" lapsed so often into French that I was disgusted but not surprised when it was suggested that I should run away and play. It was unfair. I listened to grown-up conversation, but I never interrupted. There was no valid reason for getting rid of me.

"Where is your nice governess?" said Mrs Heber.

"I don't know."

"In the village," said my mother. "She jumps on the bicycle and hares off on messages like a despatch-rider. I never saw such a girl."

Mrs Heber looked disappointed. Then I realised that she had come to see Miss Morris. It would, I felt, be bad luck in the circumstances to have to give away the birds. They had only been an excuse to see Miss Morris. And when at length Mrs Heber rose to go, I ran round the back of the house, behind the laurels, and met her at the gate. I handed her the pheasants which I had pulled off their hook in the larder.

"Please take them back," I said. "Honestly, we don't need them."

Mrs Heber gave me a look of absolute astonishment, and then the laughing look came over her face again. At that moment Miss Morris came up on the bicycle.

"What is he up to?" she said.

"I have given his mother these birds and he is trying to persuade me to take them home again," said Mrs Heber.

She was surveying Miss Morris very thoroughly, looking her all over, missing nothing. I could see this because I knew Mrs Heber's mannerisms. This was the way she looked at china or silver, about which she told me she knew a great deal.

Miss Morris, for her part, was strangely subdued. The mocking look left her eyes. She seemed to be fascinated by Mrs Heber, who was smiling at her in that way she had of seeming to offer a share in a world where everything was graceful and well ordered, where noise and trouble could never enter. Mrs Heber was more like a person in a book than a real-life character. What would happen if she met the Queen? I wondered. It was hard to imagine Mrs Heber deferring to anyone. I could imagine the two ladies approaching each other like ships in the Spanish Main, neither prepared to lower her flag.

Mrs Heber talked in her most attractive way to Miss Morris; but I was not allowed to hear all they said: as usual, I was told to go away when the conversation began to be interesting. This time the birds were used as a pretext.

"Put them back where you found them or I shall give you Hell," said Miss Morris in a cheerfully ferocious way she had. I ran off with the pheasants—wonderfully fast for me. I was a stout child, short of leg, and not a natural athlete. But fast as I ran, when I came back Mrs Heber and Miss Morris were out of sight, and the bicycle was lying against the hedge. I felt angry with both of them. I wanted to make them know how badly they had treated me. I was forbidden to bicycle on the road by myself. So, for revenge, I got up on Miss Morris's machine and rode away, unable to reach the saddle, but managing well enough. If I got into trouble my mind was made up: I would lay the blame on Miss Morris. Why had she gone away with Mrs Heber? Why had she left the bicycle on the side of the road? What else could I do but get up and go for a ride? It was all her fault.

*   *   *

There was a great deal of discussion next morning in which, as usual, except to listen, I took no part. Mrs Heber must have taken a great liking to Miss Morris, because our household was now fully in league with Drumbeg (as the Hebers' house was called). And we were giving a party for Doreen, and my parents and Miss Morris were, after all, going to the famous dinner.

Miss Morris had received a letter in the post which I noticed she did not open immediately. I thought it might be a bill. My mother never opened bills. But if it had been a bill surely Miss Morris would have tossed it aside. As soon as she saw this letter, she pushed it into her pocket. When the plans for the parties were being discussed I thought Miss Morris seemed distracted. She made an excuse and left the room. Now she is reading the letter, I thought. At eleven she said casually (but I felt that she had been preparing for some time to say it) that she had to go to visit Mrs Hone to collect a box of eggs. There was nothing surprising in this. Miss Morris was always going out on messages. But today my mother said, "Take Brian with you. The walk will do him good."

I was delighted at this; but Miss Morris looked as though she was going to object. Then she thought better of it and said: "He looks tired. Would he not be better off in the garden?"

But I chimed in at this, before anyone could prevent it, and insisted that I should be allowed to go.

"Why did you not want me to come with you?" I said as soon as we had left the house.

"I thought it would bore you," she said. She was looking about her and humming tunes to herself, which was a habit of hers when she was alone with me. It maddened me.

"No girl will go out with you if you lean on her when you are walking," she said.

I jumped away and felt foolish. I had never learned to walk beside someone without bumping them. I had a rolling way of walking as though the road was the deck of a ship in a heavy sea. When I kicked Miss Morris's ankle she said nothing, but put her hands firmly on my shoulders and led me to the far side of the road. I was tempted to turn back, but there was something in Miss Morris's manner which aroused my curiosity. It reminded me of my own feelings when the theatre goes dark just before the curtain goes up.

Not far from our house there was a turn to the right: as we came round the corner I saw a coupé of flashy design pulled up at the side of the road. A man was sitting at the wheel. He was sunburnt and he wore an army officer's moustache. When we came up to the car, he took off his hat, and Miss Morris said: "Hello, I am in charge of Brian."

"Hello, Brian," said the man. He smiled at me in too friendly a way, and I could see he was thinking about something else.

"I dropped my pipe some way back," he said, looking hard at Miss Morris.

"Bad luck," she said. "We must keep a look out for it."

"What kind of car is that?" I asked.

"An A.C.," he said. "Do you like it? Would you like to come for a drive?"

I looked at Miss Morris.

"Come in, both of you," he said. "You climb in at the back, Bill."

The back was a dickey seat greatly exposed to the air. But I enjoyed the drive. When we arrived at the Hones' house, Miss Morris asked our driver to stop. She went in for the eggs, and I was left alone with him. Then he said: "Look here, Bill. Let's organise search parties to find that pipe of mine. I will give you half-a-crown if you get it."

"Couldn't we drive along the road slowly and keep a look out?"

"That is not the way to do things, Bill. That is the lazy way. What I suggest is that we drop you at the next corner, and Miss Morris and I will drive on to the place I met you. We will start there and search back in your direction. In that way we can't miss it."

The prospect of being left alone to search while this man and Miss Morris went off in the sports-car depressed me immediately.

"What about a payment on account," said the stranger, taking a half-crown out of his pocket and pressing it into my palm. I was fond of money and very rarely handled any. I could hardly believe he was serious.

"I couldn't take it," I said. "Really I don't want anything for searching. I often look for things."

"Never look a gift horse in the mouth, Bill," he said, and turned to open the door for Miss Morris, who had come back with the eggs.

He explained his plan to her. "We put Bill down here," he said.

"Brian is the child's name," she said in a voice which confirmed my impression that Miss Morris had met this man before.

I made a conscientious search on each side of that long, dusty road. It must have taken me at least half an hour. I saw no sign of the others coming towards me; but when I got back to the stretch of road on which the A.C. had been parked earlier in the day, I saw it in the same place. The driver was apparently sitting at the wheel alone; I saw the shining black back of his head, leaning rather to one side. When I shouted at him, Miss Morris's head popped up suddenly like a Jack in the Box; and by the time I got up to the car she was getting out. She looked as though she had been sitting too close to the fire; her face, usually so pale, was flushed; her hair was untidy, and her clothes were all rumpled. It was not at all like her usual self. When she played tennis she had a most serene appearance, never showed any agitation, even when she was losing. And I never saw her with a hair out of place. Something had happened to upset her. I could see that. She hurried me away without letting me say good-bye properly. For the first time since I met her she held my hand on the way home. No one had done that to me for years. It would have seemed a very babyish thing to do. But I did not mind Miss Morris doing it. In fact, I liked it, and it seemed to give her some comfort. When we got to the beginning of the garden hedge, she turned round and faced me.

"Brian," she said. "Can you keep a secret?"

"Of course."

"Well, will you promise not to mention that man we met today? I never want to hear of him again. He is no friend of mine. I am upset that he knows where I live. And if you ever see him again, pretend you have never seen him. Will you promise? And if you keep your promise I will give you anything you ask me for. But of course we must wait to see how you keep your word."

"I promise," I said. "I won't even tell Mrs Heber."

"For Heaven's sake! Not Mrs Heber by any means, or anyone else. Promise?"

"Promise."

There must have been considerable conviction in my voice because Miss Morris suddenly lightened up. Her manner had been sad and Novemberish when we walked along hand-in-hand: now she dropped my hand; her step was lighter; her face lost its worried look; it was as if the sun had come out all of a sudden.

"And where are the eggs?" said my mother.

"The eggs! Oh damn! I left them in the——"

"They fell and broke on the road and we had to throw them away," I said.

My mother looked from one of us to the other.

"Well, you are a nice pair," she said. "But we have lashings of eggs. I couldn't make out what the attraction at the Hones' was."

"I am terribly sorry," said Miss Morris. "It was all my fault. You must let me pay you for them."

She was flushed and embarrassed, reminding me of how she had looked that morning after her ride in the mysterious coupé.

*   *   *

The night of the Hebers' dinner was intensely exciting. My mother had a new dress and Miss Morris was wearing one that she had bought for a ball earlier in the year. Doors were never shut in our house, and that night the two women talked to one another while they dressed, or rushed back and forth to assist in back-buttoning, or to consider the merits of a necklace or a bangle. My mother insisted that Miss Morris should take a loan of a pair of ear-rings. My father, looking very self-conscious, produced two little white boxes, one of which he gave to my mother and the other to Miss Morris. In each there was a rather disappointing flower. "Orchids! How heavenly," said Miss Morris. "You *are* extravagant, darling," said my mother.

She rushed away to get pins to fix the flowers in their dresses. My father stood there looking proud and rather silly.

"Kind. Kind. Kind," said Miss Morris softly.

Our house was very small. You could almost stretch your arms across the landing. I wandered round interested in the preparations. There was not space enough for me in my father's dressing-room when he was using it. My mother, who was energetic in her movements, kept bumping into me when I stayed with her, so that, after a while, she begged me to leave her. I offered to help Miss Morris, who seemed to need it (or why was she consulting my mother at every turn?), but she shoved me out of her room as if I were a straying hen. We had no motor car, but in honour of the occasion my father had hired the local taxi, a T model Ford. I was quite overcome by the grandeur of my mother in a black dress covered with sequins, my father in a dinner-jacket, and Miss Morris, like an angel, in white. The hooded Ford completed the romantic picture. I tried to imagine what the party would be like. I saw my parents inspiring enormous respect, and Miss Morris evoking raptures. There was an advertisement in our railway station depicting men in full evening dress, some with monocles, some with flowing moustaches, seated at a long table with a shining white cloth. Beside the men were ladies in dresses with muttonchop sleeves and almost naked fronts. Behind them waiters marched carrying enormous dish covers. DINE AT THE DOLPHIN was written across this wonderful picture. Some such scene was now being enacted at the Hebers', I had no doubt.

I tried to stay awake to hear about the party when the grown-ups came home. The blind was up and the curtains in my room were not drawn; a branch tapped lightly against the window pane; the moon, surrounded by a milky circle, appeared and disappeared as clouds went racing across its misty face. Down in the kitchen I could hear the comforting rumble of Jane's voice and Alice's rather dotty laugh. But I was asleep before the family came home.

*   *   *

I was up before everyone as usual and did my survey of the bedrooms. Everyone was asleep. My father snoring just a little; Miss Morris with one arm hanging down over the side of the bed looked like a picture of Chatterton, the boy poet, after he had poisoned himself. I crept very near to make sure she was breathing all right.

Bored, I went back to bed and added an instalment to the serial story which I used to tell myself, and into which I had lately introduced a Miss Morris (somewhat transfigured and much better disposed towards me than in real life). At seven o'clock there were sounds from downstairs telling that Jane and Alice had got up. At half-past seven Alice came with early morning tea. Until then I was not supposed to leave my room. We breakfasted at eight o'clock because my father had to get an early train to Dublin. This morning I was alone with him. Breakfast on trays were going up to my mother and Miss Morris. The last—an idea of my father's—was causing heavy weather in the kitchen. "Who does she think she is?" Jane was muttering to Alice (who left the talking to Jane). Alice never talked at all. She had that funny laugh instead. And she broke things.

I hated meals when my mother was not with us. My father had a way of eating porridge (which he called stirabout) that got on my nerves; and between each noisy mouthful he glanced at the paper. He was not interested in the least in my conversation.

"Did you enjoy the party?"
"Yes. Thank you."
"Who was there?"
"Just ourselves and one or two people you don't know."
"Was Doreen there?"
"The party was given in her honour."
"Was it what you would call a family party?"

"Yes. No. What are you talking about? Can't you see I'm trying to read the paper?"

"Mrs Heber said it was only a family party. And she wasn't going to ask you and Mummy to it."

"Wasn't she?"

"What do you mean exactly by a family party?"

"One that your family comes to, I suppose. Eat up your stirabout."

"It's lumpy."

"You are making excuses."

"I think Mrs Heber didn't think you were grand enough to meet Lord Swords. Why did she change her mind, I wonder?"

"You are not to talk like that, Brian. This comes from hanging round the kitchen."

"I never talk about Mrs Heber in the kitchen."

"You are forbidden to go into the kitchen."

"Did Lord Swords propose to Doreen?"

"Not in my hearing. Damn it, boy. Eat up your breakfast. It is getting cold."

And when I tried to talk about the party again, he said I had egg all over my mouth.

As I climbed the stairs I heard my mother talking to Miss Morris, who, I could see, was sitting at the end of my mother's bed, wrapped in a pink dressing-gown, cuddling the cat.

"How would you like to wake up in the morning and find that face beside you?" my mother said. Mrs Heber used to draw herself in like a cat that has stepped on wet grass when my mother spoke like that. But Miss Morris laughed and said: "Love is blind."

And my mother said: "Wait until you are married. I don't think I could have done it even for a title. He is so plain. God love him."

I knew they were talking about Lord Swords without Miss

Morris saying: "Prenez garde à l'enfant" when she saw me on the stairs.

But my mother was in her most ebullient mood, and I heard all about the party. Lord Swords's shirt stud had come adrift. He was pink underneath. Mrs Heber had looked marvellous, quite subduing her niece who wore a string of real pearls. The soup had been cold. A glass of brandy after dinner had made my father very talkative. Mr Heber had taken Miss Morris into his study to show her his snuff-boxes.

"It was very cold," she said.

"Irish Protestants always economise on fuel," said my mother.

"He told me the history of every box. I think he has about sixty. All locked away in a cabinet. I thought we should never get back to the drawing-room."

"I am always suspicious of connoisseurs," said my mother. "You will find that where there is too much attention paid to the silver and glass there is usually a saving on the dinner. Grandeur is all very well, but I like my comfort."

"Lord Swords wants me to play with him in the Malahide Tournament," said Miss Morris, lifting up a foot and examining it with an air of great concentration.

"What will Doreen say? And Dick will be furious. You did so well together yesterday."

"Will Mr Allen mind? I wish I could learn to say 'no'. I say 'yes' to everything. Should I try to get out of it?"

"Why should you? Dick can play with Doreen. I wonder if Mrs Heber would give me the recipe for that pudding."

"Wasn't it good!"

"I was longing for a second helping."

"Well, Brian. What have you been up to?"

It always ended like that.

*   *   *

"Be a sport, Bill. Tell her I'm out here."

I had been fast asleep, lying against the haycock. My book had fallen out of my hand. A great black figure came between me and the sun. He was bending towards me, his hands on his knees, looking down at me as if I were a fish at the bottom of a pool.

"My name is not Bill."

"I call you Bill. I call all my friends Bill. Will you tell Miss Morris I am here? Quietly, mind you. Tell her I want to see her. Here's something for the money-box."

"But she is not here. They went off hours ago to the tennis tournament in Malahide. I couldn't go. I had a pain after lunch. Miss Morris doesn't want to see you."

"How do you know?"

"She told me. She meant it, too."

"She did, did she? Well, when you get to my age, Bill, you will discover that women say one thing and do another. Give her that letter. Don't forget."

"Did you come in the A.C.?"

"I did."

"May I have a look at it?"

"Yes, if you hurry. I am not supposed to be here."

In our neighbourhood only four people had motor cars. And none of them were new. I had never seen anything so dashing as the A.C. It almost endeared its owner to me. But he was in no mood to discuss motor cars with me today. He was very jumpy and nervous.

"I must be off. Get in if you want a drive. But you will have to walk back."

We roared along the Dublin Road, skilfully avoiding pot holes. I was exhilarated by the speed, 50 m.p.h. I wanted to go on, but when at last I was put out on the side of the road, I was further from home than I had ever been before. I got back tired and cross and dusty a few minutes before the tennis players returned.

The tournament had been a disaster. The switching of partners had been bad for everyone's game. Personally, I was sorry for Doreen who had been left with my father. He was not much good; old, married, and not even a lord. I thought Lord Swords had behaved very badly. From what my mother said that was the general impression. What Miss Morris thought I could not discover. She was very silent. When I got the chance to see her alone, I gave her the letter. She snatched it from me.

"Where did you see him? When did he come? Oh, this is too much," she said.

I wanted to comfort her, to tell her not to be so sad, to plan some way of keeping this bothersome man away from her. But I could not get near Miss Morris now or ever. And when she was unhappy she was so far out of reach that it was hopeless to try even to talk to her. She was away in another place. She did not see me. Shouting would be no use. She would not hear. I gave her the piece of sponge cake I was eating. When I came back it was lying on the table where I had put it down beside her. I threw it away. I hadn't the heart to eat it.

*   *   *

"Lindy is coming," said my father.

"Oh, not now. He would choose the most inconvenient time. Trust Lindy," said my mother.

"He says: I have two days off and will come down this evening. Don't let me be a nuisance, or change any of your plans on my account. And any corner of the house will do me. I only want straw to lie on and a place to rest my head."

"Who would think," said my father, putting down the

letter, "that should come from the arch-grumbler of the western world?"

"Prenez garde à l'enfant," said my mother.

"Is Uncle Lindy coming?" I said, feeling that I had in a sense been included in the conversation.

"This evening. If you are good you may come down to the station to meet him," said my mother.

Uncle Lindy was my father's half-brother and his senior by fifteen years. He was an inspector in the Bank of Ireland. Worrying bank managers was a task for which he was eminently suited. Uncle Lindy was a born worrier. I did not greatly care for him because he never gave me anything when he came to see us. And he was a fearless critic of my way of life.

Disapproval hung about him like a cloud. But he never depressed us because my mother made a butt of him, laughed at his jeremiads, and held him up to me as a warning and not as an example.

"Stop making faces. You don't want to grow up looking like your Uncle Lindy," was a remark which frequently recurred in my home education.

A problem arose immediately as to where he was to sleep. The hypothetical figure sleeping in the straw would have to remain a hypothesis. But it was not immediately apparent what the alternative was. For the fact had to be faced that Miss Morris occupied the spare room to which Uncle Lindy considered he had a prescriptive right. The usurpation of his bed by a young woman, my governess by courtesy, but discharging no official duties, was something that he would fail to understand. It was a new situation; but it was characteristic of the sort of situation into which my parents' cheerful nature often led them. The room which former governesses had occupied had been converted into a workshop, apple-store and left-luggage office. My room was an attic in which Uncle Lindy could never have stood at his full height.

The problem was easily solved when Miss Morris heard us talking. She came up to my room. I went in with the apples. All traces of feminine occupation had to be removed from Uncle Lindy's room, and the large steel engraving of 'The Retreat from Moscow' restored to its former site over the chimney.

Miss Morris, who had a wonderful faculty for throwing off sadness as though it were a passing shower, resembling in this my mother, whose moods had the characteristics of the Irish climate—Miss Morris was intrigued by the onset of Uncle Lindy, and insisted that we should all go to the station to meet him.

"It's no use setting your cap at Lindy," my mother warned. "He is a confirmed misogynist."

I happened to be passing when this remark was made, and it gave me something to puzzle over for the afternoon. Miss Morris had no cap to my knowledge. She was very quick to clear me away when she found me in her room, and, perhaps, there were things there that the phrase "Prenez garde à l'enfant" applied to. Assuming that she had a cap, how did she set it? I thought of a hen hatching eggs—my mother went in for poultry in a small way—but that made no sense. *Misogynist* baffled me completely. I tried to look it up in the dictionary but having no idea how to spell it only added to my confusion. The mystery added greatly to Uncle Lindy's prestige. Hitherto there had been nothing mysterious about him except the fact that he was only half an uncle and therefore different from ordinary uncles. Now he was involved in some way in Miss Morris's private world. Everything to do with her had a fascination for me.

The train was late. In those days the railway system was disorganised. Railway bridges were blown up from time to time. Everyone worked under difficulties. Ten minutes after the appointed time our anticipation, whetted by delay, was rewarded by the sight of the familiar figure climbing down from the carriage wearing as always the disgruntled expression of the ugly sisters in Cinderella. Whenever Uncle Lindy used anything, even a step, he gave the impression of someone who was being put upon. He was very tall and thin, dressed always in black: and the appearance of an undertaker which he gave at a distance was modified on closer inspection. He wore pince-nez with a ribbon attached to them. Perched on his thin and prominent nose these gave him the air of a bird, not an eagle or a vulture; a secretary bird, perhaps. Out of a nostril grew a solitary whisker.

"Lindy has bought himself a new hat," said my father. My uncle was famous for his economy, and any sign of a relaxing of purse strings was always hailed by my parents with amused surprise. He had indeed bought a hat. It was large and grey. Coming down the platform he looked a little like pictures of President Wilson at the Peace Conference.

"He must be *much* older than you," said Miss Morris to my father (to his obvious satisfaction, I noticed). Miss Morris had a talent for pleasing people by the things she said. She could have thrown me into raptures had she bothered to talk to me.

"Hello, Lindy," said my father.

"Lindy!" said my mother.

"Hello, Uncle Lindy," I said.

Miss Morris said nothing. Uncle Lindy relaxed his expression of pained concentration as an acknowledgement of our welcome, and then his eyes were fixed on Miss Morris as though she were an error in a statement of account which required an immediate explanation.

"This is Miss Morris, Lindy, Brian's new governess. She has been a great help to us this summer."

"How do you do, Miss Morris," said Uncle Lindy.

I expected him to treat Miss Morris with the severity with which he treated me and, indeed, anything in life that savoured of youth or freedom or pleasure; but I noticed with astonishment that he attempted to look gay. I was as much surprised as if a preacher put on a false nose in the middle of a sermon.

Instead of rushing into complaints, Uncle Lindy talked to Miss Morris all the way home. Perhaps because he was not used to conversing with young women he used me as the subject of his conversation. 'How is Brian getting on?' 'What do you teach him?' 'Has he started Latin yet?' 'I hope you will make him write a legible hand.' 'Does he give you a lot of trouble?' 'I hope you give him a leathering when he deserves it.'

Uncle Lindy was about a foot taller than Miss Morris; and each time he made a remark he bent his head down to her, lifting it up again as though consulting the sky about her answers. From behind he looked like a hen at a feeding trough: down to peck an answer; up again to swallow it.

After dinner the four grown-ups sat down to bridge. I hid myself in the armchair and kept very quiet. On these occasions an hour beyond my bed-time could sometimes be snatched by prudence.

My father was a bad bridge player, being both slow and unenterprising. My mother was better, having a flair for most things. But Miss Morris was in Uncle Lindy's class, that is to say she was the first good player he had encountered in our house, where the bridge like everything else was more casual than serious.

"If I had known you had the ace of diamonds . . ." said Uncle Lindy with an aggrieved air to my mother after one hand.

"There would be no game if you knew where every card was," said my mother, by no means perturbed.

Uncle Lindy sniffed and shuffled the pack with excessive thoroughness like a man who does his duty in circumstances of exceptional difficulty.

Miss Morris and my father were winning. Instead of despairing of him as my mother did, or getting angry like Uncle Lindy, Miss Morris made an imaginative allowance for his shortcomings.

'I guessed you had the spades.' 'When you said two diamonds I knew you held every club in the pack.' 'Trust you to have the good old King of Hearts'—by saying things like this Miss Morris showed that she could play for my father as well as for herself. He looked very happy. He loved getting the better of Uncle Lindy. And the way Miss Morris went on gave the impression that my father was positively brilliant, incapable of making a mistake.

At ten o'clock Alice brought in tea and cake on a tray. Very foolishly I made my presence known by asking for a piece of sponge cake. I could not resist it. It was quite fresh and had a lovely smell.

"Do you mean to say Brian stays up to ten o'clock?" said Uncle Lindy.

"I must confess I forgot he was there," said my mother.

I was very sleepy but I noticed the way Uncle Lindy looked at me and then at Miss Morris as much as to say, 'What had happened to the regulations!'

"Off you hop," said Miss Morris.

As I went out of the room I heard Uncle Lindy say: "I suppose he is old enough to put himself to bed." And then my mother said something, and my father said: "Dorothy, you are dreadful," and Miss Morris laughed in a shy way, and Uncle Lindy said: "Well. Let's get on with the game."

When I was in bed my mother came up as always and tucked me in and kissed me and asked if I had said my prayers. I usually chose this moment of the day to ask whatever seemed to me the most pressing question of the moment. Tonight I said:

"Is Miss Morris setting her cap at Uncle Lindy?"

"I'll ask her," said my mother and left the room laughing. I heard the murmur of voices in the drawing-room suddenly louder as the door downstairs was opened and my mother saying: "You had better look out, Lindy——" Then the door shut. A concerted yell of laughter in which I could hear Miss Morris and my father distinctly told me that my question had been repeated. A blush of shame made me hate my mother for a moment. And then I experienced a quite new feeling, a complacent awareness that I could make people laugh by what I said. Perhaps it was the most effective way of attracting attention. Devotion seemed to count for very little.

* * *

'They can't see me' was my first thought when I heard Uncle Lindy's voice, high and hard, a corncrake's voice, coming down the garden, punctuated by my father's, softer, more doubtful notes; dissenting, but gently: a warble against his brother's croak. I sat up in the chestnut tree, in the place I had found quite recently—for I had been far from a precocious tree-climber, being heavy, clumsy, and therefore, by nature, earthbound. I lay back on the wide stout branch and propped my feet firmly against the fork. They were underneath me now. I looked down on the priest's tonsure on the top of Uncle Lindy's grey head and my father's very black but thinning hair. They walked very slowly; my father's hands behind his back; Uncle Lindy holding a lapel of his coat with one hand and using the other like a flail. It went up and swept down, a threat to any arguments in his immediate vicinity. Under the tree they paused. Then my father said: "Let's sit in the shade here. If we go up to the house we will have to be civil to Miss Tite, and I don't feel up to it at this time of day, decent woman though she is."

Miss Tite was a neighbour who had a moustache and several dogs that rushed out, barking, when you passed her house.

My father and my uncle sat down on the grass bank at the foot of the tree. My father was smoking a pipe, and Uncle Lindy one of my father's cigarettes. (It was a family joke that Uncle Lindy never produced any of his own.)

Neither spoke at first. My father lay comfortably on his side, propping himself on an elbow. Uncle Lindy sat bolt upright, like an Indian chief. You could never imagine a comfortable Uncle Lindy. He was all bones and corners and edges. He seemed to be looking out for something, expecting trouble to loom up. There they sat while I waited wondering who would speak first. I might have guessed.

"All I can say is: Thank God the governor didn't live to see it," said Uncle Lindy.

"How old would the governor have been if he were alive now?" said my father. He wanted to head Uncle Lindy off. I knew it from the way his tone of voice suggested some new and interesting topic.

"Eighty-five," said Uncle Lindy quickly. He never liked to have conversation taken out of his control. "It would have killed him," he continued in a tragic tone.

"I am sure he would have been grateful for that extra twenty years," said my father dryly.

"I don't know. I don't know. The suffragettes. Lloyd George. The War. And now this Sinn Fein horror—I think the governor was lucky to have gone when he did."

"We have survived them, Lindy. I suppose we will survive this present trouble; but I must say I sometimes wonder what is going to happen to loyalists in this country."

"Oho. I know what is going to happen to them; that little Welsh rat will sell them up the river. Mark my words. And when he hands us over to de Valera & Co. we will be lucky if they don't cut our throats. Mark my words."

I waited breathless to hear what my father would reply to this. Was this what my parents were so anxious to keep from me?

"I must say you always take the gloomy view of things, Lindy."

"I only speak the truth. I face facts. People don't like it. But I can't help that."

"I think there will be a split in the coalition. The Unionists will form a government. They will give this problem to the Army to tackle. A firm hand would settle the hash of these ruffians in six months. You wait and see."

"I expect we shall all be murdered in our beds whatever happens," said Uncle Lindy with a certain relish.

"I don't see much future for Brian," said my father.

I felt queer inside at hearing myself being talked about. It was exciting but not natural. I should have called out when I saw them, but I hesitated. Now it was too late.

"I don't see much future for any of us. The Sinn Feiners will take the Bank for their parliament house. And the country will be bankrupt in any case," said Uncle Lindy.

"You ought to get one of the Chancery men to write you an opinion that you are a Bank fixture. Then you could pass with the building. Would you like to be Speaker of the Sinn Fein House of Commons, Lindy?"

"Joking costs nothing," said Uncle Lindy sourly. I could see that he thought my father was not taking him seriously enough. This is what always happened in our house to Uncle Lindy.

"Talking about the boy—you know I never interfere, Dick.

I live on the principle that we all have enough to do looking after ourselves without trying to look after other people's business—but I think I owe it to you to say I am worried about Brian. Why is he not at school? He is too much with old people. And what in the name of all that's wonderful is the idea of this governess? She is a charming young woman. I have eyes in my head. But she is as fit to teach that boy lessons as I am to teach her the fox-trot."

"Get her to teach you, Lindy."

"I have no doubt it would be an agreeable experience. But seriously, Dick. What does it mean? What are people going to say? How long will Dorothy put up with it? Is it fair to Dorothy?"

"Is what fair to Dorothy? What are you driving at? Dorothy suggested Miss Morris. I had nothing to do with it. I agreed. That's all."

"No one is going to think that, Dick. And Dorothy is going to forget it pretty soon. Mark my words. I know the world, and I have some experience of women. And I am telling you, if you don't stop this nonsense now, you will live to regret it."

"What are you implying?"

I had never heard my father sound like this before. His voice had become cold. It seemed to belong to some other person.

Uncle Lindy wavered. Then he went on with a forced air, as though he was defying my father:

"What I say is: If you want a governess by all means get a governess—personally I think the boy is too old for governesses; but that is only a private opinion. I don't interfere in other people's concerns. And if you want a doxy, get a doxy. But don't . . ."

"Damn it all Lindy. How dare you say that. You ought to know me."

"You were always very susceptible, Dick."

"But I mean to say . . . a girl of two-and-twenty . . . at my age. And it's an insult to her. She is a thoroughly nice girl. It's damnably insulting. You go too far, Lindy. I don't mind you being a killjoy about most things; but when it comes to taking away a young woman's character, I draw the line."

"It is not I who am taking away her character. Believe you me, killjoy or not, I am only saying now what everyone will be saying tomorrow. I am your brother, Dick. I am fifteen years your senior, I think I have the right to speak when I see you making a fool of yourself."

My father jumped up. I could see Uncle Lindy had really upset him.

"Miss Morris stays here as long as Dorothy wants her to stay. And she goes when Dorothy wants her to go. And if you don't like it, Lindy, I won't compel you to distress yourself by staying in our house against your will. And if you please, keep your pleasant ideas to yourself when Dorothy is around. She will like them rather less than I do. Let's go in. It must be nearly lunch-time."

"Come on, Dick. Don't lose your temper. God knows I am only concerned for your welfare. Sit down and smoke another pipe. I want to talk to you about Aunt Tina's house in Dalkey."

My father sat down reluctantly. Then, in a voice I knew very well, he said: "Have you a cigarette on you, Lindy?"

Uncle Lindy slapped his pockets. "Damn it. I left them in my room," he said.

"It's all right. Don't worry. I think I have some of my own," said my father.

He did not offer one to Uncle Lindy. I think this was his revenge. He did not grudge the cigarette. But he wanted Uncle Lindy to know he had noticed one of his stingy ways.

It was because he was miserly and always complaining that Uncle Lindy had no authority in our house. He was really quite a clever man. But my mother used to say, 'What use are his brains to him? He lives like a charity child.'

After a while my father melted. He always did.

"Have a cigarette, Lindy," he said.

Uncle Lindy slapped his pockets once again.

"Thank you, Dick. I left mine inside. I have a match, though."

"Splendid," said my father.

I had been fairly uncomfortable for some time and was pressed, for a necessary purpose, to get down from the tree. Each time the conversation lagged I prayed: "Please God make them go in. Don't let them start talking again, please God." But God did not heed my prayer. At last I could stay no longer. "Prenez garde à l'enfant," I shouted and slid down the trunk, almost landing on top of Uncle Lindy.

"What the Hell!" he shouted.

"God in Heaven!" said my father.

But I did not wait. I ran as fast as I could towards the house.

*　　　　*　　　　*

Uncle Lindy stayed for two days. On the second day there was a tennis party at the Hebers'. My mother rang up to ask if Uncle Lindy could come. I heard her say to my father: "I hope he won't threaten Mrs Heber with his false teeth." He had an absent-minded habit of getting his tongue behind his teeth and pushing them forward with a grimace. It was alarming to strangers.

Left to myself when the family went to the party, I wandered off to the forge to talk to Freddy Doyle. Freddy was the blacksmith, but there were very few horses in the neighbourhood, and as no one allowed him to shoe valuable horses, he had an abundance of leisure to dispose of. Had I any choice of company I would not have seen much of Freddy, but there were no children in the immediate neighbourhood with whom I was allowed to play; and Freddy flattered me by listening to my conversation, asking me questions, and treating me with deference. I had been told to keep away from the forge. My parents did not care for Freddy. "As crooked as a ram's horn," my father said he was. "A sly-looking divil," said my mother. He was a notorious borrower. And I had to admit to myself that I could see reason in my parents' attitude. Freddy had a curious smile. It was a smile that did not believe in itself. He was always looking for something or asking for something. But I was not able—when I was lonely—to resist the lure of the forge.

Of late I had been a provider of wonderful gossip. Freddy wanted to hear about Miss Morris, about the parties, if 'his lordship' had been at the Hebers', and anything else I could tell him. Freddy shared my mother's view that Doreen Hailey had come to the Hebers with matrimonial intentions. Indeed, so excited did he become about this that nothing would content him but that I should go as far as the house, peep through the hedge and see if Lord Swords was at the tennis party. Freddy had a vaguely sinister authority over me. I went off at his command and trudged along the road against my will. The Hebers' garden was protected by a hedge and ditch on the road side. The hedge was of thorn bush, overgrown on the road side, but there were holes through which I could peer.

Four people were playing on the court. Miss Morris was playing with the parson who had lately arrived and who, according to my father, was mentally deficient. He certainly cut a strange figure on the court, missing every shot, and apologising almost simultaneously. Miss Morris wore a resigned expression which I knew only too well. Their opponents were Mr and Mrs Hone, who were swearing all the time in warm, strong voices. Mr Hone called the parson 'Padre', a word that I had not heard before, and which I assumed from the way in which he said it was derisive. I was sorry for Miss Morris to have to be running all over the court trying to hit balls which the poor parson with a cry of 'Sorry, partner', swiped vainly at, and missed.

On the far side of the court, spread out in a line on chairs and garden seats, I saw my mother talking to Miss Tite, and Doreen to Lord Swords (who lay on a rug and smoked a cigarette), and my father looking very serious, as he always did when making polite conversation, was seated beside a large woman in white. Mrs Heber, chin in hand, was smiling and talking to Colonel Clitheroe who called children brats and whom I was in some awe of. Uncle Lindy was making frightful faces at Mrs Clitheroe who stared into vacancy. I got the impression that no one was much interested in what was going on except, perhaps, Mrs Heber who was probably wondering how matters were faring on the rug. I could have told her that Doreen was not putting a spell on Lord Swords. I had seen the way the man with the A.C. car—the one who called me Bill—looked at Miss Morris. Anyone could tell that he was keen about her. There was something too peaceful about Lord Swords's manner. I knew he was not interested in what Doreen was saying. Freddy Doyle was far more interested in my conversation if it came to that.

I was distracted from the figure on the rug by Mrs Clitheroe who had caught sight of Uncle Lindy's teeth and watched him now with a horrified fascination. When at last he shut his mouth, she looked so relieved I almost burst out laughing.

"Tea," said Mrs Heber in her happy voice, getting up and smoothing her white dress with her long hands. Everyone got up and followed her in a slow procession, except Lord Swords who delayed to watch the tennis game.

He poked fun at the parson and cheered Miss Morris on. She laughed. Gone was her bored look and her mechanical gestures. Now she flew about the court and said encouraging words to her partner whenever he piped 'Sorry, partner' and hit the air.

I saw Doreen standing at the french window looking back. After a few minutes she, too, went into the house. I longed to follow her, knowing that scones and home-made jam and fruit cake and sponge cake and chocolate cake and coffee cake lay on the white table-cloth. (Mrs Heber laid out tea on the dining-room table for tennis parties.)

"Game, set and match. Bad luck, padre," said Mr Hone.

"That's a damn queer racquet you have. Who could play with a thing like that?" said Mrs Hone examining the parson's equipment with a critical eye. He had taken off his gold-rimmed spectacles and was rubbing the lenses with a red pocket-handkerchief.

Miss Morris had somehow got away ahead of the tennis players; Lord Swords had taken her racquet, and they were walking together into the house.

I ran back to Freddy to report.

*   *   *

I was not supposed to know that we lived in a time of political disturbance. Sometimes lorries swept by full of Black and Tans who sat with rifles in their hands under a wire cage. Freddy told me about the Black and Tans. He said they skinned babies alive. They murdered anyone they took an objection to. They made the man who owned the garage in Malahide sing *God Save the King* and then beat him until he was unconscious. Malahide was only a few miles away. I never talked about Sinn Feiners to Freddy because my father said: 'I am sure he is an out-and-out Sinn Feiner.' To be a Sinn Feiner meant to wear a black felt hat and trench coat (indoors and out regardless of the state of the weather) and to shoot people from behind hedges, and to burn down their houses. Black and Tans could be seen, but one could only guess who were Sinn Feiners. I believed that Black and Tans were a necessary evil, but that Sinn Feiners were anathema to all nice people. They 'drove everyone out of the country'. If Sinn Fein had its way there would be no more visits to Mrs Heber, no more tennis for Miss Morris, no Bank for Uncle Lindy, no job in Court for my father, no King, no Queen, no Prince of Wales, no visits to Dublin to buy Christmas presents and have tea at Mitchells in Grafton Street. Everything would be given up to men in black hats and trench coats with badges in their button-holes and cigarettes behind their ears.

*   *   *

The Café Cairo in Grafton Street and the Elysée in Dawson Street had *thé dansants* to which I knew Miss Morris sometimes went. I heard her discussing it with my mother. It was now October, and tennis parties were over.

"I don't like *the sound* of the Café Cairo, my dear," I heard my mother say.

One day to my intense surprise my mother said at breakfast: "We must let Brian come. He can keep me company." They had been discussing a party for Miss Morris's birthday. It was to be held at the Elysée and my father was to join us there as soon as he left the Courts.

"Will you dance?" I said to him.

"I can't do this fox-trotting," he said.

"Then why are you going to the party?"

"To pay for it," he said.

The Elysée was a long narrow room with tables at the sides

and a pianist and a violinist at the top. Large, fair-haired girls—they seemed to me in my excited state to be dreams of beauty. A waitress with a very friendly manner and a way of winking that I tried in vain to copy, brought us tea and scones, cakes and ice-cream. I was so pleased with it all, I could hardly bring myself to concentrate on the cakes, even on one iced in green.

Neither my mother nor Mrs Heber had been to this restaurant before. My mother seemed almost as excited as I was by the couples walking (as it seemed to me) face to face round the room. How, I wondered, did the girls prevent themselves from falling backwards? Mrs Heber had an expression of amused interest as if she were in the Zoo. She said something in a low voice to my mother.

"*I don't think they come here*," said my mother in her best attempt at a whisper. "They go to the other place. They say this is quite respectable."

"It would be so awful if someone started to throw bombs," said Mrs Heber.

"Prenez garde," said my mother quickly.

All our party was dancing: Mr Hone with Miss Morris, Lord Swords with Mrs Hone (who smoked while she danced and almost blinded him several times). My father had not yet come. I sat beside my mother who talked all the time to Mrs Heber.

"The poor child doesn't know what proper cakes are. Do you remember the cakes in Mitchell's before the war?" My mother did not wait for an answer, but continued, glancing in all directions.

"There is my dentist, the man with the toupée. It must be uncomfortable when he hots up. Have you seen any yet? Everyone looks very harmless. There! I see one. I am sure he is a Black and Tan—the one over there with the black moustache. I think I can see a gun in his pocket."

I was listening with one ear to the conversation at the table, with the other to the music; my concentration was spread over the cake plates and the couples on the floor. I was in a state of pleasant confusion. At my mother's last remark I looked up to see whom she was talking about.

Standing in the doorway with a girl who leaned her head against his shoulder as if to protect herself from a sudden shower, was the man with the A.C., the man who called me Bill. I wanted to shout a warning to Miss Morris. She had not seen his entry, being half-buried by Mr Hone who danced very awkwardly. To avoid constant collisions, he confined his manœuvres to a half-circle at the further end of the ball-room, near the band. When the music stopped he came back with Miss Morris to our table. They were laughing at something Miss Morris was saying. The Bill-man had his back turned. He was pulling up a chair for his partner who swayed as though she was unable to stand without a prop of some kind. I made signals to Miss Morris. She saw me but pretended not to. I caught her arm when she came near enough.

"Look out," I said. "He's here."

Everyone heard me. I did not intend that they should, but excitement must have intensified my whisper. Miss Morris was not impressed. She shook off my hand as she had shaken off my signal with a humiliating indifference. But at that moment the enemy turned round and looked in our direction. He saw Miss Morris and she saw him. He gave a playful wave to her and winked at me. Miss Morris blushed. Then she sat down and turned her back on the room. She was now quite pale.

"May I have a cigarette, Ossie?" she said to Lord Swords.

I saw Mrs Heber watching her with the close scrutiny that she had given her at their first meeting. She had seen the sudden change of colour. She looked with reflective disapproval at the cigarette. She was thinking very hard about Miss Morris. I could see that. If I needed further proofs I had them when my mother, who had a voice as loud and clear as a bugle, had to repeat a remark twice before Mrs Heber heard it. And when my father came in and stood before her, Mrs Heber gave a sudden gasp of recognition as if she had been woken out of sleep.

"Ah, Mr Allen. How nice to see you. Come and sit here beside me," she said, recovering wonderfully quickly. She patted an empty chair beside her and looked up, smiling at my father in her eager manner. When Mrs Heber was talking to my mother she had a way, as I have said before, of making my mother diminish in importance. But when she spoke to my father he seemed to swell a little. I looked at him with her eyes and saw that he did compare very favourably with Mr Hone, who looked grizzled, and with Lord Swords who reminded me of a poached egg. I looked at Miss Morris and saw that she was talking to Lord Swords in a way that was making him laugh. And he was looking at her as though it was a very hot day and she was a jug of lemonade. On the other side of the room sat the man with the A.C., his elbows on the table, smoking a cigarette. The tilting girl was leaning towards him. The way she did this reminded me of a teddy bear I had given to me when I was three. As the years went by it lost its stuffing and when it was placed in a chair it slumped like that girl forwards or backwards, whichever way it was pushed. But it never sat straight up. The man was talking very fast. But the girl said nothing. Perhaps she was afraid to open her mouth in that cloud of smoke.

I could only hear little bits of Miss Morris's conversation. She was more excitable than I had ever seen her before. It may have been the restaurant and the music, or it may have been fear of the man across the room; it was not, I was sure, on account of Lord Swords. The Hones were talking to my mother. They had very loud voices.

"A Black and Tan, did you say?" shouted Mrs Hone.

"Hush," said my mother.

"I can see his gun in the seat of his trousers," said Mrs Hone.

"That is a cigarette case," I said. "I saw him put it there."

"Prenez garde," said my mother.

Mrs Heber was talking very confidentially to my father who was leaning towards her and looking down at his chest. I knew from the way he looked up suddenly that Mrs Heber was telling him about the Black and Tan. After a while he leaned across to my mother and said something. She said, "Oh, I don't think so." "It would be fun," said Mrs Heber to my mother.

"Well, ask her," said my mother, looking at Miss Morris.

My father walked over to Miss Morris and said something which I could not hear. Her face was red again.

"I hardly know him," she said. "We are much better as we are."

I could see my father was pleased. I don't think he really liked Miss Morris to care too much for other people. I was just like that too. I wanted her to be happy with us, to stay with us always. When I was twenty-one we could get married. I happened to catch her eye at that moment and she beckoned to me. I went over at once.

"I will tan the hide off you," she whispered.

Even that, I thought, would be better than nothing. Lord Swords gave me a vague smile.

"What has the young man been up to?" he said.

"Oh, that is a secret," said Miss Morris.

I liked it when she said that. It gave me a comfortable feeling. I could see I was not wanted, so I went back to my tea. As no one bothered to talk to me I might as well eat as much as I could. I loved bought cakes. They were much more tempting to look at than home-made. But sometimes they disappointed. That sawdust taste was peculiar to them. I never got it in the jam sandwich or sponge cake at home.

"Come on and show these young people how to dance," said Mr Hone to my mother. She, to my dismay, having gone red, and protested that she had not 'put a leg under her' for ten years, gave in. I could see she was quite pleased by Mr Hone's compelling manner. He put his arm round her shoulders and guided her to the floor. My mother! At her age!

Uncle Lindy looking quite pleased with himself—he had been asked in despair when Mr Heber steadfastly refused to join the party—had Doreen cowering in a corner while he lectured her in his most vigorous manner, waving his arms and shooting out his teeth and crying 'Oho' or 'You don't need to tell me' in a loud and self-satisfied tone. My father looked at them and then at Lord Swords and then at Mrs Heber. But she pretended not to notice his dilemma. So he called out: "Miss Morris is not dancing. Take her round, Lindy. It will do wonders for your rheumatism."

Uncle Lindy, who hated interruption, acknowledged this instruction with a glare, and lectured Doreen more vigorously than before. It was Miss Morris who made the guests circulate. She jumped up and actually took Uncle Lindy by the hands and led him on to the floor. He looked very funny. But Miss Morris had a way of coping with everybody when she wanted to. And it was wonderful to see how she managed to get the two of them round the room, Uncle Lindy towering over her, on his face the expression a member of the audience wears when called up to assist a conjurer—sort of proud and silly. He was dancing to walking time although the band was playing a two-step. Lord Swords was very much amused by this. But I knew Miss Morris had been kind and only took Uncle Lindy away so that Doreen might dance with Lord Swords. I thought it was horrible of him not to understand. I saw Mrs Heber looking at him. I could only think of one thing to do. I had never learned to dance, but I could not make a worse attempt than Uncle Lindy's. It was only a matter of putting the invitation in suitable words. I ate up the cake I had in my mouth at the moment, and when I was able to speak I got up and went over to where Doreen sat. She looked quite unperturbed. Nothing seemed to please her very much or to make her sad either.

"Would you like to put a leg under you with me, Miss Hailey?" I said. We always called her 'Doreen', but when it came to the point I got shy about using her Christian name. She was, after all, thirteen years older than me.

"I'd love to," she said. "But since when have I become Miss Hailey?"

"This is rather a formal occasion for me," I said.

This reply seemed to please her. She led me out of the chairs and tables to the dance floor. But when we got there I was quite bewildered. Every time I moved, I kicked her or stood on her feet. And, worse still, people kept on crashing into us. I felt very hot. I hated it. I wanted to cry.

"You are doing splendidly," said Doreen. "Come on again. One. Two. One. Two. One. Two. There's no need to hop between the steps. Take it quietly. One. Two. One. Two. Don't worry about that. They are only an old pair. One. Two. Oh, I am so sorry. . . ." The last remark was made to a couple into whom we had backed at a corner.

"Steady, Bill," said the man to me.

I remembered what I had promised Miss Morris and I gave him a look of complete non-recognition. "And how is your Majesty this evening?" he said, with a big grin.

"George, you're awful," said the unstuffed girl in a terribly Dublin accent. It surprised me that the Black and Tan (of course I knew he was a Black and Tan) could have such a smart car and yet take out a girl who talked like that. I could quite understand why Miss Morris was ashamed to be a friend of his.

Then the Black and Tan gave me a smack on my behind. It knocked me head foremost into Doreen's stomach. But he gave such a loud laugh as he did it, I knew it was meant to be friendly.

"I am afraid he is a rough diamond," I explained to Doreen. But she had got so used to my way of dancing that I don't think she noticed that anything had gone wrong.

We stopped when we had made one round of the floor. My father must have said something to Lord Swords because when we came back to our table, he came over to Doreen and said: "May I take you away from your cavalier?" I was quite delighted. I hated every moment of the dance, and I had only offered myself so that Doreen should not feel neglected.

"Thank you very much, partner," she said.

"Well done, Brian," said my father.

Mrs Heber did not say anything. But she gave me a smile which told me she was very pleased. I felt quite a hero.

I could see that my father enjoyed his talk with Mrs Heber. He was like me in one thing. He was pleased when people made a fuss about him. I mean people like Mrs Heber and Miss Morris. Who would want Miss Tite to fuss over them? And I could see that she was happy, too. She said 'No, thank you,' very firmly when he asked her to dance. I wished my mother had been as sensible when Mr Hone jollied her into drawing attention to herself. I could hardly bring myself to look at her, although I could hear her laughing and Mr Hone chortling in his fog-horn voice. Mrs Hone shouted encouragement at them from the table. She sounded like a man

I heard at Baldoyle races cheering a horse when it took the lead near the winning-post.

"Good for you, Dorothy," she roared.

How different was the atmosphere Mrs Heber created! Even in that noisy room she had a ring of calm around her. Her voice never rose. She seemed oblivious of everyone except my father, because she was talking to him as if they were in her drawing-room, alone.

"I have such an amusing book for you," she said. "*Eminent Victorians*. I persuaded Harry to buy it at last. It is quite shocking. Such awful revelations about General Gordon. And you will love the Cardinal Manning bits. Rather catty. But one feels he deserved it. Cardinal Newman was *such* a pet."

"I read the reviews when it came out. I thought it might be too up to date for my liking."

"I can't get Harry to read it either. He says Strachey was funny about the War and wears queer-coloured clothes and a beard. But I don't think that matters. Do you? if he can write. Is not that what one asks of an author? I mean it is not as though one had to marry him. Harry is so funny about it. He mutters at me every evening, 'Still reading *that* fellow?' Then he gets down Lord Macaulay's essays which bore him to death, if the truth were known. 'When I want to read history, I read history,' he says. I know from the way he sucks at his pipe that it is costing him an awful effort to concentrate. To tease him I say that I suppose if I had read Macaulay long ago, he would have said much the same thing, and taken down Gibbon."

"And what answer did Harry give to that?" said my father.

"He said, 'Because your friend was a conscientious objector doesn't necessarily mean he is a conscientious historian. I prefer the old and tried.'"

"That was hardly an answer."

"I agree. But there is no use baiting Harry beyond a certain point. He just digs his heels in. I have asked Mr Nairn in Combridges to find out if Mr Strachey has written other books. It will be great fun keeping Harry with his nose in Macaulay until Christmas. Serves him right."

I could not understand why Mrs Heber wanted to talk like this, or why my father seemed to be interested. It bored me stiff. I took another cake and watched the dancers. My mother was begging Mr Hone to stop. She was fanning herself with her hand. He looked an old fool. As for Uncle Lindy—I felt more ashamed of my family that day than I had ever felt before. It was fortunate that my father was keeping up our dignity. I was too young. It was no use my trying to make up for my mother *and* Uncle Lindy. I preferred everyone in their usual surroundings where they looked natural. Miss Morris and Lord Swords and Doreen were of a suitable age for this place, but the rest of the party in my opinion were out of place. And, to be candid, when I had eaten as much as I could manage, and watched the dancing for a while, I began to feel bored.

I was offered an ice-cream after tea and I was sad at having to refuse it. When I had got to that stage it was time for me to give up. But I had to sit and watch the grown-ups for at least an hour. I half-hoped that someone would ask me to dance again. I was tired of just sitting there. If anybody had I should have been miserable on the dance floor. But when one is bored one will do anything for a change.

At last it was time to go. Everyone crowded out together. There was scramble at the cloakrooms. I heard Uncle Lindy complain loudly about the madness of dancing in October; the modern craze for pleasure; and the difficulty of finding his hat. Someone was looking after my hat for me, and I was not involved in the scramble. I stood at the street entrance because the passage was crowded. Miss Morris was standing outside in the street, and the Black and Tan was talking to her. He had left his friend behind. I could see her looking for him in the mill at the cloakroom door. Whatever it was he said, Miss Morris did not seem to argue. They only spoke for a few seconds. I was more than ever puzzled. If they were friends, why had Miss Morris told me they were not and made me promise to pretend I had never seen him? And why had she refused to ask him to join us? Perhaps she disliked the look of the girl with the Dublin accent and would have been ashamed to be seen in her company. And why was Miss Morris cross with me for having drawn her attention to the Black and Tan? Was she ashamed of having a Black and Tan as a friend? Was he a guilty secret? But if he was her friend, how could he be friends with that other girl? I could guess what Mrs Heber would think of *her*.

Lord Swords had a car, and so had the Hones. But we could not all fit in. An argument began as to who should go by train. In the end it was decided that my father and Miss Morris and I should. I thought Lord Swords looked very sulky as Mrs Hone climbed in beside him. He would have preferred Miss Morris.

My father became a new person when he was with Miss Morris. He joked with her and with me. He made all sorts of wild suggestions that he would never have made had my mother been there. He bought a bag of toffees, and we ate them as we sat on the outside-car which drove us to Amiens Street Station. I think it was Miss Morris who suggested that we play Beaver, but he entered into it with great enthusiasm and said in future we should carry field-glasses so as to play the game properly. There were marks for each kind and colour of beard. The highest mark of all Miss Morris said went to the person who spotted a man with a red beard, riding a green bicycle and carrying a step-ladder. I looked out for such a person with the greatest care and missed a great many points which the others scored by shouting 'Beaver' at bearded men on the footpath.

In the train my father told us stories about Uncle Lindy which sometimes made me laugh. Miss Morris almost died laughing. "You are funny, funny, funny," she said. It was strange to hear someone so gay as Miss Morris was, finding my father funny. I thought of him as serious and rather sad. But it was true that Miss Morris brought out an unexpected side of him. I had seen her with the Black and Tan and Lord Swords and my father (I don't count Mr Hone or Uncle Lindy). And I think she was happier with my father than with anyone else. And, strangely enough, each of them was nicer to me when the other was there.

When we got home there was tea ready for us, and my mother made pancakes. We sat in the kitchen (the maids were out for some reason) and I thought we had never been so happy. It is never lucky to notice happiness. The moment you do, it flies. And if not then, very soon afterwards.

I don't exactly remember what happened. It was something almost imperceptible. My father was still in his gay spirits. He was chaffing us all, and he and Miss Morris were both laughing a lot. My mother had been in her best humour when we came in. But the more my father joked and Miss Morris laughed, the quieter she became. She had said nothing for some time—I wondered what was wrong—when, suddenly, she paused at the range (she was dishing out the pancakes) and said 'Dick', just the one word, my father's name. That was all. He seemed to stumble in his manner, to be taken off guard, as it were, and to have to collect himself in a moment: there was a long pause before he said, 'Yes. What is it?'

My mother made no reply. She went on spooning out the pancakes, but more slowly than before. My father and Miss Morris exchanged anxious looks. The evening seemed to die. We ate the pancakes slowly. My mother began to eat, and then pushed her plate away. No one said a word. I found myself growing more and more sad. It must be like this in a house when somebody died, I thought.

I got up from the table and went round to my mother. "It is long past your bedtime," she said very gently, as if she wanted me to know that I was not responsible for whatever had happened in the room. I was glad to go to bed. But I was puzzled and gloomy. Why did it make my mother so unhappy—I knew she was desperately unhappy—to see my father in such a cheerful mood? I, too, noticed that he had changed. He was not the father that I knew. But I must confess I had enjoyed the journey home, the jokes and the games until I saw how much my mother was upset.

I was in bed for some time when I heard her come slowly up the stairs. She always came in, tucked me up, kissed me, asked me had I said my prayers, pulled the curtains, and said good night. It was always the same. And it never took long. Tonight was different. She did the same things but she did them slowly. And when she kissed me I thought she was crying. It made me want to cry too. I never cried when I hurt myself. I was quite good about pain. But if anyone got sad, or even said something sad to me, I became sad as well. I heard her go into her room and, for the first time in my life, heard her shut the door. I was so surprised by this, I stopped crying.

Downstairs I could hear voices. My father and Miss Morris had not come up to bed with my mother. I lay without moving, waiting for something to happen. At eleven o'clock the maids came in. I heard the back door open and shut and the noise of their feet in the kitchen and Jane's flat voice. After a while the door of the maid's room shut with a bang. (That was the only way it could be shut.) Then I heard the continuous murmur of the voices in the room below. But I was more conscious of my mother's door and the thought of her in there alone, shut off from us all. Nothing happened. The hall clock struck twelve. I could not bear to wait any more. I slid quietly out of bed, and without dressing-gown or slippers, crept out on to the landing. I wanted to open my mother's door. It looked so still and dead. I listened outside. I could hear no sound. The door of the drawing-room was slightly open. It was more inviting than my mother's. Had I heard her crying, I would have gone in. But there was nothing. The hall was lit, and the sound of voices in the drawing-room made it seem more cheerful downstairs. I started to go down quietly, not quite certain what I wanted to do, but anxious to do something to break the spell. Why did my father not go up to my mother and tell her to be happy again? Had he been alone I would have asked him to, but with Miss Morris there, I felt shy about it. I would feel that she was laughing at me for being a baby. Grown-ups, I had noticed, are not as anxious to prevent unhappiness as children are. They get cross at the least opportunity. They do things they don't like doing. They go to parties that bore them. They spend their time with people they are not fond of. And they have forgotten how to play. Miss Morris was rather exceptional in that she had a gay manner (except when she was with me). She seemed to be happy and to make other people happy. But tonight I was sure that in some way she had helped to make my mother unhappy. And I was afraid that my mother would never be friends with her again.

Having come so far I could not tamely retreat to my room. I had to do something, so I went into the drawing-room.

Miss Morris and my father were standing at the fireplace with their backs half-turned to the room, looking into the empty grate. They did not hear me—I was bare-footed—and when I said 'What time is it?' they jumped with fright. But they did not look angry. That was a relief.

"Why aren't you asleep?" he asked.

"You will get your death of cold," she said.

"I can't get to sleep," I said, looking hard at my father. I wanted to talk to him alone.

"Well, perhaps, we should all be in bed," he said, but more to Miss Morris than to me.

She said nothing. Her back was turned again. He yawned.

"Mummy has shut her door," I said.

Miss Morris looked up at this, but quickly looked down again. My father blushed.

"Come on. I will go up with you," he said, taking my hand.

"Good night. And don't worry, please," he said to Miss Morris.

She said, "Good night."

She, too—I knew from her voice—had been crying.

When I got into bed, quite cheerfully now, my father sat down on the end of it. He only did this when I was ill. "Please tell Mummy you are sorry and make her happy," I said.

"But I don't know what has upset her," he said. "It is hard to apologise when you have done nothing wrong."

Sitting there with his hair untidy he looked young. I saw him as a man, and not just my father. I realised that he had worries and problems like mine, like Miss Morris's, and not as I had been told, just special office worries which were not like other people's and which no one could discuss. I felt nearer to him than ever before, and much less frightened of offending him.

"I think it is on account of Miss Morris. You were so much

jollier with her than you ever are with Mummy. You had more fun with her. I think that is what upset Mummy."

"Did your mother say this to you?"

"No. But I knew from the way she went on. It has been much more fun at home since Miss Morris came, but everyone joined in it. Tonight Mummy seemed to be shut out of it. I noticed it, so I suppose she did as well."

My father said nothing. He blew on his nails, a way he had when he was trying to make up his mind about what he should do. Then he threw back his head and looked at the ceiling. But I knew this was only to gain time while he screwed himself up to a decision. Then he came closer to me and put an arm round my shoulders. "You shouldn't be worrying about these things, old chap," he said (his voice was very friendly). "You haven't had a chance, cooped up with old people, with no one of your own age to play with. That is the worst of this district. We have been selfish about you. But we must do something to put it right. You are a decent little skin. Go to sleep now. In the morning we will all be as right as rain."

Then he went out.

I heard him pause for a moment on the landing before he opened their door. But he shut it when he went in. I heard their two voices (much more of his than hers) for hours into the night. Then I heard snores. My father had a loud, sad snore: my mother a much smaller one, more like a kettle. Miss Morris had not gone to bed when I fell asleep. She was walking up and down her room. The sound of matches striking told me she was chain-smoking. I heard her push up the window in her room. It made a creak followed by a loud rattle. Now, I knew she was leaning out, looking into the garden and up at the sky, thinking. . . . Of what? I wondered; for I knew that she, too, was sad. And I would have liked to go into her room and offer to keep her company if she was lonely. But tonight I could not because, even if she were unhappy, she had made my mother unhappy. And yet that was unfair. She had done nothing against my mother. It was not her fault if my father enjoyed her company. If anyone was to blame it was he, because he could have tried to be gay when Miss Morris was not there. It would have been more polite to my mother. Was Uncle Lindy right? I could not understand everything he said, but I had gained a clear impression that he thought it was wrong to have Miss Morris as my governess. He said it would lead to trouble. And now it had. Would my mother send Miss Morris away? Could I bear it if she did? Why could we not all be happy together until I was old enough to marry Miss Morris? Perplexed by all these thoughts, I grew more and more confused, and eventually fell asleep.

* * *

I was last down to breakfast next morning. My father had left for Dublin, my mother was picking flowers in the garden. Miss Morris was in her room. I felt shy at meeting anyone, but no one seemed to have changed very much. Miss Morris surprised me by suggesting that we should do lessons. "You will have forgotten everything by next summer," she said.

I was pleased with this. "What shall we do?"

"Whatever you are worst at. Sums?"

"Don't let's do sums. I am rotten at them. And you will get cross. Let's do reading."

"But you can read perfectly well."

"History then. I know all the Kings of England."

"We must practise the Queens of Ireland. Do you know Latin?"

"Almost."

"What do you mean by *almost*?"

"I was just going to begin Latin with the last governess. But she went before the book arrived."

"Let's get the book. Did it ever arrive?"

The book had come. I found it under my bed. *First Steps in Latin*. Miss Morris started to read the first page with her forehead wrinkled. I think she had forgotten all about Latin and was finding it more complicated than she had expected.

"There are five declensions," she said at last, but she didn't look very happy about it.

"Yes," I said.

"Do you know what a declension is?"

"Well, it's a sort of a . . ."

"Sort of a what?"

"I don't know exactly."

"And how could you? God help you," said Miss Morris, reading on and looking more puzzled the further she went.

"Let's drop Latin. It sounds very boring," I said. I was thinking as much of Miss Morris as of myself.

"You could learn Amo Amas Amat," said Miss Morris. "I love, thou lovest, he loves. That would be something to be getting on with."

Very patiently for her she taught me the whole verb. I had not the least idea what it was all about. Alice brought in a cup of tea and a glass of milk during the morning, but my mother did not appear until it was lunch-time. By then we had given up Amo Amas Amat and Miss Morris was reading *Treasure Island* out aloud. Luncheon was not very pleasant. Everyone was too polite. Everyone in turn said 'Oh, yes' or 'certainly' or 'exactly' to whatever anybody else said. No one laughed. I was very glad when we were interrupted by Lord Swords coming back from Dublin in his car. He wanted to know if Miss Morris could go to the castle that afternoon and play tennis. Miss Morris asked my mother very formally for permission before she accepted. It meant that I would be alone—my mother was going to Malahide—but I announced that I was going to tea with Mrs Heber. I had in fact decided to have a long talk with her about the troubles at home. I needed help. I wanted to know how I could bring everyone together happily. Mrs Heber who was so superior to everyone else in the neighbourhood was the obvious person to give advice. I would go very early to ensure a long session before the inevitable arrival of Mr Heber and his ironical greeting. It had always the effect of spoiling the day. I wondered why so magical a person had such a depressing husband.

It was raining when I left home, so I ran all the way. It seemed at the time to be less trouble than going back for a mackintosh, but it left me quite breathless. I stood, red in the face, covered with sweat and rain drops, panting, and unable to talk coherently beside Mrs Heber, who today was sitting on the sofa with her feet up, and a grey Persian cat, Haig, lying at her feet like a cushion.

When at last I got my breath I explained that I had come on a visit and particularly wanted a talk. Mrs Heber asked the maid, Maud, to get a towel and when she brought it, Mrs Heber herself rubbed my hair. I liked standing close to her. She had a marvellous smell of some curious scent. I was surprised how strong she was and how thoroughly she rubbed.

"There," she said, handing me the towel. "Look at yourself in the glass. You look like Struwelpeter with your hair all on end. Go up to the bathroom and brush it and leave the towel on the horse there."

I spent some time in the bathroom. I found a razor and tried to use it. But nothing happened. The soap just rubbed off. And I had to lather my face again and again. Perhaps there was no blade in the razor. I saw weighing-scales beside the bath. We had none at home. First I weighed myself with all my clothes on. Then I took off my coat, then my shoes. Having gone so far it seemed silly not to make a thorough job of it, so I took all my clothes off. I had forgotten to lock the door. And one of the maids came in while I was doing my final weigh. She gave a scream and rushed out of the room shouting "Holy Angels deliver us." A few minutes later I heard Mrs Heber saying from outside, "Are you all right, Brian?"

I felt very awkward then. But I said, "I will be quite all right in a minute or two. Don't worry. I'll come down."

It was going to be difficult to explain why exactly I had taken all my clothes off. If Mrs Heber thought I was feeling sick, it was much easier to fall in with that idea. Children are very often sick. I could be sick one minute and well the next. But taking off all one's clothes—that was rather dotty.

"You are covered with soap," said Mrs Heber when I came down at last.

"Please don't bother about it," I said. Then, so as to get away from the bathroom at once, I told her that Miss Morris had gone out to play with Lord Swords. I saw the faintest trace of shadow on Mrs Heber's eyes as if the light there had gone out for a fraction of a second. Then she said: "Doreen is at Lord Swords's today. I didn't know it was a party."

"I hope Doreen won't be jealous when she meets Miss Morris," I said. "Miss Morris seems to make so many people like her. And I suppose she ought to leave Lord Swords for Doreen."

This time the shadow was on Mrs Heber's voice when she said: "Doreen's life is spent in London. I think she would be quite lost in Ireland. And I don't think Lord Swords or your mother would be pleased if they heard you talk in that way about Miss Morris. Lord Swords is a very kind young man. Miss Morris is quite presentable and remarkably good at tennis. It is very fortunate for her that Lord Swords has so few neighbours of his own age and in his own class of life. Before the war the idea of Miss Morris at Raheny Castle would have been quite out of the question."

"Would Doreen have been out of the question before the war, too?"

Mrs Heber gave a very gentle smile. "She will laugh like anything when I repeat that remark. You say very amusing things, dear. I hope you were not too tired after all the excitement of yesterday."

Tea came before I had even begun to tell Mrs Heber about our troubles. Getting wet, and fooling round in the bathroom, and the way I seemed to irritate Mrs Heber with the things I said at the beginning of our conversation, set me back. I found it hard to get going. And in no time I was sitting on the pouf with my hands round my knees while Mrs Heber told me all over again about her childhood in Ely Place and some old man called George Moore who lived close by and who was supposed to be an ogre in disguise. Mrs Heber had been forbidden to go into his house or to play in his garden. He used to take his hat off to her on the road, but she looked the other way and pretended not to see him.

"Was he really an ogre?" I said, excited in spite of myself.

"I don't think so. I think he was really quite harmless. But he used to growl and pretend to be fierce. And he had the reputation of being dangerous for girls especially."

"Was he not dangerous for boys?"

"I don't think he was dangerous for anyone. But he pretended to be dangerous for girls."

"That's funny."

Then tea came. Maud, the housemaid, looked as if she was going to laugh when she carried in the tray. Her face was swollen like a balloon and it was very red. She went out of the room rather quickly, and I could swear I heard a sort of snort before the door was shut. She must have been thinking about me on the weighing-scales.

Mrs Heber always gave me nice scones and she had a sort of biscuit made of oatmeal and honey which I ate a lot of. And there was a chocolate cake with almonds in it.

We had but a short time to talk before Mr Heber came in, so I began as soon as tea was over and told Mrs Heber all about the journey home and my mother getting sad and my father talking to Miss Morris for hours and my mother shutting the bedroom door. I must say Mrs Heber made a wonderful listener. She never once interrupted me. But when I had told her everything, she said: "I don't think you should tell me any more, dear. Your mother and father wouldn't like it. These are things families keep to themselves."

Then I felt guilty. I had only wanted to get advice from Mrs Heber. I had not thought it would do harm if she knew. After all she was fond of my parents—fonder of my father than of my mother, I think—and people always wanted to help their friends. Besides, how could I get advice if I didn't tell what the trouble was? But in spite of all these reasons, I had a horrible feeling deep down that I had done something wrong. The more I felt this the more certain I became that my parents would rather be in trouble than that Mrs Heber should know about it. There were things that I would die rather than that people should know about them. I felt utterly miserable. Why had Mrs Heber not stopped me in the beginning? It was not much help to anyone pulling me up when it was all over.

I must have looked as unhappy as I felt because Mrs Heber lost the eager look she had when I was talking; her eyes became soft again. She took my right hand and held it between hers, and rubbed it in a soothing way. Her hands were long and white and covered in rings.

"Don't worry, Brian. Your mother and father will be very happy together. These misunderstandings occur in marriages. Look at all the times you have made your parents cross with you. But they love you still. I think Miss Morris may not be the ideal person to have in charge of you. But you may be quite certain that your mother has reached the same conclusion. So don't worry. You will be grown up soon enough. Enjoy your childhood. What about that last cake? You will have to eat it up before Mr Heber comes home."

And now for the first time, now when she was meaning to comfort me, I became frightened of Mrs Heber, and wondered was she my friend.

"But I don't want Miss Morris to go away. I want her to stay with us always. That is why I am so worried. I am afraid Mummy does not like her any more."

Mrs Heber said nothing. She stopped rubbing, and held my hand more firmly.

"It will be all right. You will see. Sometimes when we are young we don't understand why people have to do certain things. But we are grateful when we grow up and look back on it."

This was too vague. I could not see any comfort in it. But there was Mrs Heber holding my hand, talking in her gentlest voice, her special good fairy voice which she always used when she told me stories about herself when she was young. I had to try to see if she could understand, because if she did not, who would?

"Do you think it is foolish for a boy my age to think of getting married—I mean, of course, when he grows up, when he is twenty-one?"

"There's no harm in it, dear. But I don't think it sounds very sensible."

There was no malice in her voice. But her answer was too pat. God knows what it cost me to ask the question: she answered it without a moment's consideration, I would have to try again. But she saved me that by saying, not with any real feeling:

"Why? You were not thinking about it, were you?"

"I thought if Miss Morris stayed with us that I could marry her when I was twenty-one."

Mrs Heber pulled out her handkerchief and used it while she had a sudden violent attack of coughing and sneezing. Then she took my hand again and began in her brisk voice, the voice she used when tea was taken away and it was time to go home:

"The girl you will marry, Brian, may not be in the world yet. And if she is, she is a tiny, little person. You will want to marry lots and lots of girls before you meet the right person."

"I will never want to marry anyone except Miss Morris. But I can't tell her that. I don't think she would be bothered. That is why I want her to stay. When I grow up it may be different. I am bound to change, and she may grow to like me."

I found myself becoming sad. The room had gone darker. Mrs Heber seemed, for all her talk, to be just another grown-up. She was not really my friend. What friends had I? Freddy Doyle? He would listen to me, but never for my sake. He was just collecting the things I said as if they were stamps for his album. Now the maid came in and took away the tray. She was no longer laughing to herself.

"Put a match to the fire in the dining-room," said Mrs Heber. "It has become quite chilly."

"Yes, Ma'am," said the maid.

Soon Mr Heber would appear on the avenue. I would see him before he got to the gate because he had to cross the road. Slowly he would walk towards the house, stopping now

and then to look at something that caught his attention—
usually something out of order, for he was a fault-finding
sort of man. As he approached the house he would lift his
head very slightly as if to see whether Mrs Heber was waiting for him. But it was hard to think of him giving up his
pride to that extent. Before he turned the front-door handle
I had said 'good-bye', and left by the french window. I
avoided Mr Heber as much as I could. We had nothing in
common. I did not even feel that he was fond of his wife
in the special, exciting way that I was. He sounded always
so cold and even, and so indescribably slow and old. Nothing
and nobody excited him. Sometimes I resented the way that
Mrs Heber went on, fussing about him, ordering the maids
to get out this or that for him (having his slippers at the fire
in winter, for instance); being so ready, in fact, to end our
conversations in order to concentrate on his dull, grumpy,
everyday talk. I could never understand how they had got
married. It gave me heart, in a way. Miss Morris (if she waited
until I was twenty-one) was bound to find me more agreeable
than Mr Heber.

I was thinking this to myself as I strolled along, and feeling in rather better spirits, when a voice made me jump.

"What's the hurry, Bill?"

I stopped but did not turn round. The voice came from
the lane over which the branches hung so low that at this
time of year, in autumn leaf, they acted as a curtain. I could
go on without turning round. It would save trouble in the end.
But I was not used to avoiding people, especially grown-ups
who spoke to me. It was rude.

Another thing—the Black and Tan did not seem unlike
other people to the extent I would have expected. Miss
Morris said she was frightened of him. But she did not act
as if she were. I had no objection to him personally. His

manners were not up to much. But that was probably due to the fact that he was not a gentleman. Freddy Doyle, for instance, blew his nose with his fingers. Our garden boy, Jimmy Cody, spat. It was not their fault. So long as one did not imitate them it did not matter. And no one was going to correct them for it. But it annoyed me that he called me 'Bill'. The way he said it had a common sound. It was from this that I first realised he was a common man. Miss Morris would never marry him. But his being a Black and Tan made him very interesting. And his car was a sort of racing car like nobody else's in our neighbourhood. And his following Miss Morris made him like the Sheriff of Nottingham in Robin Hood stories.

I would not run away.

The car, tucked against the wall, under the branches, was almost invisible from the road. The Black and Tan lay back in the driver's seat with a cigarette in his mouth. I never saw him without one. And they made his fingers brown as if he had been using paint and forgotten to wash himself. There was a particular smell from the Black and Tan which I rather liked—it partly came from the stuff he put on his hair (my father used water). I could see that this might fascinate Miss Morris, too. At Christmas I was going to buy myself some brilliantine.

He opened the door of his car, inviting me to come in. It was really very decent of him. I tried to keep off the subject of Miss Morris by asking him questions. He told me what each of the things in the front of the car was called.

"Here," he said. "Get into the driver's seat and I will teach you how to start a car."

It was so cramped in those front seats that we had the greatest fun changing places. I had to walk over him in the end. As I snuggled down into the driver's seat, I bumped up against his side and hurt myself.

"Mind yourself, Bill," he said. "That is my revolver."

"May I see it?"

He pulled the gun out of his pocket—I had never seen a real one before—and showed it to me.

"Is it loaded?"

"I hope so, Bill."

"Isn't it very dangerous?"

"It's more dangerous to leave it at home, Bill. We need our friends when we least expect it."

Then he put the gun back and began to explain about the car.

I did not notice time passing. I was far too interested. And to be quite truthful if it had not been for the fact that he wanted to take Miss Morris away—I knew this without being told—I should have made the Black and Tan my friend. He was far nicer than Freddy Doyle who had no gun and no car, and spent his time asking me questions about 'the quality'. But when I had time to think about it, I realised that if the Black and Tan could seem so nice to me, how did he appear to Miss Morris? He had the enormous advantage of age. Might she not start to like him? I was terribly afraid. But these thoughts only came when I left him. That was when I heard my mother calling for me: "Brian, Brian. Where has the child gone to?"

"I must go," I said.

I tried to get out of the car so quickly that he would not have time to mention Miss Morris. But, of course, it was hopeless. Before I could get the door open, he said, "Tell Katy—tell Miss Morris that I will wait until eight-thirty. But don't tell another soul you saw me, pal, will you? Cross your heart." I had never heard that expression before.

"Oh, all right," I said. Then I remembered that Miss Morris had gone out. "She is playing tennis with Lord Swords," I said. "He has a hard court."

This did not seem to please the Black and Tan. An expression came into his eyes extraordinarily like Mrs Heber's when I told her the same thing.

"She is, is she?" he said. "She won't be playing tennis all night, I suppose. I don't know his lordship's habits."

"She will be back for supper," I said. And then I bit my tongue. If I had said she was going to spend the night with Lord Swords the Black and Tan would have gone away. But it was too late to help her now.

"Thank you for showing me the revolver, and for teaching me how to drive," I said, trying to edge away.

"Anything to oblige a pal," he said. "Don't forget the message, Bill, or I shall have a crow to pluck with you." He gave me his big smile, showing all his teeth which, like his fingers, were brown-stained. When he smiled like that his moustache reminded me of the wolf in Red Riding Hood, a child's story that I had not read for years. But I never forgot pictures. I just waved. I was at a loss for words.

I looked back before I climbed through the hedge into our garden. I could not see the car. The branches hid it from here, but on the far side of the lane, leaning against the wall, I saw Freddy Doyle. He was smoking his little black pipe and watching the lane. He must have heard every word we were saying. He was as bad as the rest of them, spying on me like that.

"Where *have* you been?" said my mother in an angry voice. "I have been ringing up the entire neighbourhood. Mrs Heber said you left her hours ago. Were you at the forge? I told you you were not to go near Freddy Doyle."

"I was not at the forge," I said indignantly. "I never went near Freddy Doyle. If it comes to that I saw Freddy Doyle just now and I never even spoke to him."

"There is no need for you to get cheeky about it."

"I am not cheeky. But it's not fair for people to go around accusing me of going to the forge when I haven't been to the forge."

"No one is accusing you."

"You went for me about Freddy Doyle the moment I entered the house."

"Stop arguing. And go and wash your face and hands. I am sure they are filthy."

I went slowly upstairs. Through the window of the half-landing I could see my father rolling the tennis-court. Whenever he helped in the garden it was always a sign that my mother was cross with him. When she was pleased, he sat down and read.

Miss Morris was in the bathroom. I could hear the water plashing against the sides of the bath as she turned round in it. She liked deep baths. And so did I. Whenever we got the chance to have them someone had to go and pump water into the tank. I could see that my father would do this when he had finished rolling unless my mother made friends with him. If she did, we could all cut out baths until Jimmy Cody came in the morning. (He came at half-past seven, cleaned shoes, pumped water and brought coal and sticks. Then he worked in the garden until one o'clock. He had half an hour for lunch in the kitchen. Then he worked until six. His wages were ten shillings a week.)

"May I come in? I have a message for you," I called through the bathroom door.

"Not on your life," shouted Miss Morris. It was hard to hear because she had the hot tap running. I wondered whether she sat at the tap end which was deep or the other, narrow end. Personally I sat at the tap end, even though it meant sometimes knocking my back against the taps and getting burnt by the hot one. All the governesses I disliked made me sit at the narrow end. They were the ones who put milk in their cups before pouring the tea in. And they stuck out a little finger when they were drinking from the cup. It was funny that I had never thought about Miss Morris in connection with bath ends. It was not the sort of question one could shout through the door. It would sound silly. I wondered if I could see through the keyhole. At that very moment the bathroom door opened. Miss Morris was standing there with a bathing cap on her head and the big turkish towel (kept for visitors) round her.

"What are you up to?" she said.

I was terribly embarrassed. It seemed even more silly to ask the question now. I wished I had never thought of it. But she was smiling at me in a funny, friendly way. I was greatly relieved.

"The Black——" I began. Then I remembered we were not supposed to know, so I began again. "The man in the motor car, the one who has the A.C., is out in the lane. He says he will stay there until half-past eight."

Miss Morris stared hard at me as if she was thinking.

"He can stay all night for all I care," she said.

Then she shut the door. But she did not get back into the bath. I would have heard the splash if she did.

Mother and father made it up. I came to know this one night when after I was sent up to bed—Miss Morris was out —I started to roam round the house. I often did this when I did not feel sleepy. Rooms look so different when the people they belong to are out of them. The furniture and their various belongings take on a life of their own, but it, in a way, is a reflection of the person. Uncle Lindy's room (in his own house) for instance is very neat. But even sunlight looks sad in it. Miss Morris's room gave the impression that she had left in a hurry. Not because it was untidy, but there was always something—a single shoe, a box of powder with the lid off, a cigarette smouldering in a tray—that suggested a sudden departure in answer to a call of impatience. She had, which seemed odd for such a very unsentimental person, a doll sitting in the armchair in her room.

My father's dressing-room was small and almost filled by a mahogany wardrobe. Unlike Miss Morris's his room gave the impression that he checked over an inventory before coming out of it. His shoes, in trees, stood on a shelf. His ties hung on a rail inside a wardrobe. His ebony-backed brushes lay evenly apart on the small dressing-table so that without looking he could stretch out his hands and find a brush for each. He brushed his hair every morning with the patient intensity of a groom preparing a horse for the show ring.

My mother was more like Miss Morris. She proceeded at top speed with great vigour. I never knew anyone to plunge their face in cold water with such relish as she did. And she tackled her hair as if the brush was a harrow. I never knew whether my father was in his room or not. He moved quietly like Kitchener our cat. But everyone in the house knew where my mother was, she was always calling out to someone, and if no one was in ear-shot, she sang to herself, or talked to the cat. The cat (who was called Kitchener because he was once going to be drowned) had a mysterious personality. He had no interest in the outside world, and (resembling Mrs Heber in this) reduced physical movement to the minimum. When he was not cleaning himself or asleep, he lay in whatever was the most comfortable place in the room, and stared with mild hauteur at all of us. I think he resented being under an obligation to us. It was my mother who saved him from Miss Tite's duck pond. He never relented or allowed himself to show gratitude for any attention. He took what came as matter of right. Once or twice he may have rubbed against my father's trouser legs: but if he did, when he left off he arched his back, yawned and shrugged as though to make it clear that he had not intended any demonstration of affection.

And then Miss Morris came. She paid him no particular attention, tickled him once, I think, behind the ear while talking to my mother, gave him in fact a mere passing acknowledgement; but whatever happened, he became her slave, followed her like a dog, and could always be found wherever she was, apparently asleep, but with eyelids trigger-quick to open at a move from her. Frightened by Uncle Lindy's voice, he remained at the top of a chestnut tree during my uncle's visit.

On this particular evening, having explored the rooms, I sat down on the window-seat in my mother's room. The window was open. Underneath the sill a climbing rose cut off the downward view and made an awning under which, in summer, my parents sometimes sat after dinner. From there the small garden could be seen, the orchard, the field in which grazed the poor solitary cow, and away in the distance the Hill of Howth and the sea.

I had been taught and believed that it was wrong to listen to other people's conversation or to read their letters. It was wrong to give way to curiosity. It was not polite to show an interest unless one was really indifferent. And conversation must avoid the asking of questions, religion, politics, people and money.

I was always conscious of these rules, but somehow I was always breaking them. The old rules spoiled the pleasure I might have had because they weighed me down with guilt afterwards, even if they did add greatly to the excitement at the time. I never planned to listen to anybody talking. I just found myself there when they were at it. To announce my presence then would give the impression that I had been there for some time. It would leave an uncomfortable feeling in the speaker's mind, an unease about how much I had heard. It was easier to lie doggo and hope not to be discovered.

"Well, ask her to go then," my father said.

"I shall do nothing of the kind," said my mother.

"Do you want me to do it?"

"I think that would look distinctly odd. We said she could stay until Brian went to school."

"Tell her we have changed our plans. Tell her whatever you like. But don't let her stay if you dislike her. It was your idea she should come in the first place."

"Oh, of course. But I don't dislike her."

"Find her an irritation, then?"

"She is pleasant and amusing. She doesn't irritate me."

"Then what are we talking about? What has upset you?"

"We must divide the dahlias this year. They are crowding out the border."

"Dorothy, I asked you a question."

"I would rather forget it. There are some things it is good to talk about, and others that talking about only makes worse. I am going to scrap the Michaelmas daisies. There is something frugal about them that gets on my nerves. Let's flood the place with chrysanthemums. That golden one lasted until Christmas last year."

"You only talk about the garden when I want to talk about ourselves."

"Have you noticed that? Perhaps I do. I did not realise it. I should die without the garden."

"I don't know how I am expected to take that remark."

My mother made no answer. And there was silence. I could hear my heart beating. It was certainly the sort of conversation that would have been turned into French had either of them known where I was.

"I think it is unfair to go on like this, to wear a grievance and be a martyr. I have done absolutely nothing that gives you the right to be offended. If you insist that I like Miss Morris, I make no secret of it. I do. But so do you. So does everyone. Poor Brian follows her round like a spaniel. When he goes to school we have no excuse for keeping her. So let him go. And then she goes. If that is what you want. But if you don't want it, please don't persist with this martyred air."

"You are not very subtle, Dick."

"I don't pretend to understand women, if that is what you mean."

"I don't think that is something to boast of. You married one, you know."

"I don't want to quarrel, but you are forcing me to."

"Just leave it alone, Dick. Just leave it. That's all. Must you make an issue of everything?"

"If you would only say what your complaint is. I have had rather a bad day in Court. The Judge is in one of his most infernal humours. It was not the best day to have to face this atmosphere at home."

"I did not make the atmosphere. And I am sorry about the day. I didn't think it was a good day either."

"What happened to you?"

"Nothing. The sixteenth of October nineteen hundred and twenty. I shall not forget it."

"I can't make you out."

There was another silence. Then a curlew gave a sad cry.

"It is cold. We must go in," my mother said.

"Oh, my God!" said my father. It was the voice he used when he came out without the latchkey. "The sixteenth. I don't know what put it out of my head. I never forgot before. I am so sorry, darling. Can you forgive me? It's too late to arrange anything now."

I don't know what happened then. I think he must have

tried to kiss her, because when she spoke it was in that muffled way you talk when you are pressed close to someone. She seemed to be saying 'No'. And I thought she was crying. And my father kept on saying 'Forgive me' in a way that was altogether new to me. And I felt that I had never known them. They did not know me either, and listening, when I knew I shouldn't, and which had a sort of thrill and risk of discovery, became meaningless when now I had the feeling that I just did not exist for them. It was a new form of loneliness, a shut-out sensation. And there was nobody at all for me. Suddenly I started to shiver. My feet were numb from cold. I turned away and went back to bed, not even bothering to walk on tiptoe. And I lay awake in bed shivering. And no one came to see me that night.

*   *   *

"Lord Swords wants to see Miss Morris."

"Miss Morris is in bed. She is not well."

"I told him that. He wants to know what is wrong with her."

"She has a chill."

"She hadn't one last night."

"Well, she has one this morning."

"Why can't he go up if she can't come down? Chills are not infectious, are they?"

"Young men don't visit ladies in their rooms."

"Why not?"

"Can't you see I'm busy?"

"He is waiting outside."

"Don't say *he*."

"*It* is waiting, then."

At this my mother left the kitchen and came out with flour all over her hands to see for herself.

Lord Swords sat at the wheel of his car looking uncomfortable, as if he ought not to be there.

He jumped out when my mother came and did his best to be pleasant. But he was not good at it. He was the sort of person who has to be pleased in order to look pleased. And it could not have pleased him to see my mother covered with flour when he really came to see Miss Morris.

"I was passing," he explained. "I wanted to discuss the question of a new motor car. I promised not to buy one without Miss Morris's approval."

"She is in bed today. I will tell her to ring you up," said my mother.

Meanwhile I was examining Lord Swords's car. It was a four-seater with a hood. What I liked best was a huge brass horn. I could not resist squeezing it. The effect was remarkable. It made a most unexpected noise, loud and rude. Lord Swords turned on me with a very cross face, but my mother laughed in such good humour, I think he was sorry he got cross so easily.

"How fast can you go?" I said.

"The motor car, you mean?"

I did not say "Of course". But I wanted to. I nodded.

"On these roads I crawl. If you are not doing lessons, would you like to come back with me and collect some flowers for Miss Morris?"

"I'd love to." I was amazed by the invitation from such an unfriendly character.

It was quite a job to get the car to start. It made strange noises and loud bangs. When the engine began to run the car jumped up and down like a sewing machine. We drove off in a great cloud of smoke. As we went round the gatepost I saw Miss Morris looking out of her window. When I waved at her, her head disappeared so quickly, I might have shot it off. We drove along in silence. I was delighted with the ride and soon got used to the vibration. Lord Swords was obviously not one who would talk and drive. Driving seemed to excite him. He got redder in the face than usual and blew the weird horn at the slightest provocation.

The gates of Raheny Castle were shut, and nobody appeared to open them even when Lord Swords blew a blast that sounded exactly like a lost cow in distress.

"I will open them," I said.

"Stay where you are," he replied. And blew again.

We were only wasting time.

He blew again. And again. And again. All the while his face getting redder and redder while the engine of the car hummed and throbbed. It was a question: What would blow up first? At last a miserable little girl in rags seemed to come from nowhere and be standing beside us.

"Where is your father?" said Lord Swords, very sternly. "I have been kept waiting."

"Me daddy's beyant."

"Why is there no one to open the gate?"

"The cow got took on him."

"Where's your mother?"

"Me mammy's beyant with me auntie."

"She should be here to open the gate."

"She is beyant. Me auntie is after having a little babby."

"Open the gate, please."

The girl pushed the gate back slowly. It was heavy. And I would have liked to help her. But from the way Lord Swords looked when I blew the horn without permission I guessed he would be angry now if I moved without being told to do so.

We drove round the castle to the yard at the back and walked into the walled garden. A boy who was weeding and whom I recognised as Jimmy's brother (they all have that squint and slightly open mouth) touched his cap.

"Tell Wilson to leave a large bunch of flowers in the motor car. Right away, please."

Then we went back to the castle. We went through a back door—a disappointment. I had pictured a formal entry with footmen bowing low. There seemed to be endless rooms full of harness and leather and croquet sets and tennis racquets and boots and mackintoshes and old grey hats. At the end of the passage was a door covered in billiard table cloth with studs all over it. This led into a hall.

"Like to look round?" said Lord Swords.

I thought this meant that I could go off on my own so I said "Yes, please," with great enthusiasm. But he did not mean that. Looking rather bored, he led me from room to room.

I did not know what to say. I felt I should say something, but the things that occurred to me would sound foolish. For instance: Why were there two drawing-rooms? When did twenty people ever sit at the dining-room table? How did he decide which of all these rooms to sit in? Was it lonely in such a big house? Who slept in all the bedrooms?

The pictures in the dining-room were portraits mostly. Men in armour. Men in wigs. All were fat and red-faced. All the women in the pictures had large, plain faces and wore their hair in funny ways. Some had so much on I wondered how they moved about. But some were naked almost to the waist. I had not thought such a thing possible. I was quite curious, but terribly ashamed. It was such a funny, rude thing to have pictures like that. But Lord Swords looked so bored, I could see he was used to it.

And then I realised how different life was for people like him and people like me. He had too much of everything. Nothing was terribly precious. That was why he looked so glum, perhaps. In the dining-room he poured himself out a glass of whiskey and asked me what I wanted. I do believe he would have given me some whiskey then. He was not really paying much attention to me.

"Anything," I said.

On the table I saw bottles and decanters, but they all had the look of grown-up drinks which I have always found taste horrible.

"There might be something in the sideboard for you," he said, noticing my hesitation.

Then he pulled a door open. I looked inside. There was so much of everything everywhere, so many pictures and sofas and chairs, I expected to see all the lemonade and ginger beer and raspberry vinegar in the world. I was terribly disappointed by the half bottleful of lime juice and the brown bottles of ginger-beer in stone bottles—the one drink I detest. It tastes of iced pepper. However, I took the lime juice and pretended to enjoy it.

I stared politely at the portraits in armour, keeping my eyes off the chest displays.

"That chap fought on the wrong side," said Lord Swords.

I nodded.

"Never knew the side their bread was buttered on, my family," he said.

I nodded.

"More's the pity. You seem to like the armour. There is a suit of it downstairs. Like to see?"

I nodded.

The suit of armour was disappointing. Those things are better in imagination or even in pictures. In real life it looked small and not at all frightening. It would not have fitted Lord Swords. It was as small as that. (He was fat, but not tall. His hands, I noticed, had red hair on the backs of them.)

Then we went into the library. I never saw so many books.

All brown. They were not meant to be read, I suppose.

We sat down and looked at one another. Then Lord Swords looked away as if I hurt his eyes.

"Will the Sinn Feiners take away your armour?" I said. I had to say something.

"I think they dislike distinctive uniforms," he said. And then he laughed with a high laugh which stopped suddenly as if a tap had been turned off. After he laughed Lord Swords looked sadder than ever—as if he were ashamed of himself.

"They won't get my guns. Took good care of that," he said.

I said nothing. How many had he?

"Bad luck about Miss Morris," he said.

"I don't think she has a chill."

"Why not?"

"She hadn't one last night. And I heard her talking to my mother this morning and she never mentioned it."

"I see. It may be a diplomatic illness."

"If you ask me, it's cancer. In fact, I know it is."

"Great God!"

Lord Swords spilled his whiskey all over the carpet. I never expected him to get so excited about anything.

"I think it must be. My mother was so mysterious. If it was consumption, Miss Morris would cough. Wouldn't she?"

"Did the doctor come?"

"No."

"Come along. We must get back."

He looked quite different. More like other people. Worried.

"Are you going to drive me?"

"Yes."

"Oh, thank you. Cheers."

There was a huge bunch of dahlias on the back seat. I had never seen so many flowers in a bunch.

I could see Lord Swords was worried from the way he drove. We went much faster than when we were coming out. And he blew the horn *all* the time.

My mother was waiting for us. Lord Swords rushed up to her and said something. He was mopping his forehead on which I had seen little bubbles gathering as we came along.

My mother gave one of her great, happy laughs.

Miss Morris could not have cancer. I knew that now. Even though my mother had been annoyed with the way my father took such an interest in her, she would not want her to die. My mother was always kind, even if sometimes she got angry for no reason.

Lord Swords went inside with her. They were away quite a long time. Having a drink, I suppose, to make up for the one that was spilled.

So I fooled around with the car. When he came out, he was smiling. It was a weak sort of smile, like candlelight.

"Out you get, Northcliffe," he said.

People were always calling me strange names.

"What sort of car are you getting?"

This really interested me. I had wanted to discuss it before, but I felt that Lord Swords did not want to discuss anything with children.

"I will let you into the secret. Miss Morris has a friend with an A.C. for sale. I want a sports-car. Your mother has promised to put in a word for me."

"The Black and Tan's car? Not the A.C.! He won't give that up, surely?"

"Black and Tan?"

"Don't say I mentioned it."

Lord Swords looked at me very oddly.

Then he began to crank the car. It worked quite soon this time. But even so it was long enough to make him forget me.

He got in and took the wheel and drove away without a glance in my direction. At our gate he made a tremendous blare with the horn before going out on the road. Without turning his head he put a hand up. I think that was meant for me.

"Good-bye," I said. "And thank you for the lime juice."

But he never heard. And I did not care. What did he want to take the A.C. for? The Hupmobile suited him much better. Horn and all.

* * *

It is a curious thing about life that everything gets mended at the expense of something else. It's like a leaking pipe: stop the leak in one place, it starts in another. I have found that about visits to the dentist. Afterwards there was always a new tooth aching.

My father and mother making friends again should have made us a happy household. But I soon discovered that it was far from being so. The subject of school became the main topic of conversation. My mother did not want me to go to a boarding school. On the other hand, she was frightened about the train journey to Dublin with the country in the state it was. In fact, we lived in a very quiet district. But railway bridges were blown up along the line. There was a guard always on the viaduct at Malahide. And in Dublin one never knew what might happen. An old gentleman whom my father knew quite well was pulled off a tramcar and shot dead on the street in front of the other passengers. And Mr Brooke, the secretary of the Railway, was shot dead in Westland Row station.

I knew about everything that was going on when Uncle Lindy was about. He talked so loud and in such a laying-down-the-law tone that one could not ignore him. He was, of course, Miss Morris's chief enemy, so far as I was concerned.

I heard him from the end of the garden saying: "Get him

a proper governess, Dick. I know a young woman who used to teach in the Rutland High School, her father was the parson in Drumcondra; there is no nonsense about her, I can promise you. How long is this farce going on?"

Mr Heber said I should be sent (as he had been) to a good preparatory school.

"I never heard of such a thing," my father said.

I talked the matter over with Freddy Doyle. He suggested that I should go to the National School. But when I mentioned this at home—the idea appealed to me—no one would listen.

"I told you not to go near the forge," was all my mother would say.

Finally it was decided that I should go to a private school run by a friend of Uncle Lindy's in Dublin. My father would bring me there on his way to Court and call for me again in the evening.

"It will be a tie," said Uncle Lindy, "but you have to do something."

This was not to happen until after Christmas. In the meantime it was arranged that I should get lessons from the National School master when his own classes were over. Miss Morris was to superintend my homework in the morning.

"You won't go away?" I said to her one morning.

"I must go away some time," she said.

"But why? You can stay here. It won't matter once I go to school. No one can blame you then for not teaching me my lessons. You can just be here like one of the family. Why must you ever go?"

"I can't stay here for ever and grow into an old maid. Is that what you want me to do? I'm getting on. I'll soon be on the shelf if I don't find some old fellow to look after me. I'm twenty-two."

I wanted so much to tell her not to worry, to promise that

I would marry her on my twenty-first birthday. But I found that the thought was too near my heart to be spoken. I could not tell her or anyone.

"Cheer up. We will have good times before I go," she said. My face was woebegone and she wanted to be kind. But even as she spoke I could see that she was laughing with her eyes. No one had ever made me so unhappy.

One day my father said he was going to bring me into Dublin to see the school and meet the schoolmaster, Mr Darley. He interviewed prospective pupils on Saturday mornings. When the day came some matter in Court cropped up and I was handed over to Uncle Lindy, the arrangement being that we should call at the school and my father would join us later. We were then going to lunch together. I cannot remember why my mother did not join the expedition. She may not have been feeling well. I have an idea also that Uncle Lindy was the operating force. Left to themselves my parents would have continued to dilly dally. Uncle Lindy found the school and pushed them into sending me there.

My father walked with me from the station to the Bank where Uncle Lindy worked. There we were brought into his presence by a porter in a tall hat. Uncle Lindy was in an office of his own with a large desk, a Turkey carpet on the floor and a print over the mantelpiece. His desk was very tidy. I was quite overwhelmed by the magnificence of it all and the civility of the porter, who was quite the grandest-looking person I had ever seen.

I neither liked nor disliked my uncle. His tendencies were restrictive, but I had the comfortable feeling that, in the last resort, I would always have more influence with my parents than he had. I don't suppose he was very fond of anyone. One did not associate him with warm feelings of any kind. He belonged to the surface of life and played in my imagination a place like the milkman, the postman, or Freddy Doyle. He was always complaining and praising the past to the detriment of the present, trying to make out that he had hosts of friends long ago. But I don't think friendship ever really meant a great deal to him. I could imagine him walking with those friends, arguing and laying down the law, while they hardly listened and attended to the private thoughts which nobody shared with him.

I took his hand as we started out as I would had he been my father or mother, without thinking. It quite startled him. I could see that, but he held mine until we came to the big hall, and then he pretended he wanted to blow his nose. I did not take his hand again.

We walked up Grafton Street. I tried to peep into Lawrences and Leechmans, the toy shops, as we passed them, but we were travelling so fast (I half ran to keep up) that I got only the most tantalising glimpses. Uncle Lindy took no interest in shop windows. He was talking all the time about Mr Darley, but in a way that I was quite unable to follow. They had known one another in Trinity, I gathered, and while Uncle Lindy had won a scholarship and other honours, Mr Darley had passed through without success of any kind. His qualification for teaching me was that he was a gentleman. Uncle Lindy was very keen on this. Whenever some important event happened, he used invariably to say, if it turned out well, 'I am not surprised, it takes a gentleman.' If he had fault to find, he said, 'What could you expect? The man is not a gentleman.' We walked along one side of St. Stephen's Green until we came to Harcourt Street where the school was. A tall house with no name or plate to indicate the fact that it was a school seemed to me to be confusing for pupils, but Uncle Lindy explained that this was part and parcel of Mr Darley's being a gentleman. The school was a private school, and it was intensely private. Nearby The High School had less bashfulness. Across the road the Standard Hotel had its name written up in large letters. But Mr Darley did not want the world to know about his school.

Uncle Lindy knocked. There was no reply. He knocked again. After a long time I heard footsteps dragging along an uncarpeted floor; then there was the noise of a chain being loosened, and the door opened. A very old man in a dirty suit, upon which I could see his breakfast menu marked in samples, stood there peering at us through scaly eyes, like a very old dog we had once and who was put down out of kindness.

"Is Mr Darley in?" said Uncle Lindy in a fussy voice.

"Who wants to see him?" said the old man. His voice was unfriendly. I felt that we had woken him up and this had annoyed him.

"Mr Lyndhurst Allen. I have an appointment."

Uncle Lindy sounded wonderfully impressive when he said this, but the old man still peered at us suspiciously. After a while he said, "I'll go and see if he is in." Then he turned away leaving us standing where we were on the step.

"There's a man with a boy here looking for you," I heard him growl to someone. Then I heard his steps, flap flap down a wooden staircase. A door creaked and groaned as it was pulled open. Then it shut with a heavy crash.

"An old servant," Uncle Lindy said to me with an encouraging nod. I think he wanted to persuade me that this made him in some way special and valuable. Uncle Lindy was selling the idea of this school, and I suppose he wanted me to see no drawbacks.

Mr Darley himself then appeared. At first sight he looked like a sheep. His face was long and sad, his hair was like unbleached wool and hung in wisps. He had a moustache which also drooped. He wore a black gown over brown clothes. Everything about him suggested an imminent collapse. He sagged.

"The porter should have shown you in," he said in a wavering voice. "How are you, Lindy? And is this the young hopeful? We must try to make a man of him."

Mr Darley hardly looked at me. I think he had long before lost all hope of everything.

"Come into my study. Mind that hole in the floor, young man. I told Morton to get the carpenter to put a new board in."

The study was a tiny room at the back of the hall intended as a closet. There was just room for a desk at which Mr Darley sat and two chairs which he told us to sit on. We were looking at his back, but he slewed round on his chair and talked to us in profile. There was a small window high up on the wall. This was almost obscured by old spiders' webs in which flies stuck like currants. The little wall space was crowded with school team photographs, all faded. Each team contained one or two tall boys who sat with folded arms frowning darkly, while round them were gathered little fellows upon whom the responsibility of playing for the school seemed to lie less heavily. Mr Darley stood at the side in these photographs except in one in which he stared, in a bowler hat, out of the window of the pavilion. I think this was an afterthought of the photographer's. Mr Darley must have been ill on the day the group was taken.

I looked round with timid curiosity to see if there were any instruments of torture in the room. I could see none.

"It is a long time since I have seen you, Lindy. I think we last met at Lansdowne Road. Are you still following the game?"

"I try to keep up interest. But the sort of thing that we see nowadays is hardly Rugby," said Uncle Lindy.

I was not interested in football so that I gave little attention to the conversation that followed. Why, I wondered, had everything in the world become worse since Uncle Lindy was young? I tried to make out the faces in the photographs while stray sentences reached my ears. 'Were you there in Lucius Gwynn's time?' 'We never had a centre to match J. C. Parke.' 'C. V. Rooke was a wonder. I played against him once.'

So much talk about long ago, the faded photographs, the dust, Mr Darley's air of advanced decay, above all, the neglect of me, made me feel lonely. At home my mother would be laughing wherever she was, and Miss Morris would be doing something exciting, and Jane would be making cakes in the kitchen, and nothing would be old, or sad, or dead.

I wished I could run away. I began to hate Uncle Lindy. To prevent myself from crying I tried to take an interest in what they were saying. I hoped it might remind them of me.

"You would hardly know Trinity now," said Uncle Lindy sadly. "Salmon was Provost when I went up."

Mr Darley nodded.

"Salmon was a wonderful man, a fine scholar, a great Christian. Of humble birth, I understand. But a gentleman for all that. Very different from his successor, Traill. Traill was a savage."

I saw in my mind's eye a black, naked man, all tattooed, shaking a spear. "A contrast to Mahaffy. But Mahaffy was a snob," said Uncle Lindy.

Mr Darley hardly spoke at all. He listened, polishing his spectacles with a rather dirty handkerchief, or twiddling a pencil in his ear, or scratching himself while Uncle Lindy was talking. But he seemed to be glad to listen. I could not see what any of it had to do with me. I began to feel indignant. After all, it was on my account we had come to the school.

An hour passed, then there was a ring at the door. I heard the old porter dragging his feet across the hall, and then the sound of the chain. After a while the door of our room opened and the porter said (from outside): "A man to see you."

"I am busy," said Mr Darley rather crossly.

The porter shuffled away. He had not bothered to shut the door properly. It took a long time for him to cross the hall. I could hear my father's rather high voice. He was protesting.

"That's Daddy," I said.

"What?" said Mr Darley in a vague way.

"Daddy is at the door, Uncle Lindy," I pleaded.

Mr Darley now realised the position. He wanted to suck up to my father. It had a wonderful effect on him. His gown billowing, like a black swan, he seemed to fly out of the room. I could hear him being very civil. I was greatly comforted by my father's arrival. He came in quietly with Mr Darley flapping behind him.

"I think the young man will do," said Mr Darley, baring his teeth at me. I wondered how he had come to that conclusion.

My poor father blushed with pleasure. He thought I had acquitted myself in some creditable way.

"He knows a little Latin," he said.

"We won't start him at the bottom then," said Mr Darley. "What books have you done?" He turned to me.

I stared stupidly.

"Latin books," said Uncle Lindy briskly.

I saw my father looking at me anxiously.

"Amo. Amas. Amat," I said. Miss Morris had taught me those three words. I had told all I knew.

"Excellent," said Mr Darley.

"We must walk before we can run," said Uncle Lindy.

And my father just looked pleased.

Although I was immensely relieved, my relief was accompanied by a sense of emptiness. If three words could pass for Latin, how much was there in anything? School, which I had rather dreaded, would be but a futile, time-wasting place. And my life would be empty and silly. These feelings were in part due to the hour that I had sat there while the two men ignored me, and Uncle Lindy talked, and the schoolmaster listened.

"Would you like to see round the class-rooms?" said Mr Darley to my father. I knew from the way he said it that he hoped my father would say 'no'. My father, who was quick to understand other people's feelings, hesitated and looked at Uncle Lindy.

"Desks, benches and a blackboard," said my Uncle.

I, who had never seen a school, was very curious to see these things, but I could guess that Uncle Lindy wanted to avoid the trouble.

"Nothing new-fangled," said Mr Darley.

My father suppressed a smile. The words seemed comic, spoken by one who looked so worn-out, and in this dusty little room with that hall outside and the cross, old, dirty porter lurking in the basement.

"What about you, Brian?" said my father.

He looked so kind and friendly and almost gay in these mouldy surroundings that I wanted only to please him and encourage his good mood. My intention was quite clear to me, but as always I had trouble in selecting a form of words to express it.

"I think an inspection would be superfluous," I said, after thinking a little.

Uncle Lindy reared up like a horse at this. Mr Darley just stared at me. And my father pulled out his handkerchief and started to blow his nose. I had felt rather proud of my phrase, and I could not see why it had produced this reaction.

"After that we can only take our leave," said Uncle Lindy, but not unkindly.

We all got up and trooped into the hall. My father said something to Mr Darley and laughed. I could not hear more than the sentence 'inclines them to be old-fashioned'. I had heard this before. At the door Mr Darley shook my father's hand as though he had suddenly developed a craze for him. He patted me on the shoulder. "Glad to meet you, Simon," he said. I thought it might be better not to correct him, but I was offended that even now he did not know my name. Uncle Lindy nodded good-bye. He looked more natural than anyone else. I suppose the hour's talk about Trinity and Rugby football had done him good.

I was afraid that I might be attacked for my remark which had obviously not been the right one, but when we got outside the men decided to lunch at Uncle Lindy's club and debated whether it would be all right to take me. In the end they decided it would.

"I hope some old bore won't object," said my father.

"It is always quiet on Saturday," said Uncle Lindy. "Boys are superfluous in a man's club," he added, bending down for my benefit.

I was glad enough when the two men got so involved in a conversation that they forgot me.

I had never been in a club before. It was a little like a hotel but also like a church. The porter was friendly, not at all like the old man at the school. There was a wonderful white and shiny place to wash in. Luncheon, when it came, was disappointing. In these surroundings I expected to get a banquet. Uncle Lindy ordered me a chop and rice pudding. It was the first meal, so my father afterwards said, that he had ever known Uncle Lindy to buy for anyone. He must have been in wonderful spirits because he offered to take me to a football match. Father said he would go home, otherwise my mother would be alone. Uncle Lindy said he would come back in the train with me. This was really an outstanding day.

"What is a snob?" I asked my father when Uncle Lindy was talking to the waiter.

"A person who is inordinately fond of the great," he said. "Why do you ask?"

"Uncle Lindy said Provost Mahaffy was a snob."

"Everyone is. But he made a parade of it."

"What's this?" said Uncle Lindy sharply.

"Brian says you accused Mahaffy of being a snob."

"He always looked out for the most distinguished person in the room, and then made for him. He was incessantly referring to Kings and Queens of his acquaintance. He was too worldly for a clergyman," said Uncle Lindy.

"Is Mrs Heber a snob?" I said.

"Eat up your chop and don't discuss your elders," said Uncle Lindy sharply.

"Did Provost Traill eat people? Uncle Lindy said he was a savage." I said this because I had a feeling that this was something Uncle Lindy should not have said.

"He didn't eat people. He barked at them," said my father.

"His bark was worse than his bite," I said, feeling this was a place to get that one in.

"I don't like a child to be precocious," said Uncle Lindy. "Mr Darley will have to knock that out of you."

The day which had promised so well a few minutes before had now clouded over. I began to dread the idea of an afternoon with Uncle Lindy, so bony and fast-walking, with a perpetual drop at the end of his nose, and that way of talking as if he was shouting at one from the window of a departing train. I don't know how he could even be my father's half-brother. Father was so cheerful and comfortable—it was strange how much the better half my father was.

My father knew what I was thinking. He gave me a smile of understanding. It made me feel all right again, knowing that we were in league and Uncle Lindy was outside it.

A fat man came up to our table and said something to Uncle Lindy. I could see he was looking for someone to talk to, and he began without paying the least attention to any of us. He turned his head round slowly as he talked, and his words puffed out like steam from a boiling kettle.

"How long do you give the present state of affairs, Lindy? If the Government doesn't put down the business here, it must resign. The country will be bankrupt in six months."

"It is too late," said Uncle Lindy. "They have lost control. They should let Wilson take over with the Army. Lloyd George has made a mess of it. These Black and Tans and Auxiliaries are a disgrace. I am all for shooting Sinn Feiners, but not like this. George should never have sent jailbirds over to keep law and order. Murderers and thieves, that's what some of them are. Who could have imagined this in Asquith's time? Lloyd George is not fit for office."

I had heard this before from Uncle Lindy. It was because Lloyd George was not a gentleman we were having trouble. And needless to say the Sinn Feiners were not gentlemen either. But no one had ever told me Black and Tans were murderers. I thought they were 'on our side'. We could not have jailbirds on our side. I felt an awful dropping sensation inside me as I watched this strange man's head turning slowly like a cowl on a chimney. I waited to hear my father contradict him, but all he said was: 'They have a dirty job.'

"It is no excuse," said the other. "They represent the greatest empire the world has ever known."

"It happens when great empires employ Welsh attorneys to manage their affairs. If the Duke of Wellington were alive today——" Uncle Lindy began.

"If Julius Caesar were alive!—What a fatuous observation, Lindy," said the strange man, interrupting.

I had never heard anyone put Uncle Lindy down before. It made him red in the face. "I was only thinking of the change in our rulers in the last hundred years. I don't see what is fatuous in that."

"It has no bearing on the present situation," said the fat man. "We are going to get some sort of Home Rule. They refused it to Redmond. They will give it to the Sinn Feiners. Mark my words. We shall all have our throats cut."

"The Government must restore law and order first."

The fat man, who had sat down uninvited, banged his fist on our table.

"Up Jenkins," I said without realising what I was going to say until I said it. I wanted to relieve the tension, I suppose.

"You are an impudent pup," said the fat man. His face was quite horrible, all sweaty. His eyes bulged. I was frightened.

"Apologise," said my father to me quietly.

"I am sorry," I said.

"Children are not supposed to be in the club," said the fat man.

"Oh dear," said my father.

"The boy has apologised," said Uncle Lindy.

We all got up then, all except the puffing, sweating, fat man, who had sat down at our table. He never said good-bye.

"You must keep your mouth shut when you are with grown-ups," said my father when we got outside.

"The child deserves a skelping," said Uncle Lindy. But I think he was secretly pleased I had avenged him.

"Is that a club bore?" I said to my father when I felt we had all settled down again. The word had conveyed to me a great hog-like creature just like the man who had raided our table.

"I shall fine you sixpence for each question from now on," said my father.

The football game was in College Park. Father walked as far as the gate with us. It was on his way to the station. I was sorry when he left us. Uncle Lindy gave me the feeling that he wasn't with me. It was worse than being alone to be with someone like that. They prevented one from getting comfortable inside. They were a sort of threat to one's peace of mind. I think in Uncle Lindy's case the reason was very simple. He was not happy himself and he was jealous of happiness. He wanted to criticise and complain so that the rest of the world should realise his bad luck and feel ashamed to enjoy itself.

We could have sat down for sixpence, but he said this was a waste of money, so we stood against the railings. It was all right until people who did not think it was a waste of money to do so, came and sat in front of us. I could not see over the backs of their heads. I did not want to make Uncle Lindy cross, but I did want to see the football match. I crept under the rails and stood behind the touchline seats. A nice woman who had a rug wrapped round her told her companion to 'Move up and let the kid sit down'. I thought Uncle Lindy would not mind when he found I had got a seat for nothing. He was so busy talking to someone standing beside him about the Trinity team of 1896 that he would not miss me for ages. I looked along the row to see who was there. At first I recognised nobody. Then I found myself looking straight into the eyes of Miss Morris. There she was with the Black and Tan and Doreen and Lord Swords. She did not see me.

I wanted to get up then and there, and go to her and beg her to come back with Uncle Lindy and me, and be safe, and promise me not to have anything more to do with the

Black and Tan. I now realised what the mystery had been. He was a jailbird—a thief, perhaps a murderer. I could well understand why Miss Morris had been frightened of him. But why was she with him now? She looked happy. And so did he. But Lord Swords had the bleak look on his face which he wore when he was looking for Miss Morris; and I saw that he was not happy talking to Doreen. She was all dressed up in furs and wrapped in rugs. Miss Morris looked very undressed in comparison, not half so grand. But I could see which of the two was enjoying herself the more. Lord Swords wanted to be alone with Miss Morris. I could see that. I did not want her to be alone anywhere except in our own family. But I wanted above all to rescue her from the Black and Tan. Perhaps she did not know so much about him as I did now. Women were not told things like that by men. I got so worked up that I did not notice the footballers come out on the field. Uncle Lindy's voice high above the crowd brought me back to life. He was shouting: "Pass the ball, man. Can't you see your wing beside you? Now what's he doing? What in the name of God does he think he is doing? What is he looking round for? Back him up somebody. Is the referee asleep? That man was a mile off-side. Pass. Now's your chance. What's wrong now? Scrum back. Serves him right."

Men in white shirts were running around the ground trying to knock down other men in blue, black and white stripes. No one seemed to want to kick the ball. When anyone caught it, he was knocked down or the other side tried to tear him limb from limb. They kicked him and fell down on top of him. Then a man in a blazer who was wandering round the field getting in the way of the players blew a whistle just in time to prevent the man at the bottom of the heap from being suffocated or trampled to death. Whenever the whistle blew, the men on the ground got up and put their arms round men in shirts of their own colour in a friendly way and formed a sort of battering ram. The two battering rams then charged into one another and started to push. To distract them a player who had kept out of the scramble threw the ball under their legs. When he did this, Uncle Lindy shouted, 'Heel it Trinity.'

The ball came out behind from under the legs of one side or the other, then someone picked it up and threw it to a few players who looked more civilised than the others. They had been keeping out of the fight. They ran with the ball or passed it to one another. But someone from the other side usually knocked them down before they could get far, and sometimes they got bored and kicked the ball out of the field. Whenever the running and passing began to be fun the man in the blazer blew his whistle. This stopped the game. Then the fight began again. I was sorry for the men who had to be pulled about and kicked and pushed and stood on. But one was really as bad as another. They looked hot and dirty and very fierce. I ceased to pity them. Perhaps one of them was Traill, the savage of whom Uncle Lindy had spoken. Mahaffy, I felt sure, was out with the men in clean clothes who, if they did get knocked down occasionally, did their best to avoid it. And when they were pulled on to the ground there was none of the scrambling and fighting that went on among the savages. I wondered why both sides allowed the man with the whistle to spoil the game. He was older and more important-looking than anyone else on the field. I suppose both sides were equally afraid of him. And I could see that he might prevent the savages from killing one another.

I must confess that I became so engrossed in the spectacle at first that I forgot Miss Morris's danger. But after a while, not knowing what it was all about, the game began to bore me. I looked back at Uncle Lindy and tried to catch his eye. But whenever I waved at him I saw that he was talking to the man beside him. I heard his voice very often. He seemed to be disgusted by the players, and I thought it was rude of him to let them know it. I was sure they were doing their best. One man on each side kept well back from the other players. I suppose that was part of the game, but I was ashamed for them. I began to worry about Miss Morris and wondered what would happen if I went up to her and asked her to stay with me. She was, after all, supposed to be my governess. But this was her 'day off' and she might object. I was also nervous of Lord Swords, much more than I was of the Black and Tan, really. I was only scared of him for Miss Morris's sake. I think he wanted to be my friend. At last I summoned up courage. I decided to walk behind the seats until I came to Miss Morris. Then I was going to ask her if I could stay. She could not refuse. I could then keep an eye on the Black and Tan.

I got up quietly (no one took any notice of me) and walked along. On one side people were standing at the rails looking over my head, on the other side peoples' backs were turned and they were sitting down. I took my eyes off the game.

What happened then was so violent and sudden I cannot describe it in detail. I felt a blow as something hard hit me on the side of the head and knocked me down. My head sang with pain. My eyes watered. My nose seemed to have been pushed back into my face. I felt sick. My hands and knees were dirty. I just lay on the ground too stunned to cry.

"Well fielded, sonny," said someone. I looked up. One of the savages was smiling at me. The ball lay beside me. I got up and held it. I had never touched a football before. I tried to throw it to the smiling savage, but it was quite heavy and when I threw it, fell on a woman's head knocking her hat off. I was so confused that I hardly knew what was happening, but I realised after a moment that it was Doreen's hat. I saw

Miss Morris laughing like anything. Poor Doreen looked as she always did, like a person who has heard a noise but doesn't know where it came from. Lord Swords seemed very put out.

"I'm awfully sorry," I said.

"Brian! Where did you spring from?" said Miss Morris.

"Uncle Lindy invited me. He is back there."

"Come and sit with us," said Miss Morris.

It was exactly what I hoped for. I took care to squeeze myself between her and the Black and Tan. I tried not to look at him for fear that my face might betray my feelings.

"It's Bill," said the Black and Tan in his friendly, but not very interested, way.

I apologised again to Doreen for knocking her hat off.

"It doesn't matter," she said. "What happened to you?"

"The ball knocked me down," I said. It was the first question anyone had put to me all day. I was very grateful and began to tell her all about how it happened and why I was at the match and in Dublin at all. I explained about the school idea and the reason why I had to go to school. I was quite surprised to find how much I had to say.

"We came to watch a football match," said Lord Swords in a very pointed way.

Doreen gave me a nervous smile like a puppy gives when you push a saucer at it too quickly. It was funny to see how frightened Doreen was of everyone when, according to Mrs Heber, she was so tremendously important. I shut up then, made miserable by Lord Swords who just glared in front of him, depressing everyone. The Black and Tan had a much happier manner. It was odd when he was a villain, and everyone said how good Lord Swords was.

Miss Morris seemed to know the players personally. She told me that the two best men in the Trinity team were

South Africans. I looked among the savages for black faces and was greatly surprised when she told me the Africans were white. I thought Africans were black, Asiatics yellow, Europeans (foreigners) white, but dirty in their habits, the English above criticism and inventors of everything. The English were always honourable and fought battles which they always won because the English were always in the right. Americans were white but very common, especially in their manner of dressing, and given to boasting. Australians, New Zealanders and Canadians were people who supplied troops for war and who would be English if they only knew how. Germans were pure evil.

I did not show my ignorance, but it added to the bewilderment of the game to have had my ideas about Africa so drastically upset. I brooded over this for a while. When I looked at the field again the men in stripes—'Wanderers' Miss Morris called them; but when I asked her 'Why?' she said: "Because their fathers were wanderers I suppose," and I had to pretend to be satisfied with that answer. I don't think she really knew—had gathered into a huddle as though they had got tired of football and were playing some quiet game on their own.

"What's going on?" I asked.

"Tommy Wallis has lost his bags," said Miss Morris.

I did not want to appear stupid so I said: "This is hardly the time to be looking for them."

"Bill is a dry humourist," said the Black and Tan.

I saw that I had amused everyone by what I said. I had only meant to criticise this Tommy Wallis person and had no intention of joking. When the men came out of the huddle I saw that one of them had a new pair of trousers and I saw that a man was leaving the field with an old pair. I wondered what Miss Morris thought of my asking such an embarrassing question in public. But she did not look upset. She was not easy to shock.

I wanted to whisper to her about coming home with us. It was very awkward for me having to say it with the Black and Tan pressed up against me. And what made it harder was that she was so interested in the silly old game, saying things like "Well done, Jamie" or "Crichton doesn't push his weight in the scrum", which showed me she knew a lot about it all.

At last I took hold of her arm and tugged it until she said, "What's biting you?"

I whispered: "I want you to come home with us."

"I can't hear you. Don't whisper," she said, loud enough for everyone to hear. It was maddening. I *had* to whisper.

"I want you to come home with us," I repeated.

"Your uncle is supposed to be looking after you today. And you are always being told to go before you come out," she said.

"Come along, Bill," said the Black and Tan.

"Oh, thank you," said Miss Morris, and smiled gratefully at the murderer.

To my horror I found myself being led away. I was hot and cold. How could I explain to *him*?

It meant an awful waste of time and a walk to the pavilion and back. I pretended I wanted to so that he would not feel his time was being wasted. He meant to be kind. Lord Swords would never have made that suggestion. I suppose lords are above that sort of thing.

On our way back to the field the Black and Tan gave me a shilling. This was so kind of him I found myself, before I had time to think, saying:

"Are you really a Black and Tan?"

He took the question in a funny way. He gave me a deep

look before he spoke, then he said: "Who's been talking to you, sonny?"

"No one."

"Where did you get that idea from? Did Miss Morris tell you?"

"No. I swear. I swear, honest to goodness, she never said it. Mrs Heber and my mother seemed to be quite sure you were. I thought everyone knew."

"I am an Army officer. Have you got that, Bill? An officer in His Majesty's Army. Have you got that right into your head? The next time you hear anyone say I am a Black and Tan you know what to tell them."

I said nothing.

"Did you hear me, Bill?"

"Yes."

"Don't go telling fairy stories about me or I shall send you to a place where you will live on bread and water. Get me?"

I nodded.

I should have been very glad to hear this news. But I was not. What was most extraordinary of all was that when I thought the Black and Tan *was* a Black and Tan he seemed nicer than he did now when he said he was not. I had noticed that when I told a lie (which I did sometimes) even when it worked (which it did rarely) there was a bad feeling in the air which spoiled everything, making me sorry that I had told one and that it had been believed. It was always better to face trouble and get it over. Trouble when it came was never as bad as it seemed beforehand. I knew the atmosphere of lies. I could smell it. I smelled it now. This man *was* a Black and Tan. He only did nice things for me because he wanted to please Miss Morris. Now I was afraid of him. He walked in front of me when we made our way back to the seats. I took the opportunity to slip away and go in search of Uncle Lindy. He would be no help in my present trouble, but I could trust him. He was part of home.

He had missed me and was very fussy when I found him. It was part of his general annoyance. He wanted Trinity to win easily and they were not doing this. They had only scored once. He had fault to find with everyone. The South Africans, Malan and Van Druten, were good, but not being available for the Irish team made their merit a reproach. "If Parke and Basil MacClear were playing they would walk through that Wanderers' side," he said.

"Which is Mahaffy?" I said, not that I really cared, but I wanted to see what a snob looked like.

Uncle Lindy laughed. I had never seen him laugh before. It acted on his teeth like an earthquake. He almost choked. Without considering my feelings he turned to the man beside him and said: "My small nephew wants to know which of the players is Mahaffy?"

"Why don't you tell him?" said the man. "And be sure to point out Dean Swift and Oscar Wilde when you are at it."

"Mahaffy is dead," Uncle Lindy explained.

It would have been easy to have told me that without making a show of me. I would never come out with Uncle Lindy again. I really began to hate the day. I was cold. I was unhappy about Miss Morris. I wanted to go home. Worst of all, having gone all the way to the pavilion because Miss Morris couldn't understand my whisper, I now wanted to go in earnest.

"Uncle Lindy."

* * *

Who could I tell? Who would help? I now realise that my father was the obvious person to confide in. But then it seemed like letting him know about my feelings for Miss

Morris. I did not want him to know I had planned to marry her. I knew he would try to upset it. The family always upset an ambitious plan like camping out or looking for caves. Their imagination stopped at pantomimes and games of hide and seek.

I very nearly told Mrs Heber. I would have if I thought she was really fond of Miss Morris. But I suspected that she was jealous of all the attention Miss Morris got in comparison with Doreen who was so grand (even though nobody except Mrs Heber seemed to know about it). So I talked to Freddy Doyle.

I felt I should not. I did not care for Freddy. I only talked to him ever because he seemed so pleased to listen when most grown-ups just shoo'd one away. Freddy had this advantage also. He really knew about things like Black and Tans. He told me about them when my parents, Mrs Heber and all the older people I knew used to say "Prenez garde" when the subject came up in my presence.

He knew the difference between Black and Tans and Auxiliaries. Sometimes when I was with him a lorry would go racing past with men from one or other of these corps sitting on it behind a wire cage. Freddy always went pale at the sight. Sometimes they looked quite cheerful to me. But they always sat with guns ready. I think Freddy expected them to shoot at him.

"The Auxiliaries is worse nor the Tans", Freddy used to say.

He was not in the forge on Sunday (the day after the match) so I went to see him on Monday afternoon, pretending I was going to Mrs Heber. To make that true I decided to call on Mrs Heber after I left Freddy. I was far too excited to put Freddy last on my plans.

He was in the forge filing an iron bar when I arrived. He had on his bowler hat and shiny blue serge trousers. His shirt had been white. The buttons in front were missing and showed patches of pink skin with red hair on it.

"Good-day to you, Master," he said (Freddy always called me that).

I took my usual place beside the bellows and waited for Freddy to begin his questions. There was never any difficulty about giving him information.

"What's the quality been up to?" was his first question. Then he would ask me who had invited us, where my parents visited, what my father was doing, what I had heard said by my parents or Mrs Heber. Above all he was anxious about Miss Morris. This was really the bond between Freddy and me. He never tired of talking about 'that one' as he called her.

"Has her friend in the racing-car" [he pronounced car kee-yar] "been about lately?" he said.

"I saw you looking at him one day," I said. "He was waiting for Miss Morris, but she said she would not go out to him because she was frightened of him."

"I didn't think that one would be frightened of any man," said Freddy.

Then I explained the whole situation. Freddy listened very carefully. Sometimes he asked me questions—'Showed you his revolver did he?' 'Does your Daddy know about this carry-on?'

I answered truthfully.

It was beginning to grow dark. I realised that I had stayed out far too long. Mr Heber would be back by now. There was no use in calling there now. Freddy could not have been more attentive, but I had a feeling of dismay. I knew in my heart that I should not have talked to him. I didn't really like him. The forge was forbidden. And there was something in his manner this afternoon, some almost repulsive greed for information that made me wonder was Freddy the right person to talk to. And it became clearer to me, the more he asked me questions, how little a man like Freddy could help in a problem concerning people who only knew him as a blacksmith and who said he was a born liar and as crooked as a ram's horn. If the Black and Tan knew what we talked about I felt sure he would put Freddy in jail. My father said Freddy lived with one foot in prison and one in the pub and was equally at home in either. But when I asked Freddy if he had ever been in prison he said: "It's the most atrocious lie. I was but once before the court and the magistrate said: 'You leave the court Mr Doyle without a stain on your character up to the present.'"

I told my father this but it seemed to make no difference. "I forbid you to go near the forge," he said.

"It's late, Freddy. I must go home. Can't you suggest something? I must get someone to help me."

Freddy pushed his fingers under his hat and scratched his head.

"Listen, Master. You try to find out when the Black and Tan is expected down and let me know. But you are not to go telling this to anyone. Do you mind me now?"

This was very positive. I did not see what Freddy could do. But perhaps he had a scheme to put the car out of action. Anyhow it was a relief to feel one had tried to do something.

I ran home. On my way I went in the back gate of the Hebers' house and out of the front one without being seen. I could say I had been there if the question were put.

But God, as I soon discovered, took a poor view of this stratagem. When I came home—slipping in by the back door, hoping to get my face behind a book quietly, in a corner—I heard, to my horror, Mrs Heber's voice. It came from my mother's bedroom. I had always been impressed by the range of Mrs Heber's voice: ordinarily it had a sweet sound of water running over pebbles, but it could freeze, and it had frozen now. It came in an icy flow punctuated by my mother's warmer tones. But there was no doubt that Mrs Heber was giving the lecture. I had never heard her in such a mood; and that it should have been provoked by my mother, who was in bed, made it even more extraordinary. I never thought of grown-ups lecturing one another. I believed that to be one of the privileges of childhood.

I took up the book I was reading at the time—*Old Saint Paul's*—and crept upstairs to my own room. A few moments later the bell rang. Alice came up from the kitchen and went into my mother's bedroom. There was absolute silence from the moment the bell rang until Alice left the room. Then Mrs Heber began again. (It must be exasperating for maids when conversation stops in their presence. It must have been hard for them not to listen at doors.) Alice had not shut the door properly because I could now hear every word.

"I am responsible for Doreen, and how am I to face her mother when she hears she has been careering round the country with a Black and Tan and a nursery governess?"

"But we don't know he is a Black and Tan, and we do know Miss Morris is not a nursery governess. She couldn't look after a cat."

"That is not the point. I must say I would feel my position acutely if I were you, I should have expected you to exercise some discretion. What would you say if a daughter of yours were to meet people of that kind in my house? Would you absolve *me* from blame?"

"You invited Miss Morris. And the man has never been here. If you like I shall talk to her about him. But I don't know whether I have the right to discuss her friends with her. She is twenty-two."

"The girl is living under your roof. I should think her parents—if she has any—would feel you should concern yourself about her. But that is not the point. I am responsible to my sister for Doreen. The girl has been most carefully brought up, and I have never had a moment's worry before this. Do you know the time they came home last night? Do you know where they had been?"

"But Lord Swords was with them. Why did you not talk to him?"

"I did. I spoke very sharply to him."

"Then I suppose it won't happen again."

"The fact that it has happened at all is what worries me. I am afraid I must forbid Doreen to come here or to see any more of your governess."

"By all means, if you want to."

"And may I say—it is hardly my business, I know, but I am fond of the child—that if I were you I should send Brian to a good school. I notice a marked change in him lately."

"In what way, may I ask?"

I had my usual sensations when my name was mentioned. My mouth went dry, and my heart seemed to stand still, and a prickly sensation came in my spine. It was pleasant to hear the warm way in which my mother asked the question. She was on my side.

"He is far too precocious. I don't talk to servants, but I gather he behaved in the oddest fashion one day when he visited me. Took his clothes off and ran after Maud, so she tells me."

"Mrs Heber, what do you mean?"

Now it was my mother's voice which surprised me. It was cold and angry and fearfully solemn.

"Just what I say."

I had tried to forget the awful moment when Mrs Heber's maid found me weighing myself. I had never felt so ashamed in my life. But it was a lie to say I chased her. I would have jumped out of the window to get away. But again I was heartened by the way my mother seemed to want to defend me, and I knew from her voice that she was angry with Mrs Heber and not with me.

"I should like to talk to your maid. Brian is nine years old. Do you realise what you have insinuated?"

"I have insinuated nothing, Mrs. Allen."

"Mrs Heber, neither of us is a child. And I have reason to believe you are fully aware of the implications of what you tell me."

"And what, pray, am I to deduce from that cryptic utterance?"

"As much or as little as you please. I am not going to lie here in bed and listen without protest while anyone suggests my son is a monster of depravity. I ask you please to leave. I shall tell my husband and he will talk to Mr Heber. Good afternoon."

My mouth was dry again. I could hear my heart beat like a clock. There was a silence in my mother's room like there is between claps of thunder. I pressed my hand against my ribs to see if I could quieten my heart-beats. Could they be heard? I wondered.

"I am sure Maud exaggerated. But she swears she found him with no clothes on."

Mrs Heber's voice was quite shaky now. I knew how she felt. All her pride was gone. I wondered why I did not dislike her. I think it was because she had made me sound so exciting.

"I prefer not to discuss it," said my mother. "I don't feel very well. My husband will know what to do. I can only say this: the child is very fond of you. You must know that. I wonder what sort of woman you can be to make him the victim of your malice. It is not Brian's fault if Lord Swords finds

Miss Morris more attractive than your niece. And, by the way, Doreen at twenty-five ought to be able to look after herself. So far as I can gather she was never in the slightest danger. There are compensations for not being attractive. It ought to relieve you of a great deal of anxiety. If Miss Morris were your niece you would have something to worry about. And then perhaps you would not vent your jealous spleen on a little boy."

I heard the rustle of Mrs Heber's clothes—they always rustled—as she got up from her chair and walked to the door. She paused at the door. I wondered what she would say. I knew it must have been a strange experience for her to have been talked to like this. After so long a pause that it seemed like another day Mrs Heber said, "Twenty-four." I hardly recognised her voice. I spoke like that after I had been running, and began to talk before I got my breath back.

Would she ever seem the same to me again? She went without saying another word. I heard the hall door shut. I did not move. I sat on my bed, for how long I could not say. But when I heard Alice calling my name it seemed that her voice came from a great distance.

When I went up to my mother after supper, to talk to her before I went to bed, she was the same as she always was, not at all the person who had talked to Mrs Heber. Perhaps it had been a dream.

* * *

Grown-ups give some of the game away by the questions they ask. If three or four people ask what each thinks is a cautious question, the total effect is sometimes very revealing.

This is what happened during the next few days. I will try to piece it out and set down events in their order, but I find this difficult now. So much that happened is cut sharp on my memory, I can see it as clearly as if it were happening again. But a great deal is blurred and seems to be mixed with recollections of dreams. That interview with Mrs Heber is one of the blurs. Within a few days my parents were at the Hebers'. I heard my mother speaking quite normally to Mrs Heber on the telephone. Miss Morris went out to a party at Lord Swords's where Doreen was a guest (I heard my mother asking what Doreen looked like, and Miss Morris saying 'Dressed to kill.')

But I kept away from Mrs Heber. It was not that I bore her any ill-will. She was always different from other people in my eyes, and entitled therefore to make her own laws. But she had filled me with a sense of shame. I saw myself through her eyes, running round naked, frightening maids. I was no better than Provost Traill, and fit only for Rugby scrummages. Indeed, this impression must have haunted me, because I had a dream that I was playing football with the Black and Tan, Lord Swords and Uncle Lindy. Miss Morris was watching us. We took ages to start because the Black and Tan wanted to drag a cannon on to the field and Uncle Lindy objected. Uncle Lindy was dressed in his funny pyjamas with sugar stick stripes. Lord Swords looked fatter and balder than usual in a Wanderers' jersey. When the game began, I kicked the ball away over the trees. Uncle Lindy started to complain in his strange, high voice. But the Black and Tan said, "It's all right, Bill," and began to use Lord Swords as a ball. Uncle Lindy got very excited and screamed at me:

"Get on-side, damn you."

It was then that I realised I had no clothes on. I was out in the middle of the field with nowhere to hide. I saw Miss Morris out of the corner of my eye, but she was cheering the Black and Tan who had caught Lord Swords and was trying to push him into the mouth of the cannon while Uncle Lindy was pushing against it and shouting, 'Heel it Trinity.'

I saw my moment to escape and started to run. I was almost through the rails and safe when the whistle blew.

Mrs Heber in a blazer was coming across the field towards me, blowing the whistle as if she were a train. Everyone turned and looked at me now. I saw frightful contempt in Miss Morris's eye. The Black and Tan said, "It won't do, Bill," and he was the only one who looked kind. Uncle Lindy had gathered a group of people together and I could see he was telling them about me because they were all staring in my direction and laughing without kindness. It was a horrible dream at the time, but remembered it seems funny.

I think the row with Mrs Heber was patched up by my father. I heard him say to my mother, "I think the poor fellow has never been allowed to forget he married a Castle beauty." And there was a strange meal at which most of the conversation was in French. My mother had been at a French convent for a year, but my father's French was learned at an Irish school, and I know that he was quite helpless when he went abroad. He spoke as if he were training a dog, using very few words and repeating them very often. I understood quite a lot.

"La domestique entra là—what is the word for bathroom? —et l'enfant reste la sans vestements."

Miss Morris raised an eyebrow and looked at me.

"Prenez garde," said my mother, and kicked her under the table. I could always see when people did that.

"Il rase la figure. Le visage tout couvert avec—what is the word for soap?—anyhow la domestique a peur."

"She what?" said Miss Morris.

"A peur—how do you say was frightened?"

"A pity about her," said my mother. "Eat up that Shepherd's Pie, Brian, or you won't get a bit of pudding."

I was keenly interested in what was being said and enormously relieved to find I was not in disgrace. I could trust my father to understand.

"Où est la grand dame en ce moment?" said my mother. "Comme Madame Récamier, au salon je suppose. C'est une hypocrite. Je ne voudrais pas faire de médisances, mais quand je pense à la vie que cette dame à faite à son mari autrefois, j'ai quelque hesitation d'accepter les conseils qu'elle pourrait me donner maintenant."

"Eat up your dinner, Casanova," said Miss Morris to me. She had been watching me all the time my mother was saying unkind things in French. I knew they were unkind although I did not understand them.

"What does Casanova mean?" I said.

"You must be more careful," said my mother in a cross voice to Miss Morris.

"Oh, Tom Thumb," said Miss Morris in a sulky tone. She hated being a governess.

"Anyhow," said my father. "Peace is restored, and it was a lot to get an apology from her."

"I prefer not to think about it," said my mother, looking at me.

Afterwards I got out the dictionary and looked up Casanova. I could not find it.

> *Cascabel, kas'ka-bel, n. The whole rear part behind the base ring of a cannon (sp.).*
> *Cascade, kas-kad, n. A waterfall: a trimming of lace or other material in a loose wavy fall—v.i. to fall in cascades (Fr.-It.-L. cadere, to fall).*
> *Cascara . . .*

But I knew all about Cascara.

As I had the dictionary open I looked up 'depravity'. My mother had used it. 'Monster of depravity', that is what she said Mrs Heber made me out to be. *Deprave, de-prav, v.t. to make bad or worse; to corrupt.* I looked at corrupt. It said it meant to make putrid.

Now, whenever I had played a game with Miss Morris she always got bored before long because I was so bad. And she ended by saying, "You are putrid."

I decided to warn her not to use the word in my mother's presence. I shall never forget how formidable she sounded when she said 'monster of depravity', as if that was the worst thing anyone could be. What would she have thought if she knew Miss Morris said 'putrid' (which was the same thing) over and over again?

I began my evening lessons with Mr Griffin, the national schoolmaster, soon after this. He was a sad man who looked as if his spare time was spent untying shoe-laces. His face was grey, and his voice had only one tone, a mournful one. I had heard such terrifying stories of national schools that I expected him to beat me all the time, but he was never even cross with me. He did sums in a sad, slow way, writing very neat figures. It was a different 'method' from that which I had been taught, and I inclined to fight against it, thinking it was as common as the way he wore his hair in a quiff and carried pens and pencils in his breast pocket and wore some sort of badge in the lapel of his coat. He never showed any resentment, but patiently corrected the sums. He had a nasty-looking black book with poems and prose extracts in it. He used to get me to read these and then set me exercises in grammar or explaining the meanings of the words and what parts of speech they were. He pronounced words in such a queer way (the letter 'h' for instance was 'haitch'), I suspected his capacity and was humiliated when he showed me that 'but' was not an adjective, and 'alacrity' did not mean sadness as I had supposed.

I could neither like nor dislike Mr Griffin. He was associated in my mind with cheerless things: wet days, moth balls, old newspapers, dismissed servants, last year's Christmas cards, yesterday's pudding, duty-calls, afternoon walks.

Miss Morris sat with me in the morning and superintended my home work. If I got badly stuck in a sum I would ask her to do it. I liked to watch her while she sucked the end of the pencil and her hair fell forward round her face. When I told her Mr Griffin did not pronounce words properly she said, "Doesn't he now, Mr Prig?"

I thought she meant pig. Years afterwards when I was mowing a lawn it came to me that Miss Morris had said 'prig'. Indeed, I heard her say it in my imagination, and I blushed with retrospective shame.

We both got bored with the bits of poetry I was given to learn from *The Village Blacksmith, Excelsior, The Lay of the Last Minstrel*. She flicked through the pages and read out scraps to me but stopped suddenly after a line or two as if she were betraying secrets. She seemed to be looking for something. What did she expect to find? I tried to help. "This is good," I said and began:

> "Scots wha hae wi' Wallace bled
> Scots wham Bruce . . ."

"I don't want to hear about Scots weighing hay," she would say and snatch the book back from me and go on searching with her lower lip thrust out, a way she had.

> "Annihilating all that's made
> To a green thought in a green shade.

That's better than your haymakers," she said. But I could not see any sense in it.

Then she read out a verse and said it was so beautiful it

made her want to cry. This was so strange in Miss Morris, who was always laughing, that I marked the page and asked Mr Griffin what he thought. He read the verse out aloud. But read by him and read by Miss Morris the lines were so different that I was almost reduced to tears myself. I did not quite understand them either time. But as she read the world seemed suddenly a changed place, full of wonderful lights and sounds. When Mr Griffin read, the words stayed in black print on the horrible paper in the mean little school-book. They were a part of the furniture, of the rough desk and the dirty ink well, and the green wall with the great map on it, of the picture of the Pope over the fireplace, of the blackboard with the isosceles triangle chalked on it, of the yard I could see through the window, and the outside lavatory, and Mr Griffin's bicycle against the wall, and Mr Griffin himself in his tight blue suit, with his quiff and his pens and badges, his bicycle clips and his grey wool socks. I tried to read the verse again myself at night in my own room. Miss Morris was out, and Uncle Lindy had gone for a walk with my mother as far as the letter-box, and my father was downstairs. I tried to see what it would sound like now and if I could redeem it, if I could find Miss Morris in it again and drive the dirge of Mr Griffin's voice away.

> I cannot see what flowers are at my feet,
> Nor what soft incense hangs upon the boughs,
> But, in embalmed darkness, guess each sweet
> Wherewith the seasonable month endows
> The grass, the thicket, and the fruit-tree wild;
> White hawthorn, and the pastoral eglantine;
> Fast fading violets cover'd up in leaves;
> And mid-May's eldest child,
> The coming musk-rose, full of dewy wine,
> The murmurous haunt of flies on summer eves.

" 'Tis good," had been Mr Griffin's comment. "But the likes of this would be better for you." He then pointed out a poem by Thomas Osborne Davis which went:

"Did they dare, did they dare, to slay Owen Roe O'Neill?"
"Yes, they slew with poison him they feared to meet with steel."
"May God wither up their hearts! May their blood cease to flow!
May they walk in living death, who poisoned Owen Roe!"

"Who is 'they', Mr Griffin, please?"
He smiled, and I felt ashamed. It was a smile of pity for my ignorance, but it ended with a bitter look as if he had tasted something bad.
"The English. Who else?"
It made me more depressed than ever. I wanted to get up and run away from Mr Griffin who seemed to be the silent enemy of all that Miss Morris stood for in life.

I read quietly so as not to be heard, but in our ill-constructed house, empty as it was tonight save for my father in the room below, my voice sounded to me as if I were blowing through a horn. I heard the sound of a chair being moved downstairs, then the door opening, and footsteps on the stairs.

"Were you calling?" said my father as he came into my room. I tried to hide the book.

"You should be in bed," he said.

There was nothing cross or suspicious in his manner, in fact he was so friendly and I felt so greatly cheered by his coming that I jumped into bed and invited him to talk to me.

"What shall we talk about?" he said. He always said this when I asked for conversation. I never knew what to reply because I really only wanted his attention. It would have been quite sufficient, so far as I was concerned, if he recited nine times tables or the Ten Commandments. But that, I suppose, would have been a bore for him.

The poem I was reading had been so connected in my mind with Miss Morris that I had been ashamed of having been overheard reading it. But now when my father accepted my invitation by sitting on the side of my bed and really wanted a subject to discuss, I thought it was an excellent opportunity to kill two birds, to hold my father there and at the same time go on with what was interesting me most.

"I want you to decide something," I began. "This is the book I do my English out of. I liked the look of this poem best, Miss Morris likes this one, but Mr Griffin selected another when I asked him what he thought of Miss Morris's one. And this is another of his favourites. What do you think?"

"Keats was a wonderful poet," said my father.

"Mr Griffin says it is not very suitable for me." I had been pointing to the pages in the light of a tiny lamp which burned in my room ever since, as a small boy, I had been too frightened to sleep alone in the dark. Now I began to recite:

"Full often, when our fathers saw the Red above the Green
They ran in rude but fierce array, with sabre, pike and skein.
And over many a noble town, and many a field of dead,
They proudly set the Irish Green above the English Red."

"I hope Mr Griffin is not talking politics to you," said my father.

"What are politics? Is that a Prenez Garde subject like people going to have babies?"

He took a little time before he answered, having apparently suddenly found something wrong with his spectacles. But when he had settled this, he said:

"There are things in the world which lead to fighting and all sorts of unpleasantness. Politics is one of them. Wise people keep out of them and mind their own business. At the moment this country is upside down, people are being murdered every day on account of politics. Now do you understand why I don't want you to be bothered about them? And they are too complicated to understand at your age. You have a lot of useful things to learn. You cannot afford to waste time on old men's wickedness."

"Is *Scots wha hae wi' Wallace bled* a political poem?"

"No. Certainly not." And then he added, "Not nowadays."

"I like it. I like it better than the one Miss Morris likes." But when she read it out, it sounded beautiful, like being out in the garden on summer nights. When Mr Griffin read it I thought of nothing except the smell that tweed has when it gets wet. I did not, of course, tell this to my father.

"Miss Morris has a very pretty voice," said my father.

"Do you love her?"

"I am very fond of her."

"Are you fonder of her than you are of Mummy?"

"No. Of course not."

"Than you are of me?"

"One is fond of different people in different ways. What is so nice about Miss Morris, if you must know, is that she is absolutely natural. That is the rarest thing in people. Children have it in the beginning. But they lose it. If you can remain natural you can fly through life like a bird. It disarms everyone."

"Am I natural?"

"Sometimes I think so. And sometimes I wonder. But I think you are. You bother too much about what people think of you. That is what makes most people affected. They begin to act. They go on acting all their lives. And they act so badly."

"Is Mrs Heber acting?"

"You must not ask those questions."

"Why? You say Miss Morris is natural, and now I want to know if Mrs Heber is natural. Isn't that a natural question?"

"It is. But grown-ups should not be discussed by children. And children should not be bothered with the problems which worry grown-ups. It's quite a fair bargain, as you will realise when you get older. Who would not give up gossip to be relieved of worry? Children have the best of it."

"I worry a lot. I am always worrying. Sometimes I think I shall die of worry."

"That is because you will stick your nose into other people's business. What is worrying you now? Tell me. See if I can help."

This offer, so generous, so unexpected, overwhelmed me. I cannot convey how pleasant my father's manner was when he made the effort to be nice. He had the same effect on me as Miss Morris had when she read the piece of poetry. It transformed the world. But too suddenly. I was not ready for it. It should have made me wildly happy—it did in a way —but its immediate effect was to make me want to cry; because with the sense of wonderful delight there was another that it would not last. And the feeling of delight made the world I knew so drab that the thought of coming back to it was quite unbearable. And now when my father asked me what was worrying me, I found that I did not really know what to select. Miss Morris and the Black and Tan worried me most, but Mrs Heber also worried me, Mr Griffin worried me, Uncle Lindy worried me, the idea of school worried me, the thought of Miss Morris going away worried me. Everything worried me when I came to think of it. So I began to cry.

"Come on. Come on. This won't do. Tell me the trouble."

"How can we save Miss Morris from the Black and Tan?"

I was interested to see the change this question made in

my father's manner. He had been gentle and relaxed. Now he sat up. All his creases smoothed out. Alert. Like a bird when it hears a noise.

"What are you talking about?"

"The Black and Tan. He was at that place we went to where I danced. He was there with the girl who was so unsuitable. Mrs Heber and Mummy both said he was a Black and Tan. I told him so. He said he wasn't. But I know he is. Miss Morris says she is afraid of him."

"Did Miss Morris say that?"

"She did. She said she didn't want to see him. But I notice she does."

"She isn't going to any more," said my father.

We both kept silent after that. It was as if we were in agreement.

"But if he is a friend of Lord Swords, won't she meet him there?"

"I doubt if Lord Swords will encourage him. We must take a chance on that."

"He wouldn't do for Doreen, I suppose. It's a pity, because he can be quite decent. He gave me half a crown one day, and the other day at the football match he gave me a shilling."

"Timeo Danaos et dona ferentes," said my father.

"I don't understand."

"That is one of the few tags I have kept. It means: I don't trust the Greeks even when they are giving presents."

"Is the Black and Tan a Greek?"

"I don't think so. He is not a Black and Tan. He is an officer, new style."

"I am sure he is a Black and Tan."

"Mrs Heber had the same idea, but when she found she had made a mistake, she made a handsome apology to your mother and asked him to dinner."

"And she likes him now."

"She says he is frightfully common but wonderfully cheerful. The men in the neighbourhood are a lugubrious lot when you come to think of it."

I was not going to waste this opportunity: it was not often that my father and I reached such a level of intimacy. I had too clear a picture in my mind of this man, the way he was always found lurking on the road, the suspicion he had aroused in Freddy Doyle who was an authority. (I would never forget the way Freddy had stared that day when he thought I had not seen him, the day the Black and Tan was waiting for Miss Morris.) And, above all, I trusted my own instincts about him.

"Do you think you can see wickedness in a person's eyes?" I said.

My father thought for a moment.

"Sometimes. Particularly when they are off-guard. But sometimes it is our own wickedness that we see reflected there."

"Like a face in a pool?"

"Exactly. Your mother has the sort of honest eyes that cast reflections."

"Is Mummy more honest than most people?"

"She is."

"More honest than Miss Morris, for instance?"

"I am not going to make comparisons. Your mother is older than Miss Morris."

"I know that."

"Experience keeps people back from the edge of the cliff, you know."

Whenever I went walking with anyone near a cliff they always spoilt the adventure by yelling at me to keep back when I was still miles from the edge. It really required very little experience to keep one from falling over. But I said nothing. My father was thinking about something else, I could see.

Soon after that doors opened downstairs, and Uncle Lindy's voice blasted through the house, destroying the quiet comfort of our talk.

"Send Mummy up to me."

"I will. But don't bother her about Miss Morris and the Black and Tan, like a decent man. We have to keep these worries to ourselves. And don't let it be a worry. I will keep an eye on Miss Morris for you."

I was immensely relieved. My heart flooded with gratitude.

"Do you think I could marry Miss Morris when I am twenty-one?"

"You won't want to, son."

"Oh, but I will. I am absolutely determined to do it, as a matter of fact."

"When you are twenty-one you will be thinking of girls who are only eight or nine years old now."

"That is not true."

"There are as good fish in the sea. That's a proverb you will get to learn, but I admire your taste. Miss Morris is a very attractive girl. Don't you think it is a little hard on her to ask her to wait so long? She might get tired waiting. Have you ever thought of that?"

I had. I had thought of it very often. I lived in dread of Lord Swords, the Black and Tan, and all the other grown-up men in the world who could ask Miss Morris to marry them while I was waiting to grow up. They rose up before my eyes now, an army of Greeks all bearing gifts to Miss Morris: and I was helpless to warn her not to trust them, but to wait for me.

My father must have seen my face grow sad. He put his

arm around me. "It will all come right in the end. You'll see," he said. And then he went out.

My mother came up and tucked me in with the quick method she used when she wanted to avoid talking to me. It was all over in a second. I was tight under the blankets. She had kissed me. And her back disappeared through the door, before I had time to say 'Good night'. She answered from the stairs.

The voices came up from below. My mother's a murmur, my father's a growl, Uncle Lindy's a loud bark. I could hear everything he said when I listened. It made no sense until he said:

"I am very glad you got in touch with her parents." Then after a few answering murmurs and growls, he said: "I would not take the responsibility. She is not your daughter."

After my mother came up to bed, Uncle Lindy stayed down with my father. They went out into the garden for a moment and I could hear them under my window.

"I was afraid you were going to make a fool of yourself, Dick," said Uncle Lindy.

"I told you not to mention that subject," my father said.

"I still think it is foolish to keep her. Why doesn't she stay at home?"

"She fell out with her parents over this fellow."

"Can't she get a job somewhere else?"

"As what?"

"Anything."

"We are fond of her. Were you ever fond of anyone in all your life, Lindy?"

"Of course. I should hope so. What a question to ask! But I have never made a fool of myself over a pretty face, if that's what you mean."

"Time for bed, Lindy."

"Don't say I didn't warn you."

"I shan't. I promise you that."

Was it possible that Miss Morris was not going away after all? I felt very happy. Uncle Lindy was defeated once again. I went to sleep quite soon and dreamed that he was riding a high bicycle. He wore a mackintosh and an old-fashioned top hat and carried an open umbrella in one hand. Girls were chasing him, girls with long golden hair. They were throwing things at him. But he rode along majestically without seeming to notice them.

* * *

Miss Morris stayed at home more than usual. One day I heard my mother say to Mrs Heber on the telephone: "I don't think it is wise. It seems funny that I should be telling this to you."

I knew they were discussing Miss Morris. Lord Swords came one day and took her out in his car. He said he was hesitating about the A.C. and wanted to discuss the matter with her.

Letters came for her, letters that she used to put away and read when she left the dining-room after breakfast. I saw her drop one of them into the fireplace in the school-room without opening it. It seemed to me to be an extraordinary thing to do. I told Freddy Doyle about it. He said the letters might contain threats and that I should try to get hold of one if I could. I was shocked at the idea, but Freddy assured me that if there was a Black and Tan in the case one had to stop at nothing. "They're murderous divils," he said.

Miss Morris used to rush to the telephone when it rang, but now she let my mother answer it or Alice who always mixed up people's names. Once or twice when it was a call for Miss Morris she asked my mother to say she was out.

I was not supposed to know how to talk on the telephone. I was not mechanically inclined and the family decided this without ever consulting me. But the telephone was easy. It just happened that no one ever wanted to talk to me on it, and there was no one I wanted to talk to either. I was able to call on Mrs Heber. And Freddy Doyle didn't have a telephone in his cottage. Because I was lazy, and because the calls were never for me anyhow, I used to let the bell ring until someone else came to answer it.

But one day I happened to be passing as it buzzed, and took the telephone off the hook by climbing on a chair.

"Hello," I said.

"Is that you, Bill?" said the voice.

I nearly dropped the receiver. My tongue was paralysed. For a moment I thought to say 'no', and clap the receiver back on the hook. The moment went.

"Are you there, Bill?"

He really sounded quite friendly.

"This is Brian."

"Sorry, Brian. New name, old firm. Would you like a present of a cocker spaniel puppy?"

"I'd love it. A live one?"

"Alive and kicking. I won it in a raffle. May I bring it down to you?"

"Of course. But don't stay. Miss Morris has promised Daddy she won't see you any more."

"She has, has she?"

"So you can just ring at the door and give the puppy to Alice. What's his name?"

"He's a she. I call her Sweetheart."

"That's a funny name."

"She has eyes like Mary Pickford's."

"I don't know what kind of eyes those are."

"Listen, Bill. You really want this pup?"

"Of course. I am longing for a dog. I asked for one last Christmas."

"Very well. You tell Miss Morris that I shall have the pup in my car at the usual place at six o'clock, Monday. See?"

"Why can't you give it to Alice?"

"I couldn't, Bill. Not a pup like that. It has been reared very refined. I couldn't give it to the general."

"Alice is not a general. It's very common to have a general, I believe."

"Do you now? Sorry, Your Grace, for the gaffe. You will give my message, Your Grace, won't you? Monday, six o'clock, usual place."

"I suppose so."

"No supposing. Honest?"

"Honest."

"So long, Bill. Pack up your troubles in your old kit bag, and smile, smile, smile."

Then the telephone rang off. I stood looking at the receiver in my hand for quite a long time before I put it back. It seemed almost too good to be true that I was getting a dog at last. Could there be any harm in Miss Morris seeing the Black and Tan for just one minute? He must be jolly decent really. But I was worried. I remembered how my father changed when I mentioned the Black and Tan. And what was that he said about Greeks giving presents?

I took my courage and asked Miss Morris—in the most casual way—if the Black and Tan *was* a Greek. I said it to her next morning when we were doing my lessons for Mr Griffin. She looked quite surprised.

"What Black and Tan?"

"Oh, you know. The one who drives the A.C."

"Oh, him. Whatever put that idea into your head? He does some very special job. He isn't a Black and Tan."

"And he isn't a Greek?"

"Not that I know of. Why do you ask? Have you seen him lately? Has he been looking for me?"

"Don't worry," I said.

I tried to say it in the way my father said it to me on the night we talked to one another. I even put my arm around her and gave her a hug.

"You read too much," she said, and gave me a most suspicious look.

"As a matter of fact, he did ring up. He has a dog for me, a cocker spaniel called Mary Pickford. He wants you to be at the usual place on Monday at six and he will give it to you."

"When did all this happen?" She did not look in the least pleased about the pup.

"Yesterday. Don't tell Daddy. Promise. He will tell you not to go. And then I won't get the dog."

Miss Morris said nothing. She had become sad-looking and rather distant. I knew it was hopeless to talk to her in that sort of mood. But I could not keep myself from saying when I went to wash my hands before lunch: "You will get the pup, won't you?"

"Oh, don't keep on at me," she said.

If she had discussed the difficulty of breaking a promise she had made to my father, I would have understood and tried to find a solution. But this gloom had some other reason. She must be really frightened. And why should she be if truly he was not a Black and Tan? I would have liked to discuss the problem with my father for her sake. But I was selfishly thinking about the dog and was too nervous to risk it. What would happen if he started talking about Greeks again and did me out of the present?

Then I remembered Freddy Doyle. He had asked me to tell him when the Black and Tan was coming. Freddy could lie in wait behind the wall as I had seen him do when he had not seen me. Freddy was an authority on the subject. It was a pity I did not like him better. Indeed, I always felt ashamed when I told Freddy anything. But there was no one else who seemed to be interested in my problems. Mrs Heber might tell my parents. There was no fear of Freddy doing this. He was much too frightened of them.

I had got into the habit of going to Mr Griffin on my own. It was not difficult to slip out a little earlier than usual and call at the forge on my way.

Freddy was examining old motor-car tyres when I called. (I don't think I ever saw him shoeing a horse.) Because I was in a hurry and had been running, I found it very hard to say what I wanted to say. It was really quite simple. When Miss Morris went to get the dog, Freddy was to keep watch. That was all. Of course I did want to make sure that Freddy did not try to play tricks with the car *before* I got the dog. And it seemed rather mean to suggest doing anything to the car after I had been given such a valuable present. I did not quite know what Freddy could do to stop the Black and Tan from coming. Tintacks on the road was the sort of thing I had in mind. I had once heard a tyre go pop with a wonderful noise. Freddy made me repeat the story so often I began to be afraid I might miss my lesson.

"Monday, six o'clock. There at the lane beside your place, is it?"

"The usual place, he said. I think that is where he means."

"He will come along the Dublin Road and turn off at Campion's pub, no doubt," said Freddy to himself.

He seemed to have forgotten me. And much as I would have liked to stay to impress him with the importance of watching Miss Morris carefully, I realised that I would really be late now if I did not run. Freddy did not seem to notice me any longer. He was talking to himself.

I did my lessons very badly that day. Mr Griffin did not get angry, although I expected he would. He was wonderfully patient with me, and polite. He gave me the impression that he did not regard me as a pupil so much as a customer in a sort of lesson shop. When he showed me how to do a sum for the third time, and I forgot yet again, his face wore exactly the expression I saw on a girl's face in Switzer's shop when my mother got her to take down bale after bale of cloth in search of material for a summer dress. It was a resigned patience rather than a kind patience. I did not think of Mr Griffin as kind. Indeed, I found it hard to think of him as human. He was more like a bicycle, or a mangle, than a human person.

I did not go home alone. It was dark when my lessons were over. Sometimes Miss Morris called for me, sometimes one of the maids. Today it was Jane, the cook.

Jane was a wonderful one to talk. On the road she talked to everyone she met. When we passed the forge I noticed it was shut, and for the sake of saying something I remarked on this.

"Freddy was up looking for Mr Griffin," said Jane. "I saw him skulking round the back of the place, not wanting anyone to see him. I wonder what he wants to see Mr Griffin for?"

"What is a Greek, Jane?"

"I don't know, Master Brian. A foreigner of some kind, I suppose."

"Is Mr Griffin a Sinn Feiner, Jane?"

"Isn't it a Commandant he is?" she said proudly.

I wondered if Freddy might have possibly gone to see Mr Griffin about the Black and Tan. But I did not want to let Jane into the secret.

"I shouldn't be talking about the I.R.A. in front of children," said Jane. "Don't go telling your Daddy what I said about Mr Griffin or he will be after taking you away from your lessons. I am only going by what I hear."

"Don't worry, Jane," I said.

Secretly I was pleased to think I might be able to make use of this information if lessons became unpleasant. I remembered what my father had said about Mr Griffin's choice of a poem. To be a commandant in the I.R.A. sounded very prenez garde to me. It was funny to hear Jane wanting to keep it prenez garde. As a rule the grown-ups wanted to keep things prenez garde from her. But the more I saw of life the more I noticed that everyone thinks they are different from everyone else, but everyone is really much the same. Yet some people are definitely nicer than others. I wished then that I really thought Freddy was one of the nicer ones.

On Monday morning a letter was handed in at the door by a small boy.

"Mr Griffin is not able to give you your lesson this evening," said my mother when she read it. "That means another holiday I suppose. Miss Morris might as well take advantage of it to go up to town and get her hair done."

I looked anxiously at Miss Morris, whose every movement was so important today. I could not ask her to be sure to be back in time to get the dog because I was ashamed to show my anxiety in the face of her danger. I could not really convince myself that Freddy's sly scrutiny was really effective protection if the Black and Tan had evil intentions. What might he do? Snatch her up and drive away with her?

Freddy would have to get a plan ready if that were to happen. I could get no encouragement from looking at Miss Morris. She seemed to be quite unaware of me. So I went to see Freddy. He was sitting in the forge on a bench smoking, a pipe and reading a paper. He put it down when I came in.

"No change of plan, Master?" he said.

I explained my anxiety. What would Freddy do if Miss Morris were kidnapped?

"Don't fret yourself, Master. Miss Morris will come to no harm."

"Promise."

"Be the hokey. I promise all right."

For once he did not seem anxious to detain me. He got up when I came in and walked towards the door as he talked to me, so that I was outside before I realised what had happened. He watched me from the door smiling at first (what yellow teeth he had!), but the smile left his face suddenly. Then he had a hard, sly look.

Miss Morris did not come on the train that got in at lunchtime. There was another which left Dublin at two o'clock. I went to the station to meet it. But Miss Morris did not come. I was very worried now. I could not go home in that mood. My mother would see me with nothing to do and think of some horrible task to occupy me. I decided to call on Mrs Heber.

She was laid out in the drawing-room as usual. When I came in she put down a book she had been reading and said:

"It's a long time since I have seen you, Brian."

It was true, and I was at a loss to answer.

"I have given up casting my pearls before swine," I said. "I don't mean you are swine," I added when I thought over the remark (which was one of my emergency ones and not really very suitable for this occasion).

"Are you casting your sweetness on the desert air instead?" she said.

"I suppose so."

To be quite honest I did not really know what either of

us meant. I had only one thing on my mind and found it hard to make any conversation.

"Do you know any Greeks?" I said.

She considered before answering that one.

"I don't think so. A girl who was at school with me married a banker in Paris. I think he was a Greek."

"Are they nice people?"

"I don't know. I have always heard they were very artful about money. Greeks are smarter at business than Jews. And Armenians are smarter than Greeks."

"Did you ever hear of a Greek giving a present?"

Mrs Heber, who reclined on her sofa as a rule, now sat up and looked at me.

"You *are* a Grand Inquisitor today. Why do you want to know about Greeks?"

"I was just interested. That's all. But if you don't know any there's no use in talking about them."

"They were wonderful people. Think of it. Socrates was a Greek, and Plato and Aristotle and Praxiteles and Aeschylus and so many others. But that was long ago. I can't think of any famous Armenians. I suppose they have always concentrated on money-making. That makes people dull and unheard-of."

I did not enjoy it when Mrs Heber went on talking like this about things I knew nothing about. She was apt to do it. It did not matter so much when I had nothing important on my mind. I tried to think of something else to say, something that interested me.

"Can you be sent to prison for chasing people when you have no clothes on?" I said. I was anxious to find out whether Mrs Heber still believed the maid's story.

"What an extraordinary question? What is wrong with you today, Brian? You look flushed. Are you sure you haven't got a temperature?"

"Is it a sin?"

"If it was done on purpose it would be."

"But if someone came into the room and found you with no clothes on, that would be just their bad luck, wouldn't it? I mean, it couldn't be a sin to be discovered by accident."

"Of course not."

"What sort of sin would it be if it was a sin?"

"You have me all muddled. What sort of sin would what sort of sin be?"

"Chasing people like that."

"I don't know. Why do you want to talk about it? It's not really a pleasant subject to discuss."

I wanted to let Mrs Heber know I had not chased Maud. It was funny I couldn't just say it out. I wanted her to help me.

"It isn't mentioned in the Ten Commandments."

"Not in so many words."

"I suppose *Thou shalt not commit adultery* is more or less the same thing."

Mrs Heber said nothing. She was blowing her nose.

I was determined to be forgiven by her.

"Mrs Heber," I said. "I did not commit adultery that day, I undressed in the bathroom. And if Maud said I did, it's a lie. It was all an accident."

"Heavens!" said Mrs Heber. She was now sneezing violently. And before I could make out what had happened to her she had run out of the room. I never saw Mrs Heber run before. She moved quite fast, and her clothes rustled like anything.

She came back after a few minutes. She had washed her face. It had that sort of look.

"I have a little present here for you," she said.

I was quite astonished. Why was everyone giving me presents all of a sudden?

"It's a tie-pin. It used to belong to my father. That is a real pearl. Put it away. You can use it in your stock if you ever take up riding."

She handed me a little leather box. Inside was velvet, and in a cleft there was a gold pin with a shell on it. The pearl, which was tiny, lay inside the shell.

I had never had anything before that was valuable. I had no doubt that this pin was of immense value. Mrs Heber had a bestowing sort of manner, but she rarely gave anything away. Mr Heber was the one who sometimes gave me half a crown, or sent my mother plants for the garden. The time Mrs Heber gave the birds it was only as an excuse to see Miss Morris. Now she was really giving a present—and to me! I was too excited to speak.

"Is it very valuable?" I said.

I could have kicked myself. I did not mean to say that. I don't think it pleased Mrs Heber either.

"It will be a souvenir of our friendship," she said.

"Thank you very much."

I said 'very' as though it weighed a ton.

"Now, what about tea? Or is it rather early? Would you like to look at a book?"

"I would rather talk, if you have no objection."

"I like talking to you. But let's not talk about unhappy things. I did think you had been rather rude with Maud, but now I know it was all an accident. I am very glad, because I knew you were a nice boy, and I could hardly believe my ears when Maud told me."

"Servants are inclined to gossip," I said. My mother used to say that. I now saw how true it was.

Mrs Heber began to laugh again. But I had not intended to be funny.

"And you told my mother it was an accident, didn't you?"

(Mrs Heber began to turn red. I have felt myself get like that when I was caught at something I was ashamed of.)

"Because you told her I committed adultery when I didn't. That is *Bearing false witness against thy neighbour*."

Mrs Heber was very red now.

"Is it worse to break one commandment than another?"

"I don't know. I told your mother Maud made a mistake. Oh, Brian, I do feel ashamed."

"Don't worry." I tried once again to say that in the comfortable way my father said it to me. And then because Mrs Heber was obviously embarrassed, I tried to carry on the conversation.

"If there are Ten Commandments, I suppose all are equal. But *Thou shalt not kill* sounds much more serious than *Thou shalt not take the name of the Lord, thy God, in vain*, for instance. Jane does it every day. And I am sure it would be worse if she were to murder somebody."

"I suppose some are more serious than others. But we should obey them all if we want to lead a perfect life."

"Do you think *Thou shalt not commit adultery* is more serious than *Thou shalt not bear false witness*, for instance?"

"Oh, dear. I don't know. I suppose so."

"Then if I had run after Maud it would have been worse than what you did when you told my mother I had when I didn't?"

"I thought we had agreed to forget all that. I gave you the little pin as a sort of peace offering. Grown-ups don't always behave as they should, you know. We have our off-days, our bad moments."

"Is it *Bearing false witness* to say a man is a Greek just because he gives you a present?"

"I don't think there is anything wrong in being a Greek."

"Well, to say he was a Black and Tan then?"

"Who said who was a Black and Tan? I am really worried about you, Brian. Are you sure you are feeling well?"

"Oh, yes, thanks. I feel perfectly well. Which of the Ten Commandments would you say was the most serious?"

"*Thou shalt not kill*, I suppose."

"And second most?"

"Dear me. This is like a scripture lesson. I suppose everyone has their own ideas. To me it would be not to steal."

"Some of them I don't understand. And some are rather childish, don't you think? Keeping holy the Sabbath Day, and honouring your father and mother. Everyone knows those things without being told."

"I hope not killing and not stealing are just as obvious."

"Oh, of course. But if one didn't obey the others it wouldn't be the end of the world, if you see what I mean."

"I think we have had all I can stand of the Ten Commandments for today. Ring the bell for tea, like a good boy. I have a section of honey. I know you like honey."

Somehow I could not take any interest in the honey. I wanted to tell Mrs Heber about Miss Morris and the Black and Tan and Freddy Doyle. I wanted to get her opinion about this dog business. Would Miss Morris be safe if she just went out to get the dog? Freddy said she would. But I did not like Freddy. I wished I had never talked to him. Suddenly I had got quite frightened about it all. I had a strange feeling that something horrible was going to happen. And it would all be my fault. What made it worse was the thought that the grown-ups knew how to help if they only would. But all they did was to talk about Greeks and sections of honey, or go to Dublin to get hair done.

At half-past four I got up and ran away from Mrs Heber's. I grabbed my coat, shook hands terribly quickly and said: "Thank you for tea and for the pin."

I did not wait for her to get up or for that awful Maud to open the door. I let myself out and sprinted down the avenue.

I could see the people who had come by the last train walking slowly down the hill in twos and threes. Miss Morris was at the back. She walked alone. I ran towards her shouting at the top of my voice. I was so excited, so pleased, she had come back.

"Don't rouse the neighbourhood, Brian," she said, when I came up to her.

She had a basket on her arm.

"Here's SWEETHEART," she said.

I could hardly hold the basket I was trembling so. In the end Miss Morris had to take it back and open it for me. Inside was a little, soft, red bundle.

"Be careful," said Miss Morris. "She is young to leave home."

The pup was as small as a little kitten. I had never had anything which pleased me so much. I really jumped with joy. Of course, we began to discuss a name for it at once.

Miss Morris said SWEETHEART was not a good name for a dog. DAISY would be better. I thought Mrs Heber might be pleased if I called it after her because she had given me her father's pin. But Miss Morris said there were certain objections to the proposal, and Mrs Heber would see them and not be grateful.

I suggested MONDAY because that was the day the dog came.

Miss Morris said RAFFLE would be better, because that was how the dog came into our lives. So I decided on RAFFLE. It was quite a nice name. We were home by the time we had arranged all this. I took the basket from Miss Morris and ran ahead to show the dog to my mother and to the maids. I wanted to take it there and then to Mrs Heber and Freddy Doyle, but everyone insisted that this was unfair when she had travelled so far and was still such a tiny thing.

"It was very good of you to give it to Brian. I hope he thanked you," said my mother.

Quite taken by surprise, I stared at Miss Morris. In the excitement of the dog's arrival I had quite forgotten that I was only to get it if I arranged for Miss Morris to go out at six o'clock. I was bewildered. Miss Morris saw me and must have guessed what I was thinking because she gave me a wink. It was the most wonderful wink I had ever seen. It sent her even higher in my estimation. No one had ever winked at me like that before. One eye kept absolutely open and still while the other closed very slowly. I had tried and tried, but whenever I winked with one eye, the other always blinked a little. Miss Morris was a very exceptional person. She did so many things well.

I was alone with her when we were fixing up a kennel in a tea chest.

"You don't want me to mention the Black and Tan, do you?" I said. "I am so glad he is not coming."

Miss Morris said: "When you are grown-up, I will explain it all to you."

"Will you marry me then?" I said. It seemed a funny time to bring up the subject just then, when we were putting straw into the tea chest. But I was so pleased with everything and Miss Morris had been so good to me, it kind of slipped out.

"Is that a proposal?" she said.

"Well, not exactly. I mean, it's more an idea of mine."

"You men are all the same. You shift when it comes to brass tacks. Get out of my light while I nail this board. Get back. Give me air to breathe. I never knew such a child to hang on top of one."

I was hurt by this. Miss Morris was her old self again. I don't think she can have really cared for children.

My father came home at six o'clock. I met him in the hall.

My mother was upstairs changing. I had not seen Miss Morris for half an hour. After she fixed the kennel she went to her room to sew buttons on to something. She was bad at sewing buttons, and usually my mother got so tired watching her that she took the garment away from her and finished the sewing.

I showed my father the dog. He seemed to know all about it. This was a great relief, but it puzzled me. Who had told him?

My mother called out to him as she always did when he came in. Then I heard her say: "Miss Morris, would you come here for a moment and fasten my back."

There was no answer.

"Wait a jiffy," said my father, going to the stairs.

"I wonder where she has gone to," I heard my mother say as she went into her room with my father.

I looked at the grandfather clock in the hall. The hands stood at ten minutes past six. I had kept my father quite a while explaining to him about the kennel and the dog's name. I went back to look at her. She was whimpering, and I tried to pet her into a happy state of mind. When I held her against my chest, she dived into my coat sleeve, head first.

At quarter to seven Jane chased me out of the pantry and told me to go and "wash the dirt" off myself. Dinner was at seven. My father was sitting in the dining-room on the window seat, a tumbler beside him. He was reading a paper and did not see me. My mother was in the drawing-room. She was walking about the room straightening cushions and putting up magazines. Miss Morris was inclined to drop anything she had been reading on the floor.

I began to worry about her again. I had been so pleased about the dog and so relieved that there was no need for the meeting with the Black and Tan that I had ceased altogether to worry. I had taken it for granted that the Black and Tan was not coming. Suddenly the thought came like a dart of pain: *Had he come? Was Miss Morris outside?* If that were so it was now almost an hour after the time of the appointment. She should be back. Had he taken her away? Had Freddy failed her? Perhaps Freddy (who knew everything that went on in the neighbourhood) had heard about the dog coming. He, too, may have decided that it was not necessary to keep guard. After all, I had made the same mistake.

I crept across the hall and opened the door quietly. There was a strange moon that night, a half moon with another inside it. Clouds raced across the sky. The wind was blowing thin rain which lashed my face. It was not hard to make my way. I knew the path so well, and the moon gave a fitful light. I ran down the road until I came to the corner where I had seen the Black and Tan the first time he came. There was nobody there now. I went to the wall where Freddy had hidden himself to watch. No one was watching tonight. I ran along the lane to see if the car had moved further back from the road. The clouds left the moon uncovered for a moment. I had a sudden clear view of the lane, all shining in front of me. I saw a dark shape beside the hedge. It moved in my direction. I almost yelled with fear. I turned round and started to run. As I ran, I heard footsteps behind me. I was too terrified to look back. I felt as though, at any moment, someone would put out a hand and grab me. Now I could see the friendly lights in the windows of my home. If I shouted hard enough my father would hear me. If he heard me, I was safe. But just as I opened my mouth to scream—at that very moment—I heard Miss Morris almost at my elbow say: "Brian, you must be soaking, child."

I stopped then. She was standing on the roadside in a mackintosh with a rug round her head like a shawl. She was looking at me curiously. Her eyes had a strange look as if she belonged out of doors and was not really a tame person who found it natural to live in a house. But I was so relieved to see her safe, I threw my arms round her and hid my head in her shawl. There were little drops of rain all over it like dew on grass.

"He didn't take you. I was so worried."

"He never came, Brian. I wonder what has happened? He always comes when he says he will."

The church clock struck seven. We both stood still and counted the strokes to ourselves.

"We will be late for dinner," I said.

"And what will your mother say?"

I could not think about this. After the fright I had, the comfort of finding her safe was so great, nothing seemed to matter now. I expected my mother to be just as pleased as I was. I forgot that I was the only one at home who had cause to worry.

"It may be his new motor car," she said. "It might have broken down on the road."

"Did he sell the A.C.? That lovely A.C. How could he bear to part with it?"

"He had driven it too hard. It only hangs together. I'm afraid he stuck poor Ossie with it. What could I do? I said 'never buy a pig in a poke'. That was as good as a wink, I should have thought. But Ossie thinks the A.C. is part of George's charm. And nothing would do him but to buy it. I think he only gave £100. But he will live to regret it. And George has no charm really. He has tremendous persistence."

"I am glad Lord Swords bought the A.C. He might give me a drive in it. He did in his other car."

Miss Morris was not listening to me. She stood and looked up.

"That's a wild-looking sky. And I don't like that treacherous moon. Look at it.

> "I saw the new moon late yestreen
> Wi' the auld moon in her arm,
> And if we gang to sea, master,
> I fear we'll come to harm.

"Come on quickly, Brian. Take my hand. Let's run. I have been out too long. Aren't you frightened too?"

I wasn't. Not with her.

The front door was ajar and the house was full of light. When we came into the hall my mother rushed forward in a way that was altogether unusual, as if I had risen from the dead.

"Come up and have a nice, hot bath. You are wringing wet," she said. Not a question. Not a cross word. It was quite a miracle. She put an arm round my shoulders and almost pushed me upstairs. She was talking all the time. I knew this was done to prevent me from noticing something. But all I knew was that there were men in the dining-room with my father. I saw Mr Heber looking very grave, and Mr Hone and the new parson. The door to the kitchen was half open. Jane and Alice were standing inside staring into the hall.

"A lovely, hot bath, and you can make it as deep as you like," said my mother.

"May I dive right under?"

"You may as much as you like. But try, like a good boy, not to splash."

This was the first time in all my life I had been given permission to dive. I had often done it of course. But it was a great victory to have permission at last. Something very important must be happening. The bath was turned on, and I started to undress whilst my mother went to get a clean towel from the hot press. I heard her talking to Miss Morris on the landing. Then Miss Morris began to cry. She did not cry quietly in the way grown-ups do when they have to. They were real tears, the kind that wet all your face, and get into your nose, and make your hair untidy. I have never cried more loudly than Miss Morris did.

"Come into your room, dear. Lie down on the bed. I will send you up your supper on a tray."

Those were the words my mother used before the door shut, but I could hear Miss Morris sobbing and my mother trying to soothe her.

The bath had got to the point when it was running out through the little holes near the taps. I had only once or twice run a bath so deep. The room was full of steam. I was able to write my name on the window. It did not seem very kind to be doing this while Miss Morris was crying. But what could I do? Whatever had happened she would not want me to see her like that. What had happened? Why were there so many people in the house? No one was expected this evening. Why were the maids standing in the passage? Why was Miss Morris so fearfully upset?

Someone must be dead.

It must be the Black and Tan. That explained everything. I didn't like the idea of anyone dying, but I could not help thinking that there was a lot to be said for the Black and Tan dying, if it had to be somebody. Miss Morris said she did not like him, but she did not seem able to keep him away. And she must have broken her promise today because how otherwise did she get Raffle for me?

But when I thought of Raffle I started to cry. It was very kind of the Black and Tan to give me Raffle. Really, I had to confess, the Black and Tan had always been nice to me. He showed me how to drive his car. He let me hold his revolver.

He gave me money. He walked all the way to the lavatory with me at the football match. Perhaps he was a good man at heart. Even though he was a Black and Tan—if he were dead I felt all the more convinced he must be one—why should he not be the exception that proved the rule? There may have been good Black and Tans as well as bad ones.

And then I heard the clatter and splash of a lorry rush past our gate. A few seconds later another followed. There was no mistaking that sound. No one drove lorries so fast as that except the Black and Tans. They were out looking for the person who killed Miss Morris's friend. Or had he been killed? Did he not perhaps have an accident in his new car? And why was he coming tonight if he had already seen Miss Morris in Dublin? I was longing for my mother to come back to me.

"The bath is overflowing," I shouted.

She came at that.

"Do you mean to tell me, at your age, you can't turn off the hot tap?" she said.

"Sorry, Mummy."

I had got her back.

"Now we must let some hot out to put cold in," she said. "Couldn't you have watched it? It's an awful waste of hot water."

It took quite a time to get the bath cool enough for me to get in.

"Why is Miss Morris crying? What has happened? What is going on downstairs?"

My mother looked at me for a moment as if considering something. Then she said:

"You are bound to know anyhow, so I might as well tell you. An awful thing has happened. No one can explain it. Poor Lord Swords was shot on his way home this evening."

"Was the Black and Tan shot too?"

"I don't know what you mean. Lord Swords was driving home. He was shot at the wood just before his own gate."

I had so made up my mind the Black and Tan was dead, I could not adjust myself to this. It was as if my mother wasn't paying attention, or was talking nonsense. I had not thought of Lord Swords for days. How could things like this happen to *him*?

"You don't seem to be upset, I must say. You are an extraordinary child. Here. Get out of that bath. I have a lot of things to do, and I can't stand here while you pretend to be a submarine."

She almost pulled me out of the bath and dried me in a cross, slappy way. A waste of a nice warm towel. I was feeling ashamed. I should be terribly sorry. I should be crying like Miss Morris was. But when a person has been worrying as I had been about Miss Morris and the Black and Tan for days, and thinking of nothing else (almost) it was very hard to start being sad about something I was not prepared for. And now that I knew the truth I was rather glad the Black and Tan was not dead after all. He was much more fun to be with than Lord Swords, if not so good or so grand. But, of course, I was sorry for Lord Swords. Even though he was so stuffy, he could be kind. And he was very fond of Miss Morris. I think she was his 'best girl'. I am sure he wanted her to be. It was a pity he was so fat and so bald.

And when I thought of this—his being fat and bald—it suddenly brought him to life for me. Until then he had been just something mother wanted to talk about when I was worrying about the Black and Tan. Now I thought of him, and how he used to look, and the day he drove me to the Castle when he ordered flowers for Miss Morris. He wanted to be nice and kind. But God had made him glum. Even that glumness seemed lovable now. And by the time I was dressed I was crying almost as much as Miss Morris had been.

*   *   *

"Come down when you are ready. You can stay with Alice if you like, until the men go. They are talking to Daddy. Everyone is so shocked. And they find it a comfort to talk to him. Your father is at his best in a crisis. Everyone feels that," my mother said.

Then she left me. But I was only a few seconds finishing off. There was not much sense in dressing with care when it was so near bedtime. I hated wasting time.

The stairs ran straight down into the hall, so that anyone coming down had the front door in full view. I did not hear a knock, but there must have been one because Alice was opening the door when I came out on the landing. My father came out of the dining-room to see who was there. I suppose his nerves were on edge. The lorries of Black and Tans rushing past was quite terrifying at night-time.

"Well, Doyle. What do you want?" I heard my father say, and then I saw Freddy lurking in the shadow outside the door. It was typical of him to knock and then stand back as though a dog would rush out at him. Freddy came forward fingering his hat. He had a lowly look on his face. I knew the expression.

"Might I have a word with you, Mr Allen, sir?"

The news of Lord Swords's death, however distressing, had been in the nature of a relief to my anxious mind. Had the Black and Tan been killed I would have wondered and worried. But Lord Swords had nothing to do with me, or Freddy, or anyone I knew. But Freddy's appearance at this moment filled me with alarm. He had been ordered off our premises by my father who called him a common thief. My visits to the forge were all breaches of the commandment *Honour thy father and thy mother*. Disobedience to parents, so I understood, came into that category. I was desperate for company sometimes or I would not have laid these sins on my conscience. It was, perhaps, too much to hope that I could continue this forbidden acquaintanceship without getting into trouble. And Freddy's appearance on this day had the most sinister possibilities. Was he going to tell my father about the Black and Tan? If he did, I might lose Raffle for one thing. And my father would not understand how I could go to someone like Freddy to talk about Miss Morris. Miss Morris would not understand it either. Despite her protests she seemed to be on such close terms with this George that she would probably tell him too. And, of course, Uncle Lindy would hear. I would be in disgrace with everyone. Why had I ever trusted Freddy? I knew he was not a nice man. No one had to tell me that. If wishing could kill he would have dropped down dead there at the door where he stood squirming, smiling and showing his teeth all broken, yellow and brown, playing with his fingers on the brim of his hat as if it was a flute, and begging to come in. His manner reminded me of Uriah Heep in *David Copperfield*, but he looked more like Charlie Chaplin.

"I am very busy this evening. Come and see me tomorrow," said my father.

I almost cheered when he said that.

Then Freddy saw me. I shall never forget the look he gave me. It was both threatening and sly.

"And how's the young master?" he said, as if he had not seen me for months and I had been ill in the meantime.

"Brian is very well, thank you," said my father. I could see he was itching to slam the door in Freddy's face. But he was polite to everybody, my father was.

"Could I have a word with the mistress?" said Freddy.

"Mrs Allen is busy, I'm afraid," said my father.

But Freddy made no move to go. He kept looking at me and fiddling with his hat. I knew he was thinking very hard.

"They'll have me life," said Freddy.

"Who will?" said my father. But I could sense—and my heart sank—that Freddy had made an impression.

"The Tans, Mr Allen, sir. They are rampaging round the country on account of the accident to his lordship—God rest him. If they find me alone in the house, they'll take my life."

"Come in," said my father.

Freddy hopped in sideways and fast, like a dog who has been scratching at a door.

"What is all this nonsense? Why should you be touched? You don't know anything about Lord Swords's death that you want to tell me, do you?"

"I'd like to have a word with you, private," said Freddy.

"You can say what you have to say before my friends in here," said my father, leading the way into the dining-room. "And would you mind taking off your hat," he added.

Freddy didn't mind. And the dining-room door shut. I ran upstairs and got sick in the w.c. I felt sure that Freddy was trying to save his life at the expense of mine. What was he accusing me of? Where would all this end? I went into my bedroom and lay flat on my bed. The cool of the pillow was always nice in times of trouble. After quite a long time—it seemed an age to me—my mother came in.

"There you are. I almost missed you in the dark. What's up with you, my angel? Are you not feeling well?"

The possibility that this presented was too good to be thrown away. People are usually kind to the sick.

"I have a queer pain," I said.

"Where, pet?"

"Down here. And here. It moves about. But don't worry. I'm sure it will get better. My headache is the worst. I can't bear the sound of voices. I hope I haven't got meningitis."

"You'll be better after supper. It's the shock. None of us feels well tonight. Miss Morris won't eat any supper. I never saw anyone look so upset. I think it would be a nice thing if you were just to go in a moment at bedtime and say good night to her. She is not so much older than you, poor little thing. Why have these awful crimes to happen?"

"Has Freddy Doyle gone?"

"Not him. He has talked your father round. And he is in the kitchen gossiping with the maids. I would have sent him packing, but your father can be wheedled into anything."

"What did he say?"

"Who?"

"Freddy."

"Oh, some cock and bull story that people had taken his character away and he was the person the police would light upon. And he had no one to say a word for him. If the Black and Tans found him alone they might beat him up. Anyhow, he has quartered himself upon us. I will have to count the silver in the morning."

The news came with a rush of relief. What a day I had been having. One fright after another. If that was all Freddy had to say, I was silly to be so much afraid of him. I could imagine how he and Jane would talk. The two greatest gossips in the neighbourhood! Downstairs the visitors were saying good-bye. They had come in Mr Hone's car and he was driving them home.

"I will find out about the funeral and let you all know," my father said.

"I suppose the solicitor, or someone, will get on to me about the service," said the curate.

"Of course," said my father.

I guessed that he had become so important this evening, he had overlooked the parson. That was always happening to Mr Burrowes. He had the personality of an old umbrella.

There was so much to talk about at supper that for once my parents forgot that I was present and I heard the whole story. I kept my mouth shut as I knew very well that if I reminded my father I was there he would order me up to bed.

"What happened?" said my mother.

"According to Doyle, a tree fell across the road intended, perhaps, for a Black and Tan convoy. Swords got out of his car, and they shot him to bits in the approved patriotic fashion from behind the ditch."

"Who could have done such a thing? He had nothing to do with politics. What is the country coming to?"

"You may well ask. It means the end of Raheny house. Ossie was going to open it up in the old style and give lots of employment. No one will do that now. If the blackguards who shot him are locals, as I suppose they are, they will suffer for it. It is hard to believe people could be got to do such a thing. They will all be at Mass on Sunday, I suppose. This country makes me sick."

"Do you think it was a mistake?"

"I don't know. Someone may have wanted the land. If Ossie hadn't decided to live here the place might have been split up among the locals. Who in their senses would come to live in Ireland? Land will be given away if the Government doesn't act soon. If I were the English people I would put in a proper government under Austen Chamberlain, someone whom the people can trust. Lloyd George has a lot to answer for."

I had seen pictures of Lloyd George. He looked like a cat we had which got drowned in a paint pot. I rather liked his appearance, like a conjurer's, with long hair and a cloak. But I never heard anyone speak well of him. It was comforting to be able to fix him with the responsibility for Lord Swords's death. I found it a relief. Freddy's visit had made me feel so frightfully guilty. But that was silly, when I came to think of it.

Next day my father stayed at home. He did so to please my mother who was feeling nervous. There were Black and Tans everywhere. And passengers travelling to Dublin were searched at the railway station. After lunch when I was sitting alone in the school-room I heard a car drive to the door. I ran to the window. It was a big car full of men in uniform. And as I came to the window one of them stepped out. It was the Black and Tan. He saw me and waved quite cheerfully. But I could only stand with my mouth wide open and stare. What did this mean?

I made no effort to leave the room. I heard Alice open the front door and the sound of voices. Then I heard my father's voice. Then the door of the drawing-room shut.

I sat down on a chair and twisted my handkerchief as if that would help me to squeeze out my fear. I was still at it when my father put his head round the door and called me. I came running to get whatever the bad news might be as quickly as possible. I am always like that. I prefer to know the worst. It is never so bad as I can imagine.

"Captain Wain wants you to help him, Brian. He is a friend of Lord Swords and he is trying to find out about the murder. Don't be frightened, answer his questions. The truth never hurt anybody."

I pondered long over that last remark when I had time to think things out afterwards. But, much as I respect my father's judgement, I can't think that the truth hurts nobody. If that were true lies would go out of fashion. And people in the wrong almost always find lies an advantage. I think it was one of the encouraging sayings my father had the knack of producing when they were needed. And I did completely agree that the truth, however bad, doesn't weigh on one after it is told. Lies can be an awful burden. But, on this occasion, it was no use trying to jolly me along in this easy fashion. My father had no idea (or so I thought) with whom he was dealing.

"It's the Black and Tan," I whispered.

"No. No. This is Captain Wain," he said in an almost laughing tone.

"It's the one," I said.

I tried to look darkly at my father, but he just wouldn't understand. His eyes kept their easy unconspiratorial expression. Captain Wain might have been Uncle Lindy so far as my father was concerned.

"It's the one Miss Morris knows," I hissed. I don't know whether I really hissed, but that is what they say in books.

"Come long, old man," said my father, as if he had not heard me.

"Hello, Bill," said the Black and Tan. He was sitting at my mother's writing desk, an old spinet, and he had papers before him.

"I think you two will get along better if I leave you alone," said my father.

I begged him to stay with my eyes, but he only smiled at me, that kind, uncomprehending smile which he had worn ever since the Black and Tan arrived.

"How's Raffle getting on?"

It was a relief to be asked a question like that.

"Fine. Thanks awfully for giving him to me."

"He deserved a good home. How is Miss Morris? I couldn't come last night. I ran into a road block and decided to go home."

There was a pause then. I didn't like pauses. They made me feel responsible.

"Have you sold your lovely A.C.?"

The Black and Tan looked up.

"I have. Who told you that?"

"Oh, I just guessed."

"Come on, Bill. Own up."

"Miss Morris, as a matter of fact. She told me you . . ." But at the thought of what had happened I found myself sad again.

"Don't cry, Brian. I know. He didn't have much fun with it, and I am afraid I charged him too much. It was on my conscience. But there is no use bothering about that now. He was mad to have it."

"I liked it too."

"I have a new car now, a Crossley. You must come out in it one day."

"Is that it outside?"

"No. That's an official car. It's not healthy weather for driving alone at the moment."

We sat looking at one another for a moment then.

"You didn't tell anyone I was coming out here last night, Bill, did you?"

I looked at him. His eyes were quite kind. I wanted so much to say that I had told Freddy Doyle. But if I did, what would happen? I remembered the look Freddy gave me.

"Can't you remember?"

"I told Miss Morris."

"Yes. I know that. Have you any chums?"

"What are chums?"

"Pals. Friends. Kids you play with."

"I don't play with anyone."

"Did you tell the girls?"

"Girls? What girls?"

"The skivvy."

"Skivvy?"

"The servants, Bill. Did you tell any of the servants?"

"No. I never talk to them about anything personal."

"Well. Let me see. Where were you yesterday?"

"I was at Mrs Heber's."

"Did you say anything when you were there?"

"No."

"And where else were you?"

"I went to the station to meet Miss Morris."

"Did you talk to anyone there?"

"No."

"Sure?"

"Sure."

"I gave you a buzz on Friday. Remember? So you had Saturday and Sunday to talk to people. Can you remember who you talked to on those days?"

"Only the family."

"Haven't you a teacher?"

"Mr Griffin."

"Yes. Did you see him after I told you I was coming here? Did you have lessons with him on Friday evening?"

"I did. But I never talk to him except about lessons. He is not a talking sort of man."

"Did you go to him on Saturday?"

"No."

"On Sunday?"

"No."

"Do you never go for lessons on Saturdays and Sundays?"

"Never."

"I see. What time are these lessons of yours?"

"From half-past four to six o'clock."

"You were there on Monday then?"

"No."

"Why not?"

"Mr Griffin sent a boy over with a note to say he couldn't take me on Monday."

"Why not?"

"He had business to attend to in Dublin."

"Did he ever put off a lesson before?"

"No. But I have not been going to him for very long."

"When did you hear I had sold the A.C.?"

"Last night. Miss Morris told me when we were looking for you."

"So you were looking for me, were you?"

"Yes. Miss Morris was very worried."

"Very worried, was she?"

I had a lisp and he was imitating it. I might have been offended, but he did not do it in a sneery way. Just for fun, I thought.

"And so was I."

"And why were you worried?"

"Because I . . ."

"Because you what?"

I had been on the point of blurting out Freddy's name. But I stopped myself in time.

"I was worried because Miss Morris went out at six o'clock. And she was not home. And it was almost seven. So I went out to see had anything happened to her."

"So you were worried on her account, is that it?"

"Yes."

You have no idea with what relief I said that 'yes'. It came out as if my heart had thrown it up.

My father came back. He looked at me as if to see how I was feeling. I was able to smile then.

"Bill has come clean," said the Black and Tan. "Now I must see if the usher is at home today."

I did not know what an usher was. Then the Black and Tan went away. He waved out of the car to us as if he was off on a holiday trip.

"Wellington has gone," said my father.

"That's Miss Morris's Black and Tan, stupid."

"I know. But you must stop using that expression. He is a rum sort of officer, I must admit, but that is not to say he is a Black and Tan. There are limits to everything."

"Now Lord Swords is dead, may he see Miss Morris as much as he likes?"

My father took a half-crown out of his pocket.

"Do you see that? I will give you that when a week has passed and you have asked no questions about Miss Morris, Mrs Heber or any of the other ladies of your acquaintance. Do you understand?"

"I do."

"That's a bargain then."

"Before we begin, may I ask just one question?"

"It depends on what it is."

"Do you think Miss Morris is more sorry that Lord Swords was the one to be killed than if it had been the Black and Tan?"

"Miss Morris is a kind girl. She would have been fearfully upset if either were killed."

"But would she have minded so much if it had been the other?"

"I don't know. And if you ask Miss Morris that question I'll tan the hide off you."

"I wouldn't dream of such a thing."

* * *

"I think it quite absurd of Lindy to come to the funeral," said my father.

"It is a kind thought," said my mother as though Uncle Lindy was not given to kind thoughts.

Lord Swords's funeral was a great occasion. It would have been had he died an old man like his uncle was, but this awful shooting made people twice as sad. Everyone felt they loved him, and were anxious to go to the funeral to make up to him for being shot. I don't suppose it did him much good. But it was nice to see everyone sad.

I asked Mr Griffin if he was going to the funeral. He said he was not. It was the last day we did lessons together. He paid very little attention to me. In fact, he hardly seemed to know I was there. I wrote down a wrong answer to a sum, but before I could correct it, he ticked off the answer and said "right". After that I took no trouble and wrote down whatever came into my mind. Sometimes he corrected it, but most times he just said "right". Every time we heard a motor car on the road he got up and looked out. I could feel his nervousness inside myself. We were just about to do grammar (which I hated) when the boy who left the letter when Mr Griffin put off my lesson came to the door. Mr Griffin went outside to speak to him. I pretended to look at the book, but something told me Mr Griffin was not going to bother explaining syntax to me today. I got so tired waiting for him that I got up from the desk and studied the atlas on the wall. This did not interest me for long, so I began to draw pictures on the blackboard. I drew a picture of the funeral, and then I wrote R.I.P. over it. I had never been to a funeral, but I had seen them going along the road. I was not able to draw people well, but I gave a name to each shape. For fun I put Uncle Lindy at the front of the procession. I made him chief mourner. I was going to write, in a balloon coming out of his mouth, "Funerals are not what they were in my day. They used to bury gentlemen in those days." But I decided not to, because it seemed unkind to Lord Swords.

However, I was so interested in the drawing that I forgot about Mr Griffin, and when I heard someone come into the room I remembered that I was supposed to be looking over my grammar. But it was not Mr Griffin. Two Black and Tans stood in the door holding revolvers. Outside the door I saw a truck full of them armed with rifles.

"Where's the schoolmaster, son?" said one.

"Hurry up," said the other.

I was frightened; but one of them did not look too unkind. The other had a cross, suspicious face. I looked at the kinder-faced one.

"He went out to talk to someone a few minutes ago," I said.

"Went out where?" said one.

"Quick. Hurry," said the other.

"Through the door you came in by."

"And where did he go from there?"

"I don't know. He got up suddenly. We were sitting at that desk. I thought he would come back. He never said he was going away."

Three Black and Tans ran into the room then. They opened all the drawers and presses in the room and threw papers on the floor.

"What's your name?" said the first one.

"Brian Allen," I said.

"Where do you live?"

"Kilmoylan."

"Where's that?"

"Beside the railway station."

"What's your father?"

"A registrar in the High Court."

"A what?"

"A registrar."

"Bloke that sits under a judge," said the kind one.

The cross one had been asking the questions.

"What are you doing here?"

"Mr Griffin gives me lessons in the afternoon. I am going to school in Dublin after Christmas."

"The kid's all right," said the kind one.

"Stand over in that corner and don't move for half an hour," he added.

"Or you'll get your head blown off," said the other.

I stood in the corner, shut my eyes and tried to pray. But the prayers got stuck. They got mixed up with my fright. I wanted my mother or my father. If only they would come I should be safe. God seemed a long way away.

But when the men left the room I felt a little better. I heard screams and the crash of glass breaking. There were occasional shouts when they were giving orders. Sometimes I thought they had gone away. Then I would hear them out on the road, and I recognised the sound of engines running which told me the trucks were outside. But in the end there were two shouts on the road and the noise of the trucks starting. They roared away down the road. There was absolute silence after they left. Then I heard someone crying. The man said not to come out for half an hour, but I thought it was probably safe enough now. I crept across the room. My legs felt as shaky as if I had been sick in bed for weeks.

There was no one on the road. The crying came from the house next door. All the windows were broken and there was furniture thrown out on the street. I knew a short way home across the fields. It would be safe that way. I climbed through the hedge and made my way through a clump of blackberry bushes and furze. This way meant crossing the end of the golf links. At this time, in November, there was no one to be seen.

As I stumbled and ran along, a sudden fear possessed me: I thought that Mr Griffin might be hiding somewhere on my route. And I began to dread the thought that he might suddenly grab me from behind a hedge. I suppose I should have been sorry for him. But I never thought of him as a person. And I knew now that the Black and Tan must have suspected him of killing Lord Swords. Jane said he was a Commandant in the I.R.A. I remembered how Freddy Doyle had come to see him on the same day that the Black and Tan was expected to bring the dog. I also remembered that the boy who brought us the message was the same boy who came to see him today. He must have been looking out for the Black and Tans to warn Mr Griffin before they came. But little as I liked Mr Griffin, I had no cause to hate him. I just couldn't work up any kind feelings for him. That was all. How could he possibly do anything so cruel as to murder Lord Swords on the day he had bought his new car? And when I got as far as that in my thoughts I realised everything. The trap was set for the Black and Tan. I could see Freddy as he had been that evening when he stood at the wall watching the car. The ambushers were waiting for the A.C. They did not know Lord Swords had bought it. And when Lord Swords got out, they thought he was the Black and Tan.

It was perfectly clear to me now. Perhaps I would have thought of it before had I not been hiding it from myself. Now, when I faced it, I stood still and wondered if I could go home any more. If I had not spoken to Freddy, Lord Swords would not have been shot. I was forbidden to speak to Freddy. This is what came of disobeying my parents. God had shown me. God seemed much nearer now than when I had tried to pray to him. I could almost see him glaring at me from the sky. That frightened me but not as much as my fear that Mr Griffin might at any moment jump out at me or grab me by the ankle. And Mr Griffin terrified me more now that I realised he was a murderer. If he shot other people why should he not shoot me? I was no better than Lord Swords. In fact, I was much worse, because Lord Swords had not done anything he was forbidden to. I was the sinner. *Honour thy father and thy mother*. That meant obey them and don't answer back when corrected. I had broken the commandment and Lord Swords had been killed. It was just as bad as if I had broken the other, the one that Mr Griffin broke, the one Mrs Heber and I both agreed was the most serious. And I had made little of the other. God must have been angry about that too. God was certainly punishing me today. I tried to pray. I looked up at the sky and said: "I am sorry, God. I did not mean that Lord Swords should be killed. I swear. I shall never go near the forge again. I shall never say one commandment is less serious than another. Forgive me, God. And, please God, let me get home safely. Don't let Mr Griffin catch me, God. I will always be good so long as I live, for ever and ever."

I felt a little better. If God had been frightfully angry there might have been a red glow in the sky. But the sky was misty. I was very cold now. I had forgotten my overcoat when I escaped from the school, and the mist had now turned into gentle, persistent rain that ran down my collar and made my trousers rub harshly against my cold, red legs. One of my garters had been broken and the stocking it was holding up had fallen down. I kept on trying to pull it up, but gave in at last. This leg got stung by nettles and scratched by briars. I stumbled out on the road eventually. I was less than four hundred yards from home. It was quite dark now. Once or twice in the last field I thought I had lost my way. I tripped over wire and tore my new suit. I put one foot in a rabbit-hole and twisted my ankle. I fell into cow dirt. I had begun to cry. It was silly crying. It did no good. It was babyish too. But still I cried after the last fall. I was so tired, so wet, and I had been so frightened. On the road it was better. I was still afraid that Mr Griffin might turn up, and I was also in fear that a Black and Tan lorry might come by and the Tans might take a shot at me. They had killed children on the roadside. Freddy told me so.

I came to the corner. Our home was now in sight. And I saw the blessed glow of the Aladdin lamp in the drawing-room. I began to run.

"Is that you, Master?"

It was Freddy's voice.

I ran on.

"Can I have a word with you, Master?"

But I ran faster. I did not look back. As always when I was frightened I expected a hand to reach out and catch me from behind. But when I swung round the gatepost (the gate had been left open), I felt a thud of relief in my heart. But I did not stop running until I had crossed the backyard and thrown open the door to the light and heat of the kitchen, the seat of Jane's blue skirt as she bent down to open the oven door, and Raffle, as always, asleep in her basket.

My father was about to set out to collect me at school. When I told about the Black and Tan raid, he turned to my mother and said:

"What possessed us to let him go there today?"

And my mother said: "Thank God he is back safe and sound."

Miss Morris was with them. And I must say she was very kind that day. She insisted on helping me to take off my wet things. And for the second time in three days I had a bath deep enough to dive in.

I could not sleep that night. I kept on thinking about Lord Swords and Freddy Doyle and my sin. I wondered whether God would really think it was sufficient for me just to say I was sorry. Then it did occur to me that He might because it was not my fault that He had let Lord Swords be killed. It was, when you came to think of it, rather bad luck on Lord Swords that God should have him shot just because I went to the forge when I was told not to. It would have been fairer to have shot Freddy. And Freddy knew this because he had hidden himself in our kitchen that night. I would tell the priest in confession. It would be terrible having to do it. And what would Father Murphy say? But before I went to confession I would have liked to talk about it all to someone and to make sure how bad I had been. It was wrong of me to go to the forge. But was it my fault Lord Swords was killed? I only talked about the Black and Tan because Miss Morris was afraid of him. I wanted to help her. Everything I did had been done for her sake. If I had not bothered about her and left her to her fate, Freddy would never have known; Lord Swords would never have been killed. How could I have known Freddy would tell Mr Griffin? Did Freddy ask Mr Griffin to kill the Black and Tan? It looked like it. If that was so, would Freddy ask Mr Griffin to kill me? Would he not, perhaps, arrange to have us all killed? I must tell somebody. What did Freddy want tonight? Should I have stopped? Was he now planning to have me killed too? I must talk to somebody. Could I tell Miss Morris? But what would she do? She might tell the Black and Tan and then he would arrest me for telling Freddy. If I asked Miss Morris to swear, would she keep silent for my sake? I thought she would. But what help would she be then? And my father —but I could not tell him. I could not let him know I had gone to the forge and talked to Freddy and got Lord Swords killed. I could not face that. It would be easier to talk to someone else. But who? There was no one in the world. We were quite happy really before Miss Morris came. It was duller certainly. But terrible things did not happen. Each day was the same. That was all. Now we were all likely to be killed. And I was in a state of mortal sin. If I died my soul would go straight to hell. Uncle Lindy had been right. He told my father that keeping Miss Morris would lead to trouble.

So could it be that it was really not my fault at all that Lord Swords was dead? It was just as much my father's fault for not doing what Uncle Lindy told him. But there is no commandment *Honour thy half-brother*. There should be. If your half-brother is much older than you are, and if your parents are dead, could he take their place? And if Uncle Lindy was in that position, had my father broken the same commandment as I had? When I was being prepared for my First Holy Communion by the nuns I had learnt my Catechism very well. I knew it all by heart. And, as they explained it, the Ten Commandments really covered everything from shooting people to wetting beds. Would it do if I were to go to Father Murphy on Saturday and say: "Bless me, father, for I have sinned. It's two weeks since my last confession and in that time I have broken the fourth commandment. And that is all I can remember"?

Would Father Murphy be satisfied with that? Or would he ask me how I had broken it? Well, if he did, I could say: "I went to the forge when I was told not to by my parents."

Surely that would end the matter. Would it be a bad confession if I were not to tell him about Lord Swords? A bad confession was even worse than no confession at all. It seemed unfair that this should have to happen to me and my father should not have to tell anyone he disobeyed Uncle Lindy. It had probably never occurred to him that he might be involved in the fourth commandment. He had an easier time than I had. I was the worrying type.

When you think you haven't slept at all you are really remembering the times you were awake during the night. I suppose I did sleep. I know I did because I had a terrible dream. It was all confused. The Black and Tans and Father Murphy chased me along the road, and Mr Griffin sat up in a tree firing stones at me from a catapult, and I was trying to explain to someone that I was not to blame, that it was Freddy's fault. And when I reached my house, Freddy was sitting at the table with his hat on and my father was passing round the dishes. He put his fingers to his lips when I came in. So I said nothing. I crept out of the house and ran away. The dream got very confused then. Uncle Lindy came into it, I remember. He was dancing with Miss Morris, and when I tried to attract his attention he shouted 'Heel it, Trinity,' as if I wasn't there.

Next day was the funeral. I was feeling so awful I got sick at breakfast, right in front of everyone. I was sent back to bed. Later on I got up and I was allowed to watch the procession from the window. The coffin was carried on a farm-cart. All the estate labourers marched behind it. After that there was a stream of motor cars. And then dogcarts and pony traps. A great many people had no motor cars then. Behind the last trap there was a straggle of women and children who looked as if they had no idea what was going on but were following the crowd so as not to miss anything.

Jane told me all about it. She knew who everybody was.

"There's your daddy, love," she said. "In the car with Mr Heber and your uncle.

"All the quality is there," she told me.

My mother watched with me. It was very interesting for people who had no weight on their consciences.

"I must go to confession on Saturday," I whispered to my mother.

She smiled at that. She had no idea what I was suffering.

Miss Morris stayed in her room. The Black and Tan had come to see my father before the funeral to say how sorry he was that I had been at the school when it was raided. Mr Griffin got away, he said. It looked highly suspicious. He left flowers for Miss Morris. But she did not bother to take them out of their paper. So my mother put them in a vase in the drawing-room, to save waste, she said.

After the funeral my father and Uncle Lindy came back with Mr Heber and they had drinks of whiskey in the dining-room. Uncle Lindy in his loud voice said: "Those hypocrites following the coffin knowing full well who shot him and not one with the courage to tell. Well, what of it? Soon they'll be cutting all our throats."

My mother, I am sure, raised her eyebrows as she did when people said awkward things. And I heard my father say, "Prenez garde. We don't all want to be shot."

But the maids heard every word. I was with them and I knew.

*   *   *

"But why can't you wait until next week when we can all go together?"

"I'm very sorry. But I must go to confession tomorrow."

"What's the trouble?" said my father.

It was the day after the funeral, and we were having breakfast.

"Brian insists that he must go to confession. It is very commendable, but it doesn't suit anyone to go with him and I won't have him out at night. I am trying to persuade him to wait for a week."

"I am sorry," I insisted. "I must go."

Everyone was silent then. My mother looked round the room. I knew she was trying to see if I had broken anything. Usually my confessions were hopeless. Sometimes I longed for a real sin to tell instead of endless repetitions of little things that upset nobody.

"It is very edifying," said my father. "And damnably inconvenient."

"I had the greatest trouble persuading you to come last week," said my mother.

We were not a wildly religious family, I think, not wildly anything, humdrum, to say the least, until Miss Morris came.

She had cheered up again, and I could see her looking at me too, wondering what the reason for my anxiety was. She looked at me in a way that was different from my parents. It was as though she expected the worst. My father gave me the impression that he took an amused view of anything I did. My mother was prepared to find me in the wrong, but underneath I think she believed me to be good. Miss Morris was more cynical about me. This made it easier in a way. I could tell her things I would not tell my parents. It would not surprise her or upset her. But I wanted her to love me too. And, for that reason, would not let her know how black my soul was. I envied them all their easy consciences. They were like little children, fit for the Kingdom of Heaven. I was a monster of depravity.

In a hurry for his train, as always in the morning, my father still made time to go round the house and look at the windows. I saw him giving a glance at the greenhouse in the vegetable garden. He had an obsession about broken glass, and I could see he suspected me of having broken some. I heard my mother say:

"The china seems in order. The Dresden lady has only

one arm, but she lost the other when she came to pieces in Alice's hand."

This was a pretty figure which collapsed unexpectedly and was found to be put together with soap. Alice had been accused of breaking it, but had explained that it had miraculously come to pieces "in me hand".

"Why did you stick her up with soap instead of telling me? Own up when you break things. I never say anything when people own up," said my mother.

"I would stop it out of her wages," said Uncle Lindy.

"I haven't the heart," said my mother. "And they are all the same. It's curious that telling the truth is never taught to them with their catechism. None of them tells the truth."

"If you are worried about something, Brian, don't keep it to yourself. Own up. No one will be cross with you."

"I just want to go to confession, that's all," I said.

"I shall take him," said Miss Morris. "I don't want to go to the Hebers' at the moment. I can wash my hair instead."

Keeping something to oneself makes one feel important, but, at the same time, awkward. Walking alone with Miss Morris, I felt she must be longing to know what the fuss was about. It seemed mean not to tell her. I tried to distract her attention by asking questions, silly questions really, anything that came into my mind: 'How far away is America?' 'Is an aeroplane faster than a motor car?' 'How high are the jumps in the Grand National?' 'What exactly is "the government" about which Uncle Lindy is always complaining?' 'Was everyone going to have their throats cut by the Sinn Feiners?'

Miss Morris knew some of the answers, but I could see she was not really interested in my conversation. I suppose she had thoughts of her own, sad thoughts about Lord Swords, and other thoughts about the Black and Tan. I was frightened to mention him in case she would suspect the true reason for my confession. It was never very cheerful in our church. At night it was dark and gloomy. A few figures were huddled in the bench beside the confessional, and a woman in a shawl was flitting like a bat through the dusky aisles, doing the Stations of the Cross. The silence was broken only by the noise of shoes as people came in from the street and clattered on the flags, the faint creak of benches as penitents got up or sat down, the groan as a door of the confession-box opened, the thud as it shut, the thumping of the person inside kneeling down in the darkness, the shuttle of the grille as the priest slid it to and fro between each confession, the burble of the penitent's tale, and the deeper, purring sound of the priest as he gave absolution, the rumble as the penitent got up in the box; and then the groan of the door opening as one more came out with a clear conscience. Then the people waiting pushed up a place.

I was always nervous before confession, fearing that I should forget the procedure or get lost in the Act of Contrition. I had small matters, bits of cheek, that I decided to leave out today. Had I had no new sins to tell, I might have fallen back on these. But, alas, that was not the case today.

"You go in front of me," I said to Miss Morris, just before my turn came. She was sitting on the far side of me.

"Go on out of that," she said, prodding me from behind.

I could never get Miss Morris to fall in with my plans.

The door creaked; a young man stood there holding it open politely for the next penitent (usually whoever is waiting rushes at it).

"Hurry up," I heard Miss Morris whisper. I suppose she was a little bit annoyed. I had made such a point of going to confession, and now it looked as if I wanted to get out of it.

I screwed my courage up, and went forward. Inside the box it was quite dark at first. Then, by degrees, it lightened sufficiently for me to see the closed door of the grille and the small crucifix that hung over it. I kissed the cross, as I had been taught to do, and knelt down. Nowadays (I was quite tall for my age) my face came level with the window.

I could hear the sound of the penitent on the other side of the priest. It was a woman, and she seemed to be telling a story. Now and then the priest intervened with a few words. Then the monotonous sound began again. What sin, or list of sins, could take so much telling? I was in a way glad of the respite. But after a while my knees began to hurt. I had gone over what I had to say so often in my mind, it would be a relief to get it said at last. And then the confessional, so like a coffin standing on its end, began to oppress me. If I moved I came against the walls. The opening of the aperture would be like the sight of light at the end of a tunnel. And then I heard the priest's voice, a deep, whispering, sing-song like a bumble bee as he dives into the heart of a flower. My turn was coming.

I heard the grille sliding as the priest shut it, the commotion in the box as the woman got to her feet and thumped against the sides of the narrow box, the door opening . . . then the grille shot open and I could see, but not very distinctly, Father Murphy in profile, waiting.

"Bless me, father, for I have sinned. It is two weeks since my last confession; in that time I have——" This was the moment. What I had to say sounded in my own mind so inadequate that I almost panicked. But I went on—"broken the fourth commandment." It was out now.

Father Murphy said nothing. Had he heard me? Was he considering? I waited. The pause seemed interminable. Should I repeat myself? Then he might think I had done it twice.

"Anything else?" he said at last. His face looked very tired, but his whisper was warm and fatherly.

"No, father."

"And how did you break it, child?"

His voice was still kind.

"I went to the forge when I was told not to."

"That was disobedience. You were disobedient."

"Yes, father."

"Would you like to confess any sins of your past life? Can you remember any? Have you had any impure thoughts?"

This was Father Murphy's favourite question. I never exactly understood what he meant before, but now I was so conscious of sin, I had gone over and over this business of Freddy and the forge so often in my mind, that I felt guilty about almost everything. Mrs Heber suddenly shot into my mind. I could hear my mother saying "monster of depravity". Depraved meant corrupt. But I had done nothing wrong. Was it a sin not to shut the bathroom door? Was it a sin to undress? Why had I undressed? No, I could not remember. Perhaps it had been at the dictation of an impure thought. At last I understood Father Murphy.

"I undressed in the bathroom, father."

"Yes, child."

His voice had changed. It was still kind but very sad. It was as though he had been praying and hoping I had no impure thoughts, and now he knew he was going to be disappointed. Perhaps he asked that question so often in the hope that he would find somebody who could always say 'no'. He may even have thought he had found one at last. And now I was going to let him down, as everyone had done before.

"That was all," I said.

"Were you making your toilet?"

What did he mean?

"I was weighing myself."

"What is that, child? What did ye say?"

"Weighing myself."

That was the truth. It sounded quite mad. But that was part of the mystery. Perhaps other people with impure thoughts acted in the same way.

"Were you alone, child?"

"I was. But I forgot to lock the door, and Maud—Mrs Heber—someone's maid came in."

"Yes, child."

"That is all, father."

"What happened when the maid came in?"

"Nothing, father."

"Did she stay with you?"

"No, father. She shrieked and ran away."

"And did you have impure thoughts about her, child?"

"No, father."

"Think of Our Lady, child. Think of the holy mother of God. And next time you are tempted, say a little prayer to her and to St. Joseph. Ask them to help you not to offend God."

He sighed very deeply. Then he turned his face towards me and looked at me for the first time.

"Say three Our Fathers and three Hail Marys for your penance. Now say an Act of Contrition."

He turned away, and I could see through my tears his great red face looking old and sad and gentle as he seemed to be talking to God. I stumbled through the Act of Contrition, getting confused in the words. A final humiliation. But Father Murphy had not been listening to me. Now he turned towards me again and said: "God bless you, child." Then the grille shut.

I rubbed my eyes and tried to stop crying. Outside Miss Morris would be waiting to come in, wondering what the delay was. I did not want her to see me like this.

I came out of the box quickly, keeping my head down, and did not look at Miss Morris. To say penance I always moved up to the front of the church. I found an empty pew in which to kneel. Burying my face in my hands, I repeated mechanically the prayers I had been set as penance, but all the time my mind whirled round. What had happened? I had been worried to death about the killing of Lord Swords. Nothing else was on my conscience. Father Murphy had not bothered at all about that, but he, like Mrs Heber, had been terribly upset about Maud. The things you did, meaning no harm, were perhaps the worst of all sins. It was because Father Murphy seemed so sad, I was crying. I always cried when people were sad. It was as when a band passed—I couldn't keep myself from marching along and feeling a glad thrill at the music. Sad things had the same effect. I felt miserable, but in a quiet, peaceful sort of way. Sadness seemed to fall on me like misty rain; which was almost pleasant if one resigned oneself to it, and stopped bothering about the fact of getting wet. And my sadness now was quite different from the unhappiness of recent days when I felt that something terrible was lurking round every corner. There was nothing soothing about unhappiness of that sort.

If this was what impure thoughts meant, it was much better than the other kind of sins. But, why then, did it upset Father Murphy so much? Why was he always asking about it? Did he not say it was the worst of all sins?

"Do you want to stay here all night?" Miss Morris was whispering in my ear. I was all right now. I had stopped crying. I got up and followed her. Our feet sounded slap, slap, slap on the flags. It was very cold outside. An east wind was blowing. We muffled ourselves up and ran.

"What penance did you get?" I shouted.

"Three Our Fathers and three Hail Marys."

"Same here."

Miss Morris had been so sad I wanted to be kind to her. But this was very difficult. When we got home—the maids were out—I offered to make tea. It would be nice to sit down and have a chat. If I got a chance I wanted to say how sorry I was. But this was not easy. I got no opportunity. She chased me off to bed.

"Hurry up with your bath. I want to wash my hair."

"I don't think I need a bath. I had one yesterday."

"Let me look at you. Wash your knees and your ears and the back of your neck."

I could see she was in no mood to talk to me.

In bed I had plenty to think about. I thought most about Father Murphy and how sad and confused he had made me feel. While Miss Morris was in the bathroom I could give occasional shouts to her, and even though I could not hear her replies it was comforting to know she was near. When she went downstairs I was lonely. I began to think that there were people outside the window. I heard footsteps. It was Freddy Doyle and Mr Griffin. I felt sure of that. I could imagine Freddy pointing out my window. If they had a ladder it would be easy to come up. Was my window fastened?

I did not know, and was afraid to look. I hid under the bedclothes. I started to pray. I prayed that my father and mother would come home soon. It was only when they were out of the house I got these terrible fears. The stairs creaked. I sat up and listened. There was silence. Then, after a long time, another creak. I kept my eyes on the door. It was one-quarter open. Was there someone coming?

The clock in the hall struck ten. That cheered me up. It had a friendly, purring sort of strike. Had my parents come home then, it would have been perfect. Even if they had not come up to me, I could have gone to sleep. But they did not come. Time became huge. The clock got lost. The stairs creaked again. The door, only a blur, but distinguishable to a night-practised eye, threatened across a room patch-worked with moonlight through a venetian blind. The window was too much. I could not face that. But the door, being inside the house, was a lesser horror. I crawled out of the tunnel in the close-packed bed-clothes, caught my falling pyjamas between my knees, and set out for the door. Half-way across the room my courage failed. But now my case was hopeless. To go back to bed meant looking at the window. I could, of course, make a rush for it, but if I did, I felt that I would run the gauntlet of those awful eyes. What would it be like in bed after that? The door was a lesser threat. Behind it was the landing and the stairs, the creaking stairs; but below that was the hall in which the clock (if only I could hear it) was comfortably tick-tocking, and across the hall was the drawing-room in which Miss Morris was kneeling down, drying her hair at the fire. The further I went through the door, the better for me. One step towards the window and I was lost. The stairs creaked again. The door shadow bulged. I waited. But nothing happened. If a man were coming through the door his shape would appear on the far side of the door, in the gap between the open door and the wall. And there I could see nothing. My knees were tired. The pyjama trousers gathered round my ankles and the night air grew perceptibly cooler round the uncovered space. It was a blessing in disguise. The effect of bending down and yanking up my trousers quickened me into action. It was the posture in which a sprinter starts a race. There was a chasm between me and the door, but one good jump and I would be across it. I jumped.

Now the door. I seized the edge of it and pulled it back, at the same time jumping away in case anyone was there.

No one moved. Now it required only the courage to charge through that space down to the flicker of welcoming light below. I had that courage. I rushed through, avoiding the hands that clutched me in the dark, rushed through the shadows on the stairs, thumped into the hall. I could hear the clock. It sounded so friendly, so reassuring. I opened the drawing-room door and as I did so the wretched pyjamas collapsed again. I pulled them up quickly before I ran into the lamplight. Miss Morris was not there.

I rushed across the hall into the school-room and the kitchen. There was nobody there except Raffle asleep in her basket. I had forgotten the threatening shadows in the house. I ran upstairs. I looked in every room. Miss Morris was nowhere. I was alone in the house with a dog and a cat.

It should have made me more frightened, but my immediate feeling was betrayal. Terrified in bed I had thought that at least, if only I could get there, safety waited for me downstairs. I could see where Miss Morris had been. There was an empty tea cup on the floor at the hearth and I saw a cigarette stub in the grate. And Kitchener was asleep on the sofa. How long had I been alone?

The search had shown me that the house was empty. There was some comfort in that thought. The maids were under strict orders to be in by ten o'clock. It was now half-past. They were probably on the roadside waiting. When they saw my mother coming they would run and get home a few minutes before her. I had noticed that was their habit. But where was Miss Morris? Out in that lonely lane, waiting for the Black and Tan? Driving with him perhaps in his new car? And if that were so, might she not be shot? An ambush would kill everyone in the car. Mr Griffin was on the run; Freddy acting as a spy. They had missed the Black and Tan the last time. They might not make that mistake again. But I could not go out to Miss Morris. I could not face the night and Freddy lurking in the shadows. I had never gone out alone since the evening he called out to me. I was much too afraid of meeting him.

It was nice in the drawing-room with Kitchener. The lamp on the table threw a rose on the low ceiling. The fire, banked all day, had been given its head earlier in the evening. It threw out a great warm glow in which I sat. I tried to guess the exact place where Miss Morris had been kneeling. I traced it, as best I could, by the position of the cup and the place where she threw the cigarette stub. I was not cross with her but worried, frightened for her. When I thought of it she ran more real dangers than I did. Mine were mostly in my mind. They were apprehensions, fears. Miss Morris seemed to have no fears. If she had, why did she make such dangerous friends?

The road ran quite near the house which was separated by a path and hedge. I now heard steps ringing out on the road, and the sound of voices. I listened. These were not menacing voices and the footsteps were happy ones. Now I could distinguish my mother's dear voice and my father's funny, nervous laugh. (He looked like a nice dog in trouble when he laughed.) And then—how wonderful! I heard Miss Morris. She was laughing too; a wonderful laugh she had. It did strange things to her eyes and nose. They quivered with pleasure. And her teeth were white, which is a great advantage to a constant laugher. The house lost all its terror and mystery. My fears seemed ridiculous now. Here they were coming up the drive. I was happy.

At the very moment that the key turned in the latch, I heard the back-door stair and a scurry across the kitchen as the maids made for their room. They were just in time.

"What are you doing out of bed?" said my mother.

"There was no one in the house," I said.

"How long have you been there?" said Miss Morris.

"I don't know. I was lonely. I came down. There was no one here."

My mother looked guilty and so did Miss Morris. My father was laughing.

"We must get you a cord for your pyjamas," he said.

I was holding them up by my knees.

"Are those girls in?" said my mother suspiciously.

"Yes," I said.

"Then you weren't quite alone," said Miss Morris.

I did not want to get the maids into trouble, so I said nothing.

"Run up to bed," said Miss Morris.

"Would you like me to carry you piggy-back?" said my father.

"He is too big for that," said my mother.

"I heard voices and people walking round the house," I said.

"I tell you what. I'll make you a nice glass of hot milk," said my mother.

"May I have it at the fire?"

"It's a pity to waste that fire," said my mother. "You get into the armchair and I will put on the kettle in the kitchen."

"Let me," said Miss Morris.

I snuggled down in the chair and closed my eyes.

"He will fall asleep there," said my mother. "Poor little mite. I wonder when those lassies did come in. They are so two-faced, it's absurd to rely on them. Miss Morris should have stayed in."

"We told her to come," said my father.

"It was a mistake. I must say I enjoyed the evening. Did I tell you that Mrs Heber came up to me before dinner and stated solemnly that Doreen had been privately engaged to Lord Swords, and that she was returning to London to recover from the blow?"

"That is a half-truth," said my father. "Heber told me that her parents took fright when they heard of the murder and insisted she should come home."

"It's charitable to call that a half-truth. I nearly died when I saw Captain Wain there. When I remembered how that woman descended on me when I was feeling like a wet hen and positively called me to order for daring to allow her precious niece to meet such people. And then, to have the nerve to ask us to dinner to meet him! We never let him set foot in this house until he called officially to check on the murder. It was all aimed at Miss Morris, of course. Simply jealousy on Doreen's account."

"Who invited him this evening?" said my father.

"Miss Morris swears she had nothing to do with it. I suppose Mrs Heber has come to the conclusion that any man in a uniform is better than no man at all."

"Doreen is a nice girl. She may have done it for Miss Morris's sake. But I can't understand how she got round her aunt. Did you see Mrs Heber's face each time he said, 'What does mother say?' In the end she said, 'I am nobody's mother unfortunately.'"

"And then he said, 'Sorry, Auntie.' Even Heber smiled at that. I looked at Doreen and she seemed delighted. I think she is infatuated with the man. Women like bounders. I am always telling you that. Mrs Heber's old admirer was a frightful cad. Don't you remember? And I can see a sort of attraction in Captain George. He makes you feel you are a woman. That is flattering. Most men talk to me nowadays as if they were addressing a corpse. What's the matter? You'll wake the child."

My father had started to laugh in his funny way.

"When the women left the room Heber said: 'Will you have a cigar, Captain Wain?' 'Ta. Ta. If you don't mind I'll stick to fags. Have you a fag?' 'Not since I was at school,' said Heber. 'Then I'll smoke my own,' said Wellington."

"I hope you didn't call him Wellington, darling. He is quick enough. And I am sure he would take offence."

"I don't think I did. Heber kept on saying: 'Did he who made the lamb make thee?' I thought it was unfortunate. At last Wain took him up on it. Heber said it was a line from his favourite poet, and for some reason it was running in his head. Wain took that very well and used it as a cue to tell us lines from his favourites. They were vulgar without being funny. But one of them made Heber laugh."

"You can tell me afterwards. I am nervous of the child. I wish you had been there when he started to give his George Robey and George Formby imitations in the drawing-room."

"I missed that. Heber took me aside to talk about the Swords business. The heir is shutting up the place and dismissing all the men. I must say it's the price of them. Everyone on the place must know who did the shooting."

"I wish you had been with us. I kept my eyes on Mrs Heber's face. It was a study. She wanted to laugh, but she thought it unbecoming. And then, of course, she was behaving all evening as though the family was in mourning for poor Lord Swords whom they had hardly met half a dozen times. Doreen was playing anaemic little pieces on the piano after dinner when the men came in. She became all of a flutter then, of course. Horace Hone tried to persuade her to play something, but she refused. 'I am sure George can play,' she said. 'I strum,' he said, sitting down at once and laying his cigarette on the polished top of the piano. Mrs Heber almost cried. He then gave imitations of George Robey and George

Formby. They were both called after him, he said. He sang a song of George Formby's and asked us all to join in the chorus.

> "My name is John William, the youngest of ten.
> There were five of us girls and five of us men.
> If father had liked there might have been more
> But mother ran off with the lodger next door
> When the bells were ringing the old year out
> And the new year in.

"Mrs Heber threw a desperate glance at Horace Hone. And he rose to the occasion wonderfully. In no time we were sitting down to bridge."

"Miss Morris was late for all that. But I got the impression that she hankers after that awful creature. I saw it in her eyes when she came into the room. I will never understand women. She has only to take her time, but girls can't wait. They must be married."

"Prenez garde. Are you awake, Brian? Here comes Miss Morris with your milk. Isn't she kind? Sit up, Brian, like a good boy, and try to drink without spilling any on the new covers. There's the man."

Miss Morris came in carrying a tray with tea on it and milk for me. I thought she looked very pretty and young, almost like a little girl. Only a few hours ago she had been bossy and grown-up like any other governess. But now she was a governess no longer. She was just a nice, pretty person. How happy we would all be if she could stay like that. I had heard every word of the recent conversation—grown-ups become very careless late at night—and I felt an ache in my heart when I heard that Miss Morris might marry the Black and Tan. What did my mother mean by saying women liked bounders? Nothing seemed to make sense any more. Why did Mrs Heber attack my mother one moment for allowing Doreen to meet George and then have him to dinner? Why did grown-ups go out to parties with people they did not like? I could see my mother really hated Mrs Heber. And they all despised Doreen. And they were not upset about Lord Swords. If only Miss Morris would wait for me. I would take her to live on some beautiful island where we could bathe all day and pick fruit from the trees and sleep in a tent. Far away from Black and Tans, Sinn Feiners, and Uncle Lindy, far away from Freddy Doyle and Mr Griffin. But at the thought of them I began to be frightened again. I started to cry.

"Poor little man, he is too tired to drink his milk," said my mother.

My father picked me up in his arms and carried me to bed.

"Sleep tight," he said.

"Leave the door open and the light on the landing," I said.

"We are beside you. Sing out if you want us," he said.

I went to sleep then.

*　　　　*　　　　*

I decided that I must speak to Miss Morris. I would blow up if I kept it to myself any longer. And now was the time. Lord Swords being dead removed a rival from the Black and Tan's path. If I waited, it might be too late. I found my opportunity on the day after the Hebers' party. My parents went to play bridge with the Hones after dinner. Miss Morris stayed with me. Since Mr Griffin's disappearance there had been no lessons in the evening, but I was given some in the morning by Miss Morris—she was strange and jumpy at lesson time. I think it bored her terribly—and when my father came home he looked over what I had done and corrected it.

"Paper is cheap," was one of the things he used to say. I had a habit of writing very small at the top of every page.

"Short words and simple sentences," was another of his remarks. It used to disappoint me to hear that said when I had tried to write like a grown-up. Grown-ups go on as if they were superior to children, and yet they seem to spend their time preventing children acting like grown-ups. 'Take your elbows off the table,' I was always told. But I noticed in the dining-room after dinner, most people put their elbows on the table. Miss Morris sucked the end of her pen; a thing I was never allowed to do.

I suppose because she was still feeling guilty about leaving me on the previous night, Miss Morris was very friendly this evening. She offered to play Snap with me before I went to bed. She always won at Snap. And the games lasted for a few minutes only. But it was a kind suggestion. I got out the draughts as well because Miss Morris tired very quickly of any game.

Snap gets dull when you are losing, so I stopped paying attention and started to talk instead.

"How old should people be when they marry?"

"It depends on a lot of things."

"But in your own case. What age would you like to marry at?"

"That's a leading question, Nosey."

"I only wanted to know. How does anyone learn these things if no one will talk about them?"

"It comes in time, like whiskers."

"I shall marry when I am twenty-one."

"Will you now?"

"I will."

"Good for you. I am twenty-two and I haven't married yet. So you will beat me to it."

"Is that because no one ever asked you? Or have you exercised free will?"

"Snap pool," said Miss Morris, taking all the cards up. "You are not watching the game, mister."

"Mrs Heber said Doreen was privately engaged to Lord Swords. Does that mean he proposed to her?"

"I am sure I don't know what it means."

"Mummy thinks Mrs Heber made it up."

"Snap."

She took all my cards. "I won't play with you if you don't pay attention."

"Let's have a game of draughts. Snap is silly. Did Lord Swords propose to you?"

"He did not."

"Well then, he didn't propose to Doreen either. He much preferred you. He looked dull when he was with Doreen and he got quite lively (for him) when he saw you."

"People don't always marry the girls who make them lively. I am not going to discuss my life with you, Brian. If I did, you would be off to the forge next minute to tell Freddy Doyle. I know you."

I wonder if my face showed what I felt when Miss Morris said this. It got red. I could feel it burning. Inside my head questions went off like rockets. My heart gave a jump. My eyes wanted to wander to the corners of the room, but I forced them to meet Miss Morris's. The more I blushed, the more delighted she appeared. How much did she know?

"I would die before I would talk to Freddy about you."

It was true. I do believe it was true. Anyhow, it was very nearly true.

"You and Jane provide him with all the gossip of the neighbourhood. I don't know which of you is worst."

"I promise I would never tell Freddy about you. I don't

like him. In fact, I hate him. And I am terribly fond of you."

Miss Morris blushed a little when I said that. It was the truest thing I had said to her. It made me feel better.

"I am very fond of you too," she said.

It was the first nice thing she had ever said to me. It made me blush, but not the flaming sort of blush I had just experienced. This was quite different. It was as if I were in the garden in the morning when the sun came out. It was a nice warm glow, not a sudden stabbing flame. It melted me. It made me want to do something to show my pleasure. I am sure birds feel like that when they start to sing. But when I sing everyone laughs. I had a piece of chocolate in my pocket. I gave her that.

"Mind. It has melted a bit," I warned her.

"Thank you very much," she said.

The chocolate was sticking to the silver paper, but she did what I would have done and licked it off without trying to take the paper away first. It is the only sensible thing to do with chocolate that has been all day in someone's pocket.

"Don't worry about Lord Swords, Miss Morris. I shall marry you when I'm twenty-one. I promise."

"I must have that in writing, Brian. I told you before, I know men."

"I will write it in blood if you like."

"You are beginning very young. Don't take girls too seriously. You will make yourself unhappy. The lucky ones are never the ones who bother much."

"I shall never love anyone else.

"I am as constant as the northern star
Of whose true fixed and resting quality
There is no fellow in the firmament."

"Where did you get that?"

"Julius Caesar."

"You are a caution. Let's have a game of draughts. I will give you sixpence if you beat me, and I shall play with nine men. Is that fair?"

"You play with twelve men. It's no fun if you give me odds."

"Pride. Pride. Pride. But have it your own way."

I never tried so hard as I did that time. It was partly on account of the sixpence. I wanted it badly. All my pocket money went into a money-box and did me very little good. But much more than the sixpence I wanted to beat Miss Morris at the game so that she might begin to respect me. She had not said she would marry me when I was twenty-one. But I could see she was pleased that I had mentioned it again.

I began to take her men and to guess her moves, to set traps for her. At one moment I had three kings and five men to her one king and six men.

"You have come on," she said.

In the end she won. But it was a near thing. I felt quite proud of myself. I had beaten grown-ups before, but they had never really tried their hardest. It is rather insulting to a child to let him see you have not done your best. And I always knew.

"Let's have another game. You take white this time."

"No, Brian. Enough is enough. And it's past your bedtime."

I made no fuss about going to bed. I took a bath without arguing. I wanted Miss Morris to be still in a good humour when she came up to tuck me in.

"You never said you would marry me. Will you? Or won't you?"

I put the question like that when I saw she was quite friendly.

"When you are twenty-one, I shall be thirty-three. That

is incredibly old. People will think I am your mother and not your wife."

"Thirty-three is not so old. I won't care what people think. We can go and live where there are no people."

"Let's put it this way. If you want to marry me when you are twenty-one, and if I am not married, you come and ask me then. What about that as an idea?"

"It's no good. Unless you have promised me, you are sure to go off and marry someone else. Daddy said you ought to wait, but you wouldn't have the patience."

Miss Morris said nothing to this. She looked down at her hands which were smoothing out the wrinkles in her dress. But I knew she was listening. When a person is really interested in what you are saying, you can *hear* them listening.

"He is worried about you just as much as I am. We are both afraid you will marry the Black and Tan. Mummy says women don't object to bounders as men do. And Daddy says he can't understand women. He thinks the Black and Tan is frightfully common but that you hanker after him. It's in your eyes, Daddy said."

"You must not call George a Black and Tan. Did you tell Freddy Doyle he was one?"

I hesitated. What *had* I said to Freddy? Did *he* say Captain Wain was a Black and Tan? Who began talking about him first? I had always in my mind the picture of the A.C. in the lane and Freddy behind the wall looking like our cat watching a bird on the kitchen window sill.

That is the worst of people like Freddy; one talks to them because one is lonely and they encourage it because they want to know things and to make trouble. It makes them seem so friendly in comparison with other people who are always too busy to listen and only ask questions that need short answers. Freddy's questions are like stones dropped in a pond. They make circles that get bigger and bigger. And it is all so smooth and so effortless. I could see myself talking and talking while Freddy smiled and nodded. But try as I might I could not remember who had used the expression Black and Tan first. I had a horrible feeling that it might have been me.

"He knows it. Freddy knows all about Black and Tans and Auxiliaries. He says the Auxiliaries were supposed to be toffs, but they are much worse really. No one else ever talked to me about Black and Tans except Jane, and Alice sometimes."

"What I want to find out is what you and Freddy said about George to one another?"

"I thought you were frightened of George. You said you wanted to get away from him. I was so worried on your account I did not know what to do. I knew Freddy didn't like George either. I saw the way he looked at the car. It frightened me, so it did. I told Freddy that I wanted to save you. I thought he might be able to help. But I did it for your sake. I liked George. He was kind. He explained the way his car worked. He showed me his revolver. He gave me a drive in the A.C. He gave me money."

Thinking of all the kind things George had done made me cry. Freddy had never done a single thing for me. Indeed, I strongly suspected him of pinching a sixpence I took out of my pocket one day in the forge. It was on the anvil one minute and it had gone the next. When I asked Freddy had he seen it he behaved in an extraordinary way, and would not let me leave the forge until he had searched through all the horseshoes and cart wheels stacked in corners since ever I knew him.

Miss Morris put her arm round me. "Don't cry. But don't go near Freddy any more. Your father told you he was not a good man. And don't worry about Freddy either. I think he has cooked his goose this time."

"I told it in confession."

"Told what, Methuselah?"

"That I went to the forge. I said I had broken the fourth commandment. I thought the story about the forge was a bit too complicated for Father Murphy."

"So that's what the fuss to go to confession was about."

As she said this Miss Morris gave me a long, considering look as if I were something she had forgotten the name of.

I could see she was moving off, but I wanted to keep her. I had so much I wanted to know. But she would never sit down like my father did occasionally and really open his mind.

"Is George a Greek?" I said.

"Why do you ask that?"

"When I told Daddy that he had given me money and been kind to me, Daddy said something which was the Latin for: Look out when Greeks start giving presents."

"That was very hard on George. Generosity is his best point. And he comes from Battersea. I have a crow to pluck with your father. Good night."

She left me then without kissing me or asking me if I had said my prayers. What sort of mother would she have made? But I suppose like everything else mothering requires practice. I had not felt so happy for ages. I knew I would fall asleep quite soon if I concentrated hard on the thought of waking up tomorrow morning. It always works.

It seemed in a dream I heard the sound of lorries on the road and men shouting. Then a gun fired. I jumped out of bed and ran half-asleep out on the landing. My mother and father and Miss Morris were standing there in their night clothes holding hands and listening.

"It's all right. They've gone. We can go back to bed," said my father.

"What happened?"

"Some silly man trying to wake up the neighbourhood. Drunk probably. He won't keep me out of bed," said my father. He wanted to stop us being frightened, I could see.

"Put on your dressing-gowns, all of you, and come down and make tea in the kitchen," said my mother.

It was a wonderful idea. But, of course, as soon as I got there I fell asleep again. When I woke up it was morning and I was in my own bed.

*   *   *

"Get up out of that. There's no milk. And Jimmy never came to pump the water. Your father's shoes have not been cleaned. I think the world must have come to an end."

My mother stood beside my bed, all cheerful as she usually was, and up, as usual, the first of the household.

"Run along to Miss Tite's, like a good boy, and ask her to lend me enough milk for breakfast. Tell her I will return it later in the day. Hurry up, now. Give yourself a lick and a promise as usual. Don't dawdle."

I hated when anyone said: 'Don't dawdle.' It always made me want to dawdle. But today was not an ordinary day. Something must have happened if no messenger had come to the house. It must have something to do with the shot last night. I was still dressing myself as I ran down the road to Miss Tite. She lived in a bungalow with a huge family of Scotch Terriers, and ever since I asked her why she grew a moustache, I hated meeting her. I once heard her say: "The Allens' brat has a shifty expression." But the truth was I tried to avoid looking at her face lest she should get the impression I was inspecting her moustache. I had the same trouble with our doctor's wife. Mrs Groves had once seen me putting out my tongue. Ever afterwards I pretended it was an affliction, and I did it whenever I met her. She told my mother I had adenoids. And my mother said that Mrs Groves was looking for work for her husband (which was unfair to her). But what could I do?

No one would bother about a moustache today when there were so many important things to think about, but all the same I was delighted when I saw Miss Tite hurrying towards me. It was ringing at the door and waiting for her to appear I disliked so.

"I was sent by my mother to borrow a jug of milk. Paddy never turned up this morning," I explained. "She will give it back," I added.

"I am always glad to oblige your mother, Brian," she said. "Wait there until I find some in the dairy—God save the mark!—I was coming to see your father when I met you. Did you hear the shooting last night?"

"It woke me up."

But Miss Tite had disappeared into her back premises.

She came out a few seconds later carrying a blue and white striped jug full to the brim with bubbling milk. It looked as if she had come straight from a cow.

"Come along, now," she said. Her voice was like a man's voice. Only more so. And she wore a man's soft hat, a collar and tie and thick leather brogues. She gave the impression of someone talking into a strong wind. There was something ferocious about her. But it was not frightening. She was like someone dressed up and pretending to be fierce. Deep down underneath I think she would have preferred to be like Miss Morris; but when she could not be like that she pretended to be an old farmer. It was an easier disguise. I felt sorry for her really. And when I heard she cried because I mentioned her moustache I was terribly unhappy. I was only seven at the time, and at that age one does not realise a person sometimes is ashamed of what they've got.

"What has happened?" I asked. I had to run to keep up with her.

"The whole damn lot of them are frightened out of their skins," she said.

And then before I could ask her another question, she said:

"There's an apple to stop your gob with."

It was a pippin, the best of all apples. I was deeply grateful.

"Why doesn't your mother buy you a proper pair of knickerbockers? Your knees must be frozen in this weather," she said.

I thought the word knickerbockers was a funny expression to use. It only applied to things women wear. I blushed. This was the sort of difficulty Miss Tite put one in. She had everything mixed up.

"You have a warm jacket, I see. I suppose she works on the principle, what you lose at one end you gain at the other. Take your hands out of your pockets, and don't kick stones with your shoes. But I see the warning comes too late."

Whoever heard a coat called a jacket? But I let Miss Tite go on. Never again would I run the risk of upsetting her. And somehow her criticism did not seem to matter. It was like the deep barking of a friendly dog. There was nothing angry about it. It was her way of talking to children.

"I am glad to see you are alive, Victoria," said my mother, who was waiting for us.

"Come in and have breakfast," said my father.

"I've had my breakfast. But I will take a cup of tea. Is that young play-actress out of her bed yet? I'd give her a good hiding if she was in bed at this time in my house. Oh, there you are, miss."

We were all ready for breakfast. My father had a nice way with people. He fussed over Miss Tite just as if she had been grand and beautiful. She had to have the best chair and sit nearest the fire. I could see she liked it. She felt very important this morning. On the road I sensed it. She was like a kettle coming to the boil.

"Let me tell you about the goings-on in the village," she began. "I was over with the Hones helping them to eat a pheasant and I thought I would take a walk home for the sake of my digestion. Horace always offers to drive me. But I prefer the walk. It was a damn silly thing to do at that time of night—we sat up gossiping until twelve. But one forgets that we no longer live in a civilised country. The dogs started to bark. That was the first I knew of what was happening, and then—God bless my soul!—I walked straight into a lorry-load of Auxiliaries. They had pulled across the road to stop traffic going by. I know they are supposed to be protecting us, but I declare to God I felt as if my days were numbered.

"Then I saw Freddy Doyle standing in the middle of the lorry with his braces cut. He had to hold up his breeches with his hands. They had put a pot on his head, and he was singing *God Save the King* for all he was worth. They were pretty drunk. And little as I like the same Mr Doyle, I declare I felt sorry for him.

"They let me pass. One said: 'You might be safer at home, ma'am.' I could have smacked his face. Freddy saw me then. 'They'll take my life, miss. They'll take my life,' he shouted. He was in terror. 'That man's harmless,' I said to the officer. 'Don't worry, miss. A little exercise will do him good,' said the officer. 'Would you join in the chorus?' said another. But he looked nasty. 'Hurry home,' said the first one. What could I do? I cleared off. A little later I heard a shot go off. I felt a coward. I said to myself: 'Victoria. This is where you act, my girl.' There was no reply when I rang the telephone exchange. Mrs Dillon was probably under the bed. I was going to talk to someone in the Castle. They should not give half-drunken daredevils a free hand. What can you expect of them with no proper discipline, and as likely as not to be shot at from behind the hedge at any moment? So I took a stout walking-stick—no one needs a licence for that—and an electric torch and went out again. But by this time the Auxiliaries had gone. I went to Freddy's house. The door was open. The furniture was out in the yard in pieces. All the windows were broken. And there he was down on his knees praying like a dervish. 'Are you all right, Doyle?' I said to him. But he wouldn't answer me. He was reciting a litany at the top of his voice. I wonder what God thinks of prayers like those? So far as I could see the Auxiliaries had done him no harm. I need hardly tell you that by this time the absence of braces made him an embarrassing companion for a single woman. But he had recovered his hat. So the decencies were observed to that extent anyhow."

"I hope they did no harm in the village," said my mother.

"Let me go and see," I said.

"You stay where you are," said my father.

In the end he went off with Miss Tite. We watched them stumping along the road together.

"She has great stuff in her," said my mother.

Miss Morris and I looked at one another. She said Freddy had cooked his goose. Did she know that this was going to happen? And why did she say George was not a Black and Tan? He must be. And most probably a Greek as well. What would Freddy do to me now? Not that I was afraid of him. He was a sneaky coward. But I could not be sure whether Mr Griffin had gone away. He might be hiding in the neighbourhood. The Tans were probably looking for him last night. He was a queer sort of man, but he had been very polite to me. I don't suppose he would shoot me just to oblige Freddy. And then I thought of poor Lord Swords who was so grand and so rich and so good. He had done no harm, and yet they shot him. No one was safe.

"Did the Black—did George do that to Freddy?" I whispered.

"No, you chump. I told you George is not a Black and Tan," she said.

"You said Freddy had cooked his goose."

"Did I? Well, he has. Hasn't he?"

And that was all the satisfaction I got from her.

Jane and Alice were caught listening at the door, but no one said anything. That was what I rather liked about disasters: they brought everyone together. And we knew the maids listened, whenever they got a chance. Things we are not meant to hear always sound so much more interesting than what is told to us.

Another pot of tea was made which everyone shared because there had been no milk in the kitchen—or so Jane said —but I had a feeling that this was not her first cup of tea that morning.

"Have they murthered poor Freddy, ma'am?" she said.

"No, Jane. But they must have frightened him badly. He is saying his prayers."

"He was lucky," said Jane. "Them fellows would kill their own mothers, so they would."

Jane had been my informant about what was happening since I had been keeping away from Freddy. She told me about Terence MacSwiney, the Lord Mayor of Cork, who died of hunger strike in an English prison. It was very sad, but I could not understand why anyone but himself was to blame for this. Jane would never explain anything properly. I came to the conclusion that he must have been starved to death. But she wouldn't agree. 'They are a hard-hearted lot of divils over there,' she said. 'They could have let him go free. But he was too good for the likes of them.' And then, a week afterwards, Kevin Barry was hanged. He was only eighteen. Jane said he had killed nobody. He had been found with a revolver in his hand after a Tommy had been shot. But I think what really upset her was his being so young. They might have given him another chance. 'He was not much older than yourself, Master Brian,' she said.

I saw myself being hanged. How terribly sad my mother and father would be. It made me sorry for Kevin Barry. I wished they had let him off even if he had taken out his gun to shoot Tommies. What would happen if George found out that I had told Freddy about him? Could they say I was guilty of Lord Swords's murder? Could they hang me for it? Why could I not get this out of my mind? After all, I had told the priest in confession. Or had I really? If Father Murphy was as cute as Miss Morris, he would have got me to tell him a whole lot of things. But he thinks about impure thoughts all the time. That's why people get away with murder, I suppose.

"I hope Miss Tite and Dick are safe," said my mother.

It was a relief to start fretting about that for a change. I wanted to forget my old self. I climbed to the top of the highest tree so that I could keep a look-out. One could see just as well from the gate, but it was more exciting to climb the tree and imagine I was on the top of a mast in mid-Atlantic. It was so cold that I was only able to stay up for a minute. And I tore my trousers getting down. But fortunately the wanderers had returned when I got back to the house. And nobody had eyes for me.

They were laden down with objects of various kinds. Miss Tite had another jug of milk and a loaf and *The Irish Times*.

My father had the letters, and a ham and the cat. (He had been missing.)

"I don't think anyone in the village will stir out before Christmas," said my father.

"Tell us all about it," said my mother. "But not a word until I have told Jane to put on the kettle."

"I nearly knocked the nose off her when I opened the kitchen door," said my mother on her return.

"Now, what's the news?"

"You tell them," said my father to Miss Tite.

"Go on, Dick," said Miss Tite.

But both, I could see, were longing to talk.

In the end Miss Tite told us all about it. No one in the village was hurt, but all the cottages were raided. The forge was wrecked, and the schoolmaster's house was turned upside down. Freddy was found hiding under the table in his kitchen. They took him out and threatened to shoot him. That must have been the time Miss Tite came along. In the end they shot a bullet through the door of his house. (It was lucky there was no one else living in the cottage.) Then they pulled out the furniture, and broke the windows.

Freddy had locked himself into his kitchen and refused to come out. He was drinking methylated spirits and, according to my father, would be in D.T.'s before night. Mrs Kelly, the milkman's wife, had a baby as a result of all the noise. But no one else had come to any harm. Everyone was frightened to death. We had been peaceful until now. No raids or anything until Lord Swords was shot. That had begun the trouble. It was strange that Mrs Kelly should have a baby on account of it. To be quite honest I had no idea where babies came from, but I would not have thought a Black and Tan raid could be the cause of one.

"I must say I am not sorry," said Miss Tite. "If anyone

of them had the courage of a rat he would have denounced Lord Swords's murderers. I like the natives in many ways, but I don't give them any marks for moral courage."

"Prenez garde," said my mother. "Jane is at the key-hole."

"Prenez garde, my foot," said Miss Tite. "It's time we stood up to them."

"It's all very well for you, Victoria. You haven't got a family to feed," said my father.

"My old governor always answered the door himself with a gun in his hands in the Fenian days. And there was no one the natives respected more," said Miss Tite.

"Who are the natives?" I whispered to Miss Morris. I thought of Traill, the Provost of Trinity whom Uncle Lindy had called a savage. Were there black men in the country? Why had I not seen them?

Miss Morris kicked my shin. She hated me to whisper.

Miss Tite went off at last. She forgot to take the milk and I had the fag of bringing it to her later on. But I got another pippin. I had rather hoped I would.

I was tempted to creep as far as Freddy's house and find out for myself what was going on there. I was afraid in one way, and fascinated in another. I had been told to come straight home when I left Miss Tite's; but I had not been forbidden to visit somewhere else on the way. No one thought of that possibility. I made a detour by crossing the field opposite Miss Tite's house, on the far side of the road. By doing this I could skirt Freddy's cottage (which stood beside another ruined cottage, a little way out of the village) and come to Miss Tite's house from the Malahide direction. There was a hedge behind the cottages. I could come quite close. I could see nothing and heard no sound. It was disappointing. I peered through the hedge. The cottages looked deserted. There were no windows on that side. Time was passing. I would be missed and I had had enough trouble for one day over the torn trousers. But just as I turned away, I heard Freddy's voice. It made me jump and run. Why had I walked into danger? But as I ran my fears died. The voice came from the house, through the broken kitchen windows. He was swearing, using all the bad words as well as others I had not heard before, and he was shouting, "I'll burn them all out . . . I'll shoot the lot of them . . . God save Ireland. . . . Long live Charles Stewart Parnell. . . . Hamar Greenwood, you may rot in Hell . . . I'll burn the lot. . . . Mr Allen is a decent man. I won't burn his house. . . . Who killed Thomas Ashe? . . . O'Reilly died for Ireland at the top of Moore Street Lane." Then he began his awful curses. And then—I had stopped to listen—he began to pray, "God spare me. Holy Mother of God. Blessed Saint Joseph." And then he began to cry. I was almost going to turn back. After all, Freddy had talked to me when no one else would. He may have wanted to collect gossip, but he treated me like a grown-up, which was more than I could say for most people. And it was very kind of him to speak so well of my father—and to offer not to burn our house down. It showed a good side to Freddy which most people would not have expected to find. But I hesitated. And then the most awful shrieks came from the cottage. Shrieks like the damned give in Hell in my nightmares. Worse than anything I had heard—except once when the stables went on fire at Mr O'Neill's farm and the horses got frightened. That was what Freddy sounded like. I thought someone must be trying to kill him. I was too cowardly to go and see. But who could be in the cottage? And then the shrieking stopped, and he began to use bad words again.

So I went away. I had not wasted more than five minutes. By running I made up the time. But unfortunately I spilt the milk. I spilt it on the road outside Miss Tite's own gate. I was as near as that. I tried to scoop some up, but it looked dirty from having been on the road. Two accidents today already, and it was not eleven o'clock yet!

But Miss Tite had seen me coming and came out to the gate to save me part of my journey. It was kind of her to be so considerate. She saw what had happened immediately. I must say she took it very well.

"We have been told not to cry over that, haven't we?" she said. "Come in and see if I can find you another apple. I have milk enough. So you need not go for more or confess what you did. I don't want any brat to have his backside sore on my account."

It was a rude way to put it. And my parents never did beat me; but I am sure Miss Tite meant well. It was all part of her pretending to be a man. She was quite soft-hearted really. I wonder why God gave her that moustache. If Uncle Lindy was kind he would have offered to marry her. I am sure she would have appreciated the compliment, but she was probably better off as she was.

When I got home my father was fussing because the telephone was out of order. He wanted to ring up the Courts and explain why he was at home. Sometimes the telephone worked, and sometimes it was most unsatisfactory. It was always unsatisfactory when the message was important.

It was not a good time to ask questions. There was a lot I wanted to know. And if only my father would get into a better humour it was nice to have him home for a change.

"What natives was Miss Tite talking about?"

"I haven't the least idea. Why in God's name does nobody answer this telephone?"

"Are natives and savages the same thing? Was Traill a native?"

"He was an archangel in comparison with the lady who is supposed to look after the telephone exchange. I am going to lose my job over this."

After a while all was well. Someone promised to pacify the Judge. So I began again.

"Miss Tite mentioned natives. I wondered who she was talking about."

"*Whom*, not *who*."

"She said it anyway."

"Said what? Why don't you do lessons with Miss Morris? She is supposed to be your governess."

"Miss Morris is helping Mummy with button-holes in a new dress."

"I want to look at the paper. I have not had a moment of peace to read it."

"I won't keep you a moment. I was curious when Miss Tite said something about the natives. That's all. I have never seen black people about. Uncle Lindy said Traill was a savage. And I wondered if Miss Tite knew many people like that. I would like to see them."

"Miss Tite means the poor people, the people who live in cottages."

"But they are not savages."

"She never said they were. Miss Tite means people of the working class. Her father was a big landowner."

"I don't understand."

"A native of a place is a person who has always lived there. It is the opposite to a foreigner who is someone from abroad."

"Am I a native then?"

"Not in the sense Miss Tite used the word."

"Am I a foreigner? I thought only French people were foreigners."

"In France, French people are natives."

"How can they be foreigners *and* natives if one is the opposite of the other?"

"I told you. Just work it out for yourself."

"Then I am a foreigner."

"You are when you go to France."

"What am I when I am here?"

"A pestilential nuisance. I am not going to waste the morning giving you a lecture on Irish history. And I don't think I am competent to do it anyhow."

"Are the English foreigners?"

"They are not. I dare say I shall be shot if Jane hears me say so. This country is tied to England. If England lets go, Ireland sinks. Your Sinn Fein friends want to drive the English away. If they do, we shall have a government of gombeen men. My father said that in 1912. And I think he was a farsighted man."

"Are gombeen men savages?"

"They are worse than savages. A savage is, at least, raw material."

"Are Greeks savages?"

"The Greeks were in some ways the most civilised people the world ever knew."

"Why do you say no one should take presents from them? I have been worrying about this for days."

"That is a quotation from Virgil, a Latin poet. The Greeks were fighting the Trojans all on account of a beautiful lady called Helen. It is a very exciting story, but if you don't mind I shall put off telling it to you until I have finished reading the paper. Can't you find yourself a book?"

"Was Helen as beautiful as Mrs Heber?"

"Much more beautiful."

"I don't suppose the Greeks would fight a war over Mrs

Heber. But they might over Miss Morris. After all, the Black——"

"What's that?" said my father.

He had dropped the paper. It was funny how attentive he could become all of a sudden if certain subjects were mentioned.

"I only said the Black and Tan might go to war over Miss Morris."

"You have been told not to call the egregious Captain Wain a Black and Tan."

"Does egregious mean Greek? You said he was a Greek. But Miss Morris says he comes from Battersea. Did she tell you? I think she was quite annoyed about it."

"Egregious does not mean Greek. It means unusual. I hope I offend nobody when I say Captain Wain is unusual. Please tell your mother I said you were to do your lessons. Miss Morris can make button-holes some other time."

I could see my father was fed up with me. So I went off to my mother's room. She was having a cup of tea with Miss Morris and very kindly gave me a piece of shortbread. I did not bring up the subject of lessons. Miss Morris disliked them just as much as I did.

*   *   *

Doreen was leaving on Monday. Everyone was trying to make a fuss about her, but it was difficult: she did not play up. Every year it was the same: Mrs Heber announced her arrival as if it were an eclipse of the sun, my father used to say, and her departure was given the importance of 'The retreat from Moscow'. But Doreen came and went so quietly, and made so little impression when she was here, that it was clear we were all indulging Mrs Heber in a sort of elaborate game she was playing at our expense. Perhaps because she had no children she wanted to pretend that Doreen was the wonderful daughter she might have had. I could never understand why my parents were the only ones in our immediate neighbourhood who had a child. I asked Mrs Heber what the reason was, but she became exactly like a picture of the Queen at Ascot when I pressed for an answer.

"God arranges these things, Brian."

"I know, but why did he arrange it differently for my parents? And they have only one. Jimmy Cody who works in our garden has ten brothers and sisters alive and three dead. And his parents look quite ordinary. Of course they are very poor."

"It is quite different for the poor. And look at Mrs Cody. She is no older than I am, and she might be seventy."

"Having children makes you old, then. My mother doesn't look as old as Miss Tite. And Miss Tite has no children."

"Her Scotch terriers are her babies," said Mrs Heber. "And mine are my roses and my china and furniture. If I had real babies I could not have afforded them. No one has everything."

"If it were me I would sell some of the china and get a child. A child is company."

I knew when Mrs Heber disliked a topic. And I soon learnt to avoid this one. No one wanted to talk to me about it. I got the idea that it might be the hardness of the water which was responsible. The Cody family never washed. They were not affected by it. Uncle Lindy said he could never shave himself properly in our house; the water was so hard. Perhaps that explained it. And Miss Tite's moustache may have been due to the fact that she had Scotch Terriers instead of babies. Miss Morris avoided the questions I put to her on the subject.

"You would be better off kicking a football than bothering yourself about these matters," she said.

My mother said something like that too. I asked Alice, but she got cross.

"That's dirty talk," she said.

I asked Miss Morris why Alice said that. Miss Morris said: "Ask your father. He can't pass the buck for ever."

My father said Miss Morris was forgetting herself. But he started to talk about something else.

And then the truth flashed upon me.

"I want to go to confession," I said.

"Not again. Not so soon," said my mother.

"I must," I said.

At last I could tell Father Murphy I had impure thoughts. To make quite sure I asked my mother. And the way she said: "No, dear. But don't worry about things before you have to" convinced me that everyone was hiding the truth from me. I was a monster of depravity, but everyone realised it was not my fault.

All this happened while Doreen's departure was the chief topic amongst us. We had to give some sort of party for her. And there was the same difficulty where we lived about young men as there was about children.

There were three bachelors in Malahide. But the youngest was fifty. And most of the unmarried men in the county were eccentrics of some kind or other. No wonder such a fuss was made about poor Lord Swords when he arrived.

"I give up," said my mother. "We shall have to call on Lindy. Anything in trousers. But I do want the poor girl to enjoy her last week. She has had a thin time."

The matter was openly discussed with the Hebers. And the bomb fell when Doreen herself suggested that Captain Wain should come.

"It is certainly time she went home," said my mother.

"Funny when you come to think of it. Her parents are

rescuing her from Sinn Feiners, and the girl's only danger is a Black and Tan," said my father.

"He is not a Black and Tan," I said.

"You are quite right. But you are responsible, you know. I never imagined that an Army officer could be like Captain Wain—I am behind the times. You offered a very plausible explanation."

"Will Mrs Heber mind if Captain Wain comes to the party?" I said.

"Mrs Heber has invited him to her house," said my mother. "If Doreen wants him, let's have him. You must keep an eye on the amount he drinks. Mrs Heber had a little trouble I understand."

"It's not fair to Miss Morris. After all she came here to get away from him. God knows we have had our fill of the subject."

"I think it's a thing of the past. Brian, love. Run out to Jimmy and tell him to divide the dahlias in that clump I showed him yesterday."

My mother had remembered me when the conversation began to get interesting.

"I think he is doing it."

"Go out and see."

"In a moment."

"This very minute. I must have instant obedience."

I went. Anyway they wouldn't have gone on with the subject if I stayed.

Next day everyone was in bad humour. Miss Morris got angry when Captain Wain's name was mentioned. But in the end it was agreed that my mother should write to him in a formal way and say Doreen had asked for his presence.

"Mrs Heber won't like that," said my father. "That's hitting below the belt."

I need hardly say that my visit to Father Murphy was regarded as inconvenient and unnecessary. Miss Morris went with me. But this time she did not go to confession herself. The walk gave me an opportunity to talk to her, but she was absent-minded. She said she had been invited to Kenya to look after children and to India to look after children. "You would think it was my vocation," she said.

The thought of Miss Morris in those distant places filled me with gloom.

*   *   *

I was on my way back from a short visit to Mrs Heber's. I had been sent to borrow something for Sunday's party and was hurrying past the forge which had been locked up since the night the Black and Tans came. Freddy Doyle had been locked up too. Drinking methylated spirits in large quantities is not good for anyone. It certainly had a bad effect on him. He might have been burned to death if some kind person had not told Father Murphy. He arranged the whole affair. Father Murphy was very kind, and quite sensible about many things.

Even though the forge was locked up and disused, I always hurried past it now. Freddy seemed to haunt it. Today there were signs that someone had been in the forge. The doors were shut, but they were not barred up any longer, and some of the old iron which had been strewn around was gathered into a heap. I glanced at this, but did not stop. It reminded me that Freddy might come back. When Father Murphy had him locked up, I must confess I prayed that he would never come out again. The thought made me feel guilty now, for as I left the forge behind, Freddy suddenly rose out of the ditch beside me. I gave a shout of terror.

His face was white, but his eyes were red, and his nose was

blue. It looked like the result of magic by the Black and Tans. But I did not think of that then.

"Master Brian, I want a word with you."

"I am sorry, Freddy. I'm in a hurry. I was sent on a message."

"I'll walk some of the way with ye. But don't run, Master. I'm nearly crippled with the rheumatism. Is your father above in the house?"

"No. He is at Court today."

"I wonder if he would spare me a loan of a small drop of whiskey. The doctor says I must have it, and I am short of a bob until Saturday."

"I will tell him when he comes home."

"You wouldn't slip inside yourself and see if you could find me a drop. I have a strong weakness on my chest since the Tans got hold of me."

"The whiskey is locked up now. I was caught the last time I gave you some. Did you ask Mrs Heber for some?"

"The likes of her wouldn't give you what would make a shirt for a louse. Your father is a real gentleman. I always say that. You can tell the quality."

"I swear the whiskey is locked up. There is only one bottle. And that's kept for visitors, or in case anyone gets a pain suddenly at night."

"Doesn't himself take his drop of an evening?"

"No, Freddy. Not any more. He says he can't afford it."

I tried to get away. I was tempted to run. But Freddy must have guessed this because he kept his hand on my sleeve.

"Listen, Master. I've something to tell you. Take a look down the road. Is there anyone coming along?"

"No. But Freddy, I can't wait. They are expecting me at home."

"Just a minute, Master. There's something terrible important

I want to tell you. Do you mind how you told me about your man that was coming down after the little flapper beyant?"

"I don't understand. I must go, Freddy."

He had cornered me. His face had the same miserable, beseeching look, but I could see he was determined not to let me go.

"You said she was in terror of her life of him and he was to come here at six. Do you mind that now?"

"I can't remember."

"Well, I remember. And will you listen to this now? You know what the Tans did to me—wrecked me forge and me cottage and as good as took me life. The doctor said: 'You had somebody's prayers, Doyle, or you wouldn't be alive this day.' Now the other crowd is after me. They want to know where your man lives. They have something to say to him."

"I don't understand."

"Well, I'll enlighten ye. That one can tell. She is going with the feller. You can find out from her where he lives, can't ye? That's not hard, is it? Just keep an eye out for letters. I'm sure she writes him Billy Doos. She is a flighty little one, that one, so she is."

"I can't, Freddy."

"They'll have my life, Master. I'll swear to God they'll riddle me."

"If you stay there I'll try and get you a drop of whiskey. I think I know where the key is."

"That's a decent boy. You're a kind little chiseler after all. I'll stay here handy. You can slip out by the side door. And if you can get me that address I'll light a candle for you before the altar, so I will."

"I can do that myself, Freddy. Wait there now."

I had no intention of coming out again. I was cheating

Freddy. And how was I going to avoid him in future? But I was desperate. And I was frightened.

I was glad to come home. My mother sat at her writing-table finishing her letter. Miss Morris was putting photographs into an album.

"There you are, Brian. As you are on your feet would you slip down to the pillar box and post that. You will just be in time for the post."

She handed me an envelope. I saw:

>   Capt. George Wain
>   Lower Mount Street

I read no more.

"I have a frightful pain in my tummy. I think it may be appendicitis," I said.

"Where, dear? Show me the place," said my mother.

I pointed to the middle, the place where I got pains sometimes.

"You don't get an appendix pain there," she said.

"It's over this way a bit."

"That's the wrong side."

"It's really all over. It's here one minute, and here the next."

"If you were told you need not go to the post and were offered a nice piece of jam sandwich the pain would go. Wouldn't it?" said Miss Morris.

I ignored her.

"Honest," I said, looking at my mother. "I feel awfully sick."

"He doesn't look too well," said my mother.

"Jane is going out for her half-day," said Miss Morris. "She can post it."

"Run," said my mother. "You will just be in time to catch her. I hear the back door."

"Don't."

"What's the matter, Brian?"

"Nothing. I wouldn't give an important letter to Jane to post."

"She has only to go a hundred yards down the road. She won't have time to forget it."

Miss Morris disappeared. She had gone to find Jane.

I knew what would happen. Jane would show Freddy the letter. They were both the sort of people who read any letters they could find. I once saw Jane steaming an envelope at a kettle. She told me she was cleaning an inkstain off it. But I knew what she was doing. I liked Jane. She was kind. But she had funny ways.

I should have told my mother all about it. She could have stopped Miss Morris. There was still time. But I was afraid to bring up all the Freddy business again. I was still frightened when I thought about it. And I would not go out at night by myself. Not for a fortune.

"I will go up and lie down," I said.

"Good boy. You are probably tired. A rest will do you good."

From the landing window I could see Jane walking down the road. She was wearing one of my mother's cast-off hats. It was very wide, and it made her look funny because she was small and square. I could see that she was looking at the letter. Her head was bent down. She read very slowly and always aloud. At the corner I saw her stop. She was talking to someone. I leaned out as far as I could, but I was not able to see the other person. The hedge cut him off. It was the corner at which I had parted from Freddy. And Jane stood there for ten minutes. I counted them on the hall clock.

*   *   *

On Friday George's answer came. Mother passed it across the table to my father who read it with one eye still on the newspaper.

"Does Captain Wain call you 'Bill', Miss Morris?" he said in the teasing voice he used with her.

"It's me," I said.

My father handed me the letter as if he was getting rid of a new baby, and turned back to the paper with relief.

The Black and Tan had very fancy writing. Squiggles and wriggles, and an enormous signature at the end. But in the space beneath his name he had written 'Love to Bill'.

I must say this made me feel proud. I very seldom got letters. To be mentioned in one was quite an honour.

I had been wondering what I should do about the Freddy business. I spoke to Jane. "Did you show Freddy the letter Mummy gave you to post?" I said.

"What do you take me for? I haven't laid eyes on the same Freddy this month back," she said.

So I knew she had.

I then decided to ask my mother to promise to send George up to say 'Good night' to me. As a special treat for him I would have Raffle sleeping in my room. She was such a tiny puppy she was kept in the kitchen for warmth. She should not have been taken away from her mother so soon. But I could put a hot bottle in her basket for this occasion. My mother agreed to this. She was a very agreeable woman when nothing had happened to cross her. When he was with me, I would tell the Black and Tan that Freddy had been looking for his address. That would put him on his guard. I would be happy then.

It was to be quite a large party. As well as the Hebers and Doreen, the Hones were coming, and Miss Tite, the Clitheroes and the three old bachelors from Malahide, Uncle Lindy, and a very grand old lady from Howth, who snubbed everybody except Mrs Heber. Mrs Heber was a match for her. My mother did not want to invite Miss Grieve, who looked at people when she met them as if they were meat on a slab at the butcher's, but Mrs Heber was very anxious that Doreen should give a favourable account of her visit. And apparently it would please her parents to hear she was friends with this cross and unkind old lady.

I heard all this being talked about. Nothing else was mentioned but the party. And my mother got tired of saying prenez garde. So I gathered quite a lot of interesting information.

On Saturday Jane and Alice (they were sisters) asked for Sunday afternoon off to go to the football match in Croke Park. It was Alice's Sunday out, and my mother was plucking up courage to ask her to stay in when Jane must have been plucking up her courage to ask for the day for both of them. "They say they have a gorgeous pair of fellers coming up from the country who want to take them to the match," my mother said. "But how can I give a meal to fifteen people when the staff goes off for the afternoon?"

"It is only cold supper, isn't it?" said my father, who minimised difficulties and disliked saying 'no'.

"I would like to see you prepare it," said my mother.

In the end it was agreed that a younger sister would come and help during the day; Jane and Alice promising faithfully to come back at six o'clock.

From dawn on Sunday the house rattled with preparations. Miss Morris arranged flowers and did all the nice jobs, my mother was buried in the kitchen, my father 'looked after' the drinks.

"We are short of tumblers," he said.

"We are short of silver," said Miss Morris.

"The cream has all gone sour," said my mother.

"Is there anything I can do to help?" said Uncle Lindy, who sat in the drawing-room all day reading *Daddy Longlegs*. We ate sandwiches for luncheon in the school-room. I liked that. But my mother's temper was very short.

"For the tenth time, I will send Captain Wain up to say 'Good night'," she said.

I was only wanting to make sure. Promises had been broken before now. Never important ones, I had to admit. But they did not know how important this one was.

To Uncle Lindy she said: "Would it be too much to ask of you, Lindy, to watch the drawing-room fire? I am the only person in this house who can light it if it goes out."

After luncheon I was sent out for a walk with Uncle Lindy. I hated that. He walked so fast. And out of doors a drop came on the end of his nose in winter. I wondered if it was always the same one. But I thought it was better not to ask. He did not talk to me really, although he did talk quite a lot. He pointed at things, and found fault with them. He said the roads were in a dreadful condition, the hedges were uncut, the fields undrained. He said the country was ruined and that very soon the English would hand us over to the Sinn Feiners who would cut our throats. I had heard this so often I really did not believe it any more.

"Will the Black and Tans go away then?" I said.

"Indeed they will. We shall have no protection at all then. I am glad my father did not live to see the day."

Uncle Lindy never gave me the impression that he was fond of anything or anybody. If he really thought we were all going to be killed, why did he sit all morning reading *Daddy Longlegs*? I think he enjoyed complaining. He asked me questions about my lessons.

"I can't make your father out. I shall believe you have

gone to Mr Darley's school when I see it. At your age I was reading Livy."

"Would you rather read *Daddy Longlegs* now?" I said.

He gave me a suspicious, darting look when I said that—the look of a startled bird. I knew it well.

"You are going to be very like your father," he said.

That was the end of our miserable conversation. When we got home there was consternation. The telephone was out of order, or else the whole family at the exchange had taken a holiday for the match. Kitchener, the cat, had disappeared with most of the fish. Worst of all the young sister who replaced Jane and Alice had arrived but was not very satisfactory.

"She is the imbecile one. I might have known. I might have known," wailed my mother.

Bridie (the sister) had stockings in wrinkles and a perpetual cold in her nose. She dropped everything she handled (six plates and three tumblers had fallen by four o'clock, and there were three hours to go before the party). She had been relegated to floor-scrubbing after the third tumbler fell.

"At least she can't break the kitchen floor," said my mother.

"Her inside is upset," said Miss Morris.

All the water had to be pumped by hand in our house. It was Jimmy Cody's chief occupation. On Sundays it was most important to conserve supplies. But Bridie, on Miss Morris's calculation, had visited the w.c. seven times since she arrived.

"You had better talk to her," said my father.

"It seems brutal."

"Well, send her home then. She is more trouble than she is worth."

"I will have a word with her," said Miss Morris.

She came back laughing.

"Bridie was only doing it for fun. She said she enjoyed 'them yokes' as they hadn't one in the cottage."

This amused us all. Even Uncle Lindy gave a grudging sort of laugh.

To avoid trouble I sneaked off to bed with *The Scarlet Pimpernel* and Raffle. I took her inside the clothes to keep her warm. Her life was very peaceful—sleeping, eating and making messes. She soothed me by her gentle snores. And I loved that book. I thought of myself as Sir Percy Blakeney, Miss Morris as Lady Blakeney, and Mr Griffin as Chauvelin. It was funny how great an impression Mr Griffin had made on me considering how little he said and how uninteresting he looked. It was the way he smiled that day he said "The English, who else?" that put the fear of God into me.

I forgot about the party and the preparations that were being made downstairs, and was only brought back to consciousness of life in the house by the sound of my mother, Miss Morris, Uncle Lindy and my father all talking together. Grown-ups have a way of talking when they are excited which is unmistakable. I put down the book, tucked Raffle in tight, and went downstairs to reconnoitre.

The excitement was on account of Alice and Jane, who, in spite of their promises, were not home. And it was now half-past six.

"Of course we were mad to let them go," said my mother.

"It's too late to do anything about that now," said my father.

"They respect neither God nor man," said Uncle Lindy.

But nobody paid attention to him.

In the end it was decided that my father should bicycle to Kinsaley where the family cottage was, to find out if the girls had come home.

"They leave this house tomorrow morning," said my mother.

Jane had been sacked three times, and Alice once. But

they always came back again. It was fun fixing up the bicycle for the journey. There was no oil in the lamp and one tyre was flat.

"It would be quicker to walk," my mother said.

Uncle Lindy was clever about the puncture, and we took oil from the lamp in the school-room. My father hated anything mechanical. He looked very wobbly when at last he was ready to set out.

"I don't like the look of that back wheel," said Uncle Lindy. But that was when my father had disappeared from view.

"Mind yourself, love," called my mother.

Miss Morris and I cheered.

It was a great send-off.

Kinsaley was a mile away. And it did not take long to make the journey. When my father came back he looked very worried.

"The Evans family is in a state of jitters," he said. "There's been trouble in Dublin today. Someone has come back with a report of shooting at the match. The roads into Dublin are all closed. And everyone is being searched. There is no sign of the girls. What should we do? It was madness to let them both go up to Dublin."

"I hope they have come to no harm. Try the exchange again," said my mother.

Now we were all worried and sad on account of Jane and Alice.

"I am sure the story is wildly exaggerated," said my father. "But if there has been shooting in Dublin, it may be difficult to get through."

"George will be able to help," said Miss Morris.

And now we were happy again. The Black and Tan was the very best person in this situation. He would know what had happened and he might be able to get us news of the maids.

"I hope their pair of gorgeous fellows will take good care of them," said my father.

At seven o'clock, guests began to arrive. They had all heard rumours of trouble in Dublin, but the telephone not being in order meant that no one knew for certain what had happened. It was funny when Dublin was only seven miles away. But at that time only three people in our neighbourhood had motor cars, and no one went into Dublin on Sundays. Not having maids (Bridie had been sent home when she left the bucket under Uncle Lindy's feet and gave him a very nasty fall) was rather fun. Everyone offered to help. It was like playing House. I could hear Miss Tite's voice drowning all the men's; and Mrs Heber made it pleasant for everyone by walking about and admiring out loud. The women did the kitchen part while the men went into the dining-room for tumblers of whiskey as a preparation. I heard my mother calling:

"Come here out of that, Victoria."

Miss Tite must have been trying to stay with the men.

I sat on the landing watching the hall door. As each person arrived I prayed it would be the Black and Tan. At half-past seven everyone had come. The house was almost swaying with the noise of so many people all talking together. But there was no sign of the Black and Tan. Eight struck. He had not come. I waited there, in my dressing-gown, until I was quite stiff with cold.

"I must see him. I must tell him," I kept on repeating to myself. Jane and Alice not having come home, the rumours of shooting, the holds-up on the road (as there were when Lord Swords was shot), and now the Black and Tan not coming—all gave me a mounting sense of dread. Was it too late? Had Freddy given the address?

Was I the cause of another person being killed? My father came up and found me there. He picked me up and carried me to bed. I held him tight and told him of my fears. I gabbled and gabbled. He said nothing until I had finished and was crying too much to talk any more.

"It is all imagination. Everyone is safe. You will see."

"And the Black and Tan?"

"Of course. He is not a Black and Tan. I expect he was busy today. He would have let us know had the telephone been working."

"Promise he is safe."

"Promise."

"And Jane and Alice?"

"And Jane and Alice."

"Promise?"

"Promise."

I have great faith in my father. So I went to sleep after that.

*   *   *

The household 'took it easy' next morning. Raffle had wormed her way to the end of my bed. I dug her up to give her breakfast. She licked my hand twice afterwards, wriggled back into her basket and fell asleep again. I opened the door of the room in which Jane and Alice slept. It was a joyful surprise to see them both safely home again. It was rude to look; but I was fascinated by Jane's appearance. Her mouth was wide open. A pink stays, a cast-off of my mother's, lay on top of a pile of clothes at the end of her bed. I looked away because it was a horrible colour and the clothes had a sad look.

Alice's face could not be seen. Her head was under the blankets.

I went back to bed in order to finish *The Scarlet Pimpernel*. My mind was quite at peace now. What a comfort my father was! How much wiser than Uncle Lindy who found so much fault and always predicted woe. Anyone could do that. When I had finished *The Scarlet Pimpernel* Paddy, the milkman, had come and gone. I was sorry to miss him as he always knew the news, and I wanted to find out why Mrs Kelly had a baby because the Black and Tans had frightened her. Mrs Heber was shocked by our Black and Tan, but she didn't have a baby. And neither did Miss Morris when he frightened the life out of her. So, it must have been something else, if the truth were known, was responsible for Mrs Kelly's.

When my father stayed late in bed, it meant that someone had promised him a lift into Dublin in a motor car. On those days he slept until the last moment and then cut himself shaving. Jane and Alice must have come home after I fell asleep. To put in time I went to the station to collect *The Irish Times*. It sometimes came late and I wanted to repay my father for making me happy again. I got my feet very wet taking a short cut across the field. It is curious how one always gets into trouble when one goes out of one's way to do somebody a good turn.

I kicked my shoes off in the kitchen. Miss Morris must have heard me. She came out of her room in her blue dressing-gown. She was yawning.

"Knock on the maids' door, like a good chap," she said. And then went back to her room.

I did as I was told.

"All right. All right," said Jane in a sleepy voice.

She would be out in a moment. The speed at which Jane and Alice dressed was quite wonderful. They washed themselves by some dry-cleaning method so as to save time. I never spent much time at it myself.

I put the paper where my father sat. He liked to be the first to open it.

As a rule I did not look at newspapers, except the ones which had a column for children. But today I was curious to see what had happened in Dublin, so I slipped the paper out of its wrapper in such a way that I could put it back without my father knowing he was not the first to open it. A sort of Three Bears trick, really.

I was not sure where to look. On the front page there were Births, Deaths and Marriages and Advertisements. I opened it at the centre.

DREADFUL SERIES OF MURDERS IN DUBLIN

CONCERTED ATTACK ON OFFICERS OF HIS MAJESTY'S FORCES

FOURTEEN SHOT DEAD AND MANY OTHERS WOUNDED

WILD SCENES AT GAELIC FOOTBALL MATCH

And under this in smaller print:

Yesterday morning there was enacted in Dublin a series of crimes unparalleled in the history of the city. As a result fourteen members of His Majesty's forces were murdered in their houses and a number of others seriously wounded.

The attacks, which were apparently preconcerted, in every case occurred at the same hour. At nine o'clock in the morning the houses and hotels where these officers resided were entered by civilian bands. Most of the officers were in their bedrooms.

My head was swimming. The print danced in front of my eyes. An awful feeling of black horror came. Yet I was compelled to go on to find out for sure what I knew was there.

There was so much print, small print dazzling and dancing. My eyes remained glued to the larger black headings.

THE MURDER OF CAPTAIN FITZGERALD
FIGHT IN LOWER MOUNT STREET
THREE KILLED IN MOREHAMPTON ROAD
OFFICER MURDERED IN LOWER BAGGOT STREET
OFFICER ATTACKED IN PEMBROKE STREET
COURT MARTIAL OFFICER KILLED
AT THE GRESHAM HOTEL
SEARCH AT THE CLARENCE HOTEL

It was getting more and more difficult to go on reading. I could see the Black and Tan. He was dead. But he was staring at me with accusing eyes. I was the boy who had killed two men.

I read whatever first came to my eyes.

The police found the dead body of Captain Newbury half-way through the window, covered by a blanket, which had been thrown over it by his wife.

The raiders made for the front room on the first floor, where a Mr Bennett was. They carried Mr Bennett to the room in which Mr Aimes slept. The servant was stopped as she was going upstairs. She heard shots.

The raiders then went to No. 24, the door of which they forced, and shot Captain McCormack dead as he lay in bed. His body bore five bullet wounds, one being in the head.

The raiders brought them to a spare bedroom on the upper landing. They brought Mr Smith there also, and there Captain Maclean and Mr Smith were shot dead.

It was horrible now, like looking through pools of blood. But I must be sure. I must see it as well as feel it inside.

> *They made for the Hall Porter, a well-known figure, remarkable for his courtesy to all who came in contact with him. They forced him up the staircase, and with pointed pistols compelled him to show them the rooms occupied by a Mr Wilde, and ex-Captain McCormack.*

The hall porter, "remarkable for his courtesy", made the scene more horrible. I saw him bowing graciously, and then being hurried along, with revolvers pushed into his back. All his dignity gone. All his graciousness for nothing. Only murder now.

> *The murders which occurred in the morning were followed by an unexpected fusillade at Croke Park in the afternoon when nine people were shot dead and a great many wounded.*
>
> *It is difficult to discover what actually happened, but it appears from statements of spectators that during the progress of the match armed men in uniform arrived simultaneously at four corners of the ground.*
>
> *Michael Hogan, aged 28 years, a member of the Tipperary football team, was also killed.*

Poor footballer. All blood and mud now.

SCENES IN PEMBROKE STREET
OFFICERS KILLED IN THEIR BEDROOMS

And underneath a long account in small print. I looked for names.

> *Mrs Gray, however, found further tragic evidences of the attack of the assassins. In a room on the second floor Captain Kenleyside of the Lancashire Fusiliers . . .*

Not there. And then:

Colonel Woodcock was found shot in the back.

Poor Colonel Woodcock. But still—I was beginning to hope. Had I been accustomed to reading newspapers I could have found what I wanted more quickly. But I was not, and I was trembling.

Major Dowling, of the Grenadier Guards, and Captain Price. The former, it would appear from all the evidence, was shot at his bedroom door.

Poor Major Dowling. I saw him as I had seen Miss Morris in her blue dressing-gown, yawning.

OUTWARD TRAINS STOPPED

A Military Order

INCENDIARISM IN CORK
Attempt to burn a Warehouse

I thought of Freddy when he asked for the address, his nasty little eyes, his cringing voice. 'They have something to say to him.' There must be a clue somewhere in all this. I looked at the top of *The Irish Times*. The headlines lay on the page like tombstones in a graveyard. I had not noticed the smaller heading of the paragraph on the left-hand side before. I read:

LOWER MOUNT STREET FIGHT

That was the address on the top of the Black and Tan's letter. I remembered. Now it was coming.

TWO POLICE AUXILIARIES KILLED

I heard Miss Morris on the stairs. I looked quickly at the

page again. I saw 'Morris' written quite distinctly. But I could not wait to read the other name. I could not face her. I could not face anyone now.

She must have seen me as I ran out. I heard her call me in a puzzled voice. I did not look back. I turned left at the gate and ran towards the sea. My head was throbbing.

As I passed Miss Tite's house her terriers rushed out barking and I heard them barking against the wooden gate which kept them from running out into the road. I could hear Miss Tite's voice over all the barking.

"Come here, Rover. Come back, Nell. Here, sir. Down, Bruce. Rufus. Ginger. Come here, sir."

A shaft of loneliness went through me. I thought I heard Miss Morris's voice muffled in all that barking, sounding from far away. And then I thought I heard my mother's voice. But it seemed to be close to my ear. As I ran faces came before my eyes. My mind was saying: "He broke his promise. He broke his promise." I saw my mother and my father looking sadly at me; and Miss Morris, in her dressing-gown; and Uncle Lindy as he said 'I don't like the look of that front wheel'; and Mrs Heber, in her drawing-room; and Mr Heber, walking slowly along the path; and Doreen as she danced with me; and Lord Swords at the football match; and Freddy in the hedge; and the Black and Tan. One moment the Black and Tan was talking to me, calling me 'Bill', giving me half a crown; another, he was standing in his bedroom door, yawning, while men in black hats, men in trench coats, were coming towards him, shooting, shooting. He lay in a heap on the floor, and blood was flowing slowly out of his head, over the floor, down the stairs, out on the road. It was coming towards me now. It covered the sky. And he was looking at me. And then I saw the hall porter who was 'remarkable for his courtesy to all who came in contact with him'. He was bowing very low at the foot of the stairs and I was being pushed and dragged by men in trench coats who were shouting "Show us the room. Show us the room." I did not know the room until I saw a long row of doors, all exactly alike. But from under one a trickle of blood oozed out.

I passed Freddy's cottage. I was not afraid of him any more. Like Miss Tite, he was something belonging to long ago. I saw him standing quite still beside his house, staring at the broken windows. He must have seen me too. But he gave no sign. I passed the Clitheroes' gate. I could see a maid polishing the door-knocker.

Mr Hone went past in his high two-seater. He did not see me.

A stitch had come in my side. My throat was sore. I could hear my feet go flap, flap, flap. I felt them hit the road. Each step went up my back into my head, and struck there like the clapper of a bell. My stockings had fallen down and hung round my ankles. One of my shoelaces was untied. And by degrees the shoe loosened and dragged. But I could not stop to tie it up. There was a buzzing in my ears. I seemed to hear, indistinct and far away, someone calling my name. And all the time my mind was saying: "He broke his promise. He broke his promise." The stitch went away. I had my second wind. I left the road and crossed the fields behind the village and the school. The golf-links was on my right. The grass grew shorter as the earth became sandier. I was coming near the sea.

There were three miserable trees in the corner of a field, their trunks overgrown with ivy and some of their branches dead. They looked like three witches, and they seemed to threaten me. I did not want to come near. But each place I tried to cross into the next field was too thickly wired. I tore my clothes on the pricks, and nettles stung my unprotected legs. There was a broken-down gate beside the trees. I had to go out that way. I ran along the ditch. The gate was rotten. The top bar broke under me. I fell into the next field. As I got up, I happened to glance in the direction of the trees.

A face was looking at me. Just a face. I saw it for a moment. Mr Griffin's face. Then it disappeared.

I ran. I was desperate now. I tripped over tufts. I slipped on stones. I caught my feet in rabbit holes. Briars lashed back as I pushed my way through bushes, leaving long scratches across my face. I lost one shoe.

Now I was on sand and moss. The path through the dunes was clearly marked uphill to the grey-blue line of the sky.

At the top the strand stretched out on either side; to the rocks and Martello Tower on the Malahide side; as far as I could see on the Sutton side, where the Hill of Howth curved out into the ocean. Before me lay a grey-black November sea, patched in green, and flecked with white. On the horizon a ship seemed to stand—a small, black shape. It looked lonely.

I stood for a moment there. Then I heard my name spoken quite distinctly.

I ran down the sandbank and across the wide acres of wet sand. The sea water cut like a knife. I ran at first and then had to push my legs slowly as the depth increased. The water was soon up to my knees. But there it stayed. I ploughed on. It got no deeper. Now it was at my ankles again. That strand is supposed to be ideal for children to bathe from. It is very safe.

At last the water deepened. I was up to my knees again.

I heard my name. Miss Morris was calling me. I looked back. She was standing at the water's edge, waving at me. I turned my face away and tried to go faster. If I threw myself down and kept my head under I would drown. I knew that. But I could not kill myself that way. I could swim out until

I was too tired to swim any more. Then I would go down and die in the deep water.

Miss Morris had stopped shouting. I glanced back. She was pulling off her stockings. Then she tucked up her skirt and came into the water.

I tried to run. The water was at my thighs. It had begun to get deeper. The cold which had made me breathless at first had now become a sharp pain in my hands and feet.

"Brian. Brian."

Miss Morris was calling me. Her voice sounded very sad.

I am not quite sure what happened then. I started to swim, I remember. And then my feet struck on another sandbank and I was in water ankle-deep once more. I ran on and plunged in when the water began to get deep again. But the last sandbank was fatal. Hands gripped my hair and pulled. I thought the top of my head was coming off.

She took my hand and led me towards the strand. It took longer to get back than I can tell. And neither of us spoke a word.

Our clothes clung to us, and a wind which blew along the shore cut like a whip. Still holding my hand Miss Morris began to run. She had forgotten her shoes and stockings. We walked up the crooked track which led from the shore to the road.

All wet, Miss Morris looked like a little girl. She glanced around as if trying to decide what to do. Then she took my hand in an unfriendly grip, and led me along the road towards the gate of St. Malachy's where Mr Threestar, the distiller, lived. We passed the gate, but on the right, further down the road, there was a yard. Miss Morris went in there. A woman came out of a doorway.

"Lord a mercy," she said.

Then a farm man joined her. He had a big, red, slow face. He stared at us for quite a while.

"The child fell into the sea," said Miss Morris.

They led us into a warm kitchen, and the woman undressed me at the fire. Miss Morris went into another room. When she came out she was in a man's overcoat which hid her hands in its long sleeves and touched the ground at the hem. The woman wrapped a blanket round me.

"He's Mr Allen's little boy, isn't he?" she said.

Miss Morris nodded. I think she was not able to think of anything to say.

"Joe recognised him," said the woman. "He has gone up to the house. The chauffeur will drive ye home. Are you feeling better, love?" she said to me.

She was a good woman. And it was kind of her not to ask questions. I enjoyed the warmth, but inside I was sick.

"The moty car is ready, beyant," said the woman.

"I will come back later with all these things," said Miss Morris. "Thank you very much. You are very, very kind."

As a rule I am good at thanking people. But I could not talk now.

The car was the largest I had ever seen. I sat in one corner and Miss Morris in the other. She turned her head away from me and stared out of the window. She hated me now. Sometimes she gave big sniffs. She had no handkerchief. Her sniffs may have been from cold, or because she was crying. I think they were a mixture of both.

Suddenly the driver gave an exclamation and pulled the car up with a jerk which threw me almost out of the seat. I looked up.

A lorry was parked on the roadside about fifty yards in front of us. It was outside Mr Griffin's house. I saw the berets of the Auxiliaries. If only I could have drowned myself. It would have been peaceful in the sea. One stood with a rifle. He was looking in our direction. Others stood on the lorry. Then some came running out of the house, shouting. They took no notice of us, but jumped on to the lorry and drove away. Some of them were still shouting.

The chauffeur started the car again. But he now drove at a funeral pace. Mr Griffin's house looked like Freddy Doyle's, as if a cyclone had blown through it, smashing and upsetting everything. The door was swinging in its frame. We all stared at it with the same expression. I had a book with a picture in it of travellers long ago passing a gibbet. They looked at it in the same way.

An armoured car was standing outside our house. I saw it before Miss Morris did. She was wrapping herself up in the loose overcoat. The car was slowing up gradually. I did not wait for it to stop, but jumped. I fell and cut my hands and knees, but not badly. I started to run back towards the sea.

I heard footsteps behind me. A soldier in khaki was following me.

"Come back, you little blighter," he shouted.

I knew I would be caught. I was crying. I was frightened.

When he caught me, he threw me over his shoulder and walked back quietly.

"I have the little shinner. Trying to avoid arrest he was."

Frightful as the words were, they were not spoken fiercely.

"Oh, thank you," I heard Miss Morris say. (I could only see the soldier's back and the ground. And I was rather dizzy.)

"I had better make a job of it," said the soldier.

I saw the door mat, the tiles on the porch, the rug in the hall, the carpet on the dining-room floor. Then he turned me right side up, and dropped me feet first on the floor. The room was full of people. I saw my mother and my father, and on the table, as I left it, *The Irish Times*. I could hardly take my eyes off this. But when I did, I saw, on the far side of the table, smiling and shining, the Black and Tan. It was all confusion then, all voices. I heard my mother's clearest. I think she was talking to me.

After a while that first confusion passed. I could make people out again. My eyes went back to the paper. And when they did, I could not take them off it.

My father said: "I thought so."

I looked up then and saw the Black and Tan again. He was in khaki uniform. He was a proper soldier. It was the first time I had ever seen him dressed up. He looked at the paper and then at me.

"I was one of the lucky ones, Bill," he said.

And then I knew it was all true. My father had kept his promises. And I forgot all about the awful paper. I was glad to see the Black and Tan was alive. I thought that I had never been so happy before in all my life. It was as if nothing could go wrong any more. I forgot what I really wanted most of all: that the Black and Tan should go away for ever and leave us alone, leave us by ourselves without any strangers around. And by ourselves I meant: me and Raffle and my mother and my father and Miss Morris. No one else.